CAKE ON A HOT TIN ROOF

CAKE ON A
HOT TIN ROOF

JACKLYN BRADY

WHEELER PUBLISHING
A part of Gale, Cengage Learning

Detroit • New York • San Francisco • New Haven, Conn • Waterville, Maine • London

LIBRARY OF CONGRESS CATALOGING-IN-PUBLICATION DATA

Brady, Jacklyn.
  Cake on a hot tin roof / by Jacklyn Brady. — Large print ed.
    p. cm. — (Wheeler Publishing large print cozy mystery)
  "A Piece of Cake Mystery"—T.p. verso.
  ISBN 978-1-4104-5177-4 (softcover) — ISBN 1-4104-5177-1 (softcover) 1.
Women cooks—Fiction. 2. Uncles—Fiction. 3. Money—Fiction. 4.
Murder—Investigation—Fiction. 5. Large type books. I. Title.
PS3602.R34334C35 2012
813'.6—dc23   2012026933

Published in 2012 by arrangement with The Berkley Publishing Group,
a member of Penguin Group (USA) Inc.

Printed in the United States of America
  1 2 3 4 5   16 15 14 13 12
FD298

*This one's for Valerie Sherry Brown
and Vanessa Lee Sthole.
I couldn't do any of it without you.*

ONE

"You'll be here by seven, won't you, sugar? You won't be late?"

My mother-in-law sounded so hopeful, I hated to disappoint her, but how could she ask me to leave work early on a Friday evening during Mardi Gras season? I shifted my cell phone to the other ear and glanced at the chaos surrounding me. Clutter and constant movement filled every corner of Zydeco Cakes, signs of the work overload the staff and I had been experiencing since the first of the year.

Stacks of empty boxes, all decorated in traditional Mardi Gras purple, green, and gold, teetered in every corner of the massive design room. Near the door to the loading dock, boxes filled with King Cakes awaited delivery to businesses and events. More boxes filled the other end of the room, in preparation for the walk-in customers we hoped would be coming in droves to pick them up before the season was over. And that was on top of our regular business: cakes for two weddings, a Valentine's Day party, and a fiftieth birthday party, all scheduled for delivery in the coming week.

I'd only been running Zydeco Cakes for a few months, and this was my first Mardi Gras in New Orleans. I knew the carnival season was a big deal around here, but as a recent transplant to the city, I was still shocked at just *how* big a deal it was. We were already a month into the season, but the sharp increase in business had left me off-balance and scrambling to catch up. I'd been looking forward to the celebration, but I was starting to wonder if I'd be able to find enough free time to enjoy any of it.

But that wasn't Miss Frankie's fault, and I tried not to take out my frustrations on her.

She and I became partners last year, shortly after the death of her only child, Philippe Renier, who'd also happened to be my husband — at least on paper. I was his widow on a flimsy technicality: he'd been killed minutes before he was supposed to sign our divorce agreement, though Miss Frankie liked to imagine that we'd been on the verge of reconciling when he died.

I'm the one with the training and experience as a pastry chef, so I handle the day-to-day work at the bakery. Miss Frankie offers moral support and the occasional cash infusion from the comfort of her living room. Most of the time our arrangement suits me, but today I was frustrated by my partner's lack of hands-on experience.

I'd been working alongside the rest of the staff for days, ignoring the growing heap of paperwork in my office and the even longer to-do list for tonight's Mardi Gras party at Miss Frankie's country club. The same party Miss Frankie was nagging me about at that very moment.

"Rita? Are you even listening to me?"

Her insistent tone pulled me away from my growing frustration and back to the conversation. "I'm listening," I assured her. "But I don't think you realize how crazy it is around here. We're up to our eyeballs in work. Nobody has been able to take a lunch break for two days and things are only getting worse."

"I know y'all are busy," Miss Frankie said, "but tonight's party is important."

And there it was: the crux of our argument.

"It's a *party*," I pointed out.

"A very *important* party," she pointed back. "With very important people. It's not just a social event, Rita. It's the Captain's Court for Musterion. It's crucial to the business that you be here, *and* that you show up on time."

Like I said before, I'm no expert on Mardi Gras, but over the past few months I'd learned a few things. All of the parties, parades, and balls are organized by social clubs known as krewes. There are hundreds of them scattered across the Gulf Coast region. Some krewes take themselves very seriously, others not so much. Musterion (whose membership list topped 2,000) falls somewhere in the middle. The Captain's Court was a sort of last blast for Musterion's movers and shakers, a celebration of all the work they'd done to get ready for Mardi Gras and the prequel to next week's parade and formal ball, which would be open to the entire krewe.

Carnival season may seem heathen on the surface, but it actually has deep roots in Christianity. The whole point of it, after all, is for people to stuff themselves silly on Fat Tuesday before the forty-day austerity of Lent begins on Ash Wednesday. That "last hurrah" starts all the way back at Epiphany on January 6. Which is where the King Cake gets its name — the word *King* refers to the wise men, and the traditional plastic baby figurine baked into every cake represents the baby Jesus. According to tradition, the person lucky (or unlucky) enough to get the slice of cake with the hidden baby in it is obligated to host the party next year.

Philippe, who had been a longtime member of the Krewe of Musterion, got the baby at last year's Captain's Court celebration, which put him on tap to act as this year's host. Thanks to Miss Frankie, I got custody of the baby when he died. This party was, according to Miss Frankie, a *very* big deal, which was why she volunteered me to take over as hostess. I just wish she'd discussed it with me first.

I'm all about doing what's best for the business. I just didn't happen to agree that this party she was so wound up about needed the top spot on my priority list. I'd said so about two million times in the past few weeks, but Miss Frankie wasn't listening.

"I'll get there as soon as the orders for tomorrow morning have been filled," I said, also for the two-millionth time. "That's more important for the business than me standing around with a glass of champagne in my hand." She started to argue, but I went on as if she hadn't spoken. "I don't know any of the people on your guest list.

They're not going to miss me if I'm a little late. If you need help entertaining the masses before I get there, I'm sure Bernice will pitch in."

Bernice Dudley is Miss Frankie's neighbor and closest friend. She's a sweet lady with a halo of white hair and a drawl as smooth and Southern as aged Kentucky bourbon.

"Well, of course I can count on Bernice," Miss Frankie said with a tick of her tongue. "That's not the point. A proper party simply cannot begin without its hostess."

That would be me, though not by choice. I was harboring some resentment over the way Miss Frankie had finagled me into the role, which might have been making me slightly more stubborn than usual. I still wasn't convinced that Philippe's predeath party obligations had legally become my responsibilities.

Miss Frankie let out a long-suffering sigh. "Rita. Sugar. Try to understand. This party is important. All the top brass of Musterion will be here, and that includes some very influential — and wealthy — people."

I could have refused, but I was a little concerned about Miss Frankie. Losing her only son had shaken her world to its core. She'd made a valiant effort to keep her spirits up as we stumbled through the holidays together, but by New Year's Eve she'd had enough. The idea of heading into an entire year without Philippe had crumbled her like a stale cookie. She'd spent the whole month of January in a funk, and had only started rallying again in the past week or so. I didn't want anything to jeopardize that.

"These people were friends of Philippe's," she was saying now. "Most of them were clients of Zydeco when he was alive."

"I understand that, but —"

"They'll want to meet you."

I laughed. "I doubt that."

"Why would you? You were Philippe's wife and you're running Zydeco now. Of course they'll want to know more about you. This is your chance to make a good impression. To establish yourself as one of them. Otherwise, they might take their business somewhere else now that Philippe is gone."

But I *wasn't* one of them. I knew it, and they'd figure it out soon enough. Philippe and Miss Frankie had been born into that society. Old money and the genteel Southern breeding might be in their blood, but they weren't in mine.

"I know there are a lot of potential customers on the guest list, but I can't ignore current paying customers just to play nice with people who *might* spend money at Zydeco in the future." It was a lousy excuse. Even I knew that. But the thought of trying to impress two hundred of New Orleans's most influential citizens at once was stressing me out.

"I'm not asking you to ignore anybody," Miss Frankie said. "But you work too hard. I'm asking you to take one evening to have a little fun and make an investment in the bakery's future at the same time. Is that so difficult?"

"Much more difficult than you can imagine," I grumbled, sounding like a moody teenager. Work had always been my comfort zone, and I was resisting leaving it big-time.

Over the phone, I heard the tap-tap of fingernails on a hard surface, a sure sign that Miss Frankie was processing my response and formulating another argument. "What's the matter, sugar? Why does the idea of this party bother you so much?"

She knew me too well. "Besides the fact that I don't know anyone on the guest list?" I rubbed my forehead with the fingertips of one hand as if I could scrub away my nervousness. I had half a dozen solid objections to hosting this party, but Miss Frankie didn't really want to hear any of them. "It's just that it falls at such a bad time. This carnival thing is pretty overwhelming."

Miss Frankie gave a low chuckle. "Relax, sugar. Have fun with it. That's the whole point of carnival."

Relax. Have fun. This wasn't the first time she'd given me that advice. I rotated my head on my neck and tried to work out a few of the stress kinks. "I'll try," I said. But it wasn't that simple. I'd been raised by a master worrier. My uncle Nestor didn't know the meaning of the word *relax*, and he'd taught me everything I knew about stressing out. Part of me wanted to enjoy life more — I just didn't know how.

"Will you?"

"Of course."

Miss Frankie pretended to believe me and changed the subject. "By the way, did I tell you who phoned in an RSVP this morning?"

I stopped rolling my head. "This morning? I thought we turned in the final head count to the caterer two weeks ago."

"We did, but everyone knows that for a party like this, the final head count is just a guideline."

"Not *everyone*," I mumbled. We'd hired a caterer for the buffet, but Zydeco was supplying the King Cakes and I'd been relying on those figures to plan how many we'd need.

"I'm sure we'll have plenty of food," Miss Frankie said. "Nobody expects us to turn away a guest who calls at the last minute. Now, guess who it was."

I wasn't even going to try. "Who?"

"Ivanka Hedge."

The muscles in my neck tightened up again. Ivanka Hedge was one of the wealthiest young women in New Orleans, heir to the Lafitte perfume fortune. Just a week earlier, she'd announced her engagement to Richard Montgomery III, son of an obscenely wealthy businessman with international ties. His grandfather, Richard I, had founded the prestigious Terrebonne Academy, a private school open only to those with the right family background and sufficient money to afford the astronomical tuition. Academic accomplishment factored way below the right genealogy on the list of qualifications.

The city had been buzzing with wedding talk all week, and every business that was remotely tied to the wedding industry had been scrambling to offer their services for flowers, dresses, entertainment, china, silver, and of course, the various cakes they'd need.

At Zydeco, we'd been discussing the possibility of landing the wedding cake contract — a dream only slightly less ambitious than being hired on by the White House. For the past four days I'd tried countless times to reach Ivanka personally or, failing that, to set up an appointment through her assistant. For all my efforts, I had yet to even speak to a live person.

My heart did a little pitty-pat at the prospect of actually meeting Ivanka tonight. I nibbled at the carrot cake Miss Frankie was dangling in front of me. "Are you serious?"

"Would I lie to you?" she asked.

Only if she thought the means justified the end. "How did you manage to get her to come?"

"I have connections, sugar. The Montgomery men have belonged to Musterion for six generations. Richard is on the Parade Committee this year. I knew he and Ivanka were on the guest list, but I didn't want to say anything until I knew they were coming. So you see why you have to be here on time. This really is your chance to make a good impression."

Well. That ought to help me relax. No pressure at all.

I chewed on my bottom lip and argued with myself for a few seconds. Maybe I *could* leave work a few minutes early. Someone else on staff could stick around here to make sure all the orders were filled. My staff was competent and well trained. They didn't need me to hold their hands to make sure the work was done. And if leaving early would help me land the Hedge-Montgomery wedding contract, everyone at Zydeco would benefit. Win-win.

"Fine, I'll be there by seven," I said, making an executive decision. "Should I bring anything special with me?"

"Just your sunny personality." I could hear the triumphant smile in Miss Frankie's voice. "But don't keep the staff working too late. They're all on the guest list, too, and you know Philippe wouldn't want them to miss out."

She was right about that. Philippe had loved a good party more than almost anything else. If he'd still been alive, the whole bakery would have shut down early so the staff could get ready, even if he'd lost business as a result.

I'd always been more practical. It's not that I don't like a good party. I'm fun. I just believe that work should come first, especially in our current circumstances.

Zydeco's reputation had suffered a hit because of Philippe's death. We'd lost enough business to hurt our bottom line, and new orders had been slower to come in since I took over at the bakery's helm. I guess people were waiting to see whether I could maintain the high quality and creative genius Zydeco was known for.

Eventually people would realize that the quality of our work hadn't suffered. But until then, we'd have to rely even more than usual on the income we could make during Mardi Gras. Shutting the whole operation down early and losing walk-in customers wasn't an option I would consider.

I was trying to figure out a tactful way of saying so when Dwight Sonntag looked up from his work table and gave me the stink eye. He jerked his chin toward my own station, where the work was beginning to pile up. "Hey! Rita! A little help?"

I've known Dwight since pastry school in Chicago. He's a talented cake artist with a strict work ethic, but you'd never know that to look at him. He's six-foot-nothing with shaggy hair and an untidy beard, both tucked into sanitary netting when he's working. His clothes hang off his thin frame and he slouches through life looking as if he just rolled out of bed. But there was nothing casual about the frustration glinting in his hazel eyes this morning.

I held up a finger to indicate that I'd be finished in a minute and told Miss Frankie, "I have to go."

"Trouble?"

"Nothing I can't handle."

Since I took over at Zydeco I've tried to protect Miss Frankie from unpleasant reality whenever possible. Partly because losing her only son had left her vulnerable and — let's face it — a little unhinged. But also because my life is a lot easier when Miss Frankie doesn't know about every speed bump Zydeco encounters. If it's earth-shattering, I discuss it with her, but if I ran to her every time one of my eccentric, talented, and emotional staff members got upset, I'd never get anything else done.

A momentary silence fell between Miss Frankie and me, followed by a soft, resigned sigh. "Seven o'clock," she said again. "Don't be late."

Two

Knowing that Miss Frankie would call at least once more before the afternoon was over, I disconnected and stuffed my cell phone into the pocket of my white chef's jacket. As I turned toward the bank of sinks on the far wall, Ox, my second in command, appeared in the doorway leading to the bakery's front offices. He scanned the room looking for someone, and I had a feeling that someone was me.

Ox is a big man, a dead ringer for an African-American Mr. Clean. He's deeply committed to Zydeco and willing to do whatever it takes to make the business succeed. He also has the right breeding to work with our clientele. Known to his mother's highbrow friends as Wyndham Oxford III, he's far more comfortable at society events than I'll ever be. He bucked family tradition to attend pastry school, where Philippe and I met him, and he's in many ways my closest friend. Not that that stops him from trying to prove that he'd be a better choice than me to run Zydeco.

He spotted me and plunged into the chaos, making his way across the room with dogged determination. "Got a minute?" he asked when he reached me.

I shrugged and turned on the water, then squirted soap into my hands. I could feel Dwight glaring at me, but I wasn't in the mood to deal with both of them at the same time, so I avoided eye contact with him. "A minute? Sure," I told Ox. "You have sixty seconds, starting now. What's up?"

He didn't even twitch a lip at my little joke. "Edie tells me you haven't approved the content of the web page I sent you on Wednesday. Is there a problem?"

His question made my smile fade. I couldn't believe he wanted to talk about the website *now*. Couldn't he see how swamped we were?

I rinsed the soap from my hands and used my elbow to turn off the faucet. "No problem," I said, reaching for a paper towel, "unless you count the total lack of time. I'll get to it by the end of the week, I promise."

I'd been saying those last two words far too often lately, and I knew they'd catch up with me soon. In the meantime, I just kept running from crisis to crisis, putting out the biggest fire first and hoping I could get to the smaller ones before the flames got too high.

Wrinkles formed in Ox's usually smooth forehead, and his dark eyes turned stormy. "That web page is supposed to go live today. Or didn't you bother to look at the production schedule I e-mailed you last week?"

"I looked at it," I said.

And I *had.*

Okay. So I'd skimmed it the day he sent it to me and filed it away in a folder on my computer. The point is, I'd intended to go over it in detail. Later. When I had the time.

Which probably wouldn't be until Mardi Gras was over, Lent was in full swing, and I'd had time to recover from the nervous breakdown I could feel threatening to erupt.

I shot a pointed look at the commotion all around us. "Maybe you haven't noticed, but things are a little busy right now. I'll get to it as soon as I can."

Ox folded his arms across his chest. "The web designer is waiting for it now."

He was making me feel defensive and I *hate* feeling defensive. Last fall, I agreed to hire a couple of guys to create our web presence. They were young, talented, and eager to make their mark. Most important, since they were just starting out, they were relatively inexpensive. I'd left the rest to Ox, hoping that giving him lead on the project would smooth some of the feathers Miss Frankie had ruffled when she'd passed him over and chosen me to take over at Zydeco. So far, all it had done was make him more restless.

"We're paying those guys to wait," I pointed out. "It's their job."

Ox rolled his eyes. "Very professional attitude." He glanced at Dwight's workstation with a scowl. "You wouldn't be so busy if you'd just stuck with our original recipe, you know."

It was my turn to roll my eyes. Against Ox's advice, I'd added two additional varieties of King Cake to our menu this year. He was a purist, convinced that the only good King Cake was one without filling. A large portion of the New Orleans population agreed with him, but there were hundreds of thousands of potential clients who thought a little cream cheese–cinnamon or strawberry filling made the cake better. I happened to agree with them. So far, the new varieties were selling well — a fact that made me happy but stuck in Ox's craw.

"What are you saying?" I asked him. "That the only good changes around here are the ones *you* suggest?"

"Seems to me, you're the one who feels that way."

Like anything else, there are good things and bad about hiring friends. Our friendship means that he can sometimes finish my sentences and guess what I want even before I figure it out. It also means that the lines sometimes blur and Ox occasionally forgets which of us is in charge. We were getting nowhere fast with the finger-pointing, so I pulled us back to the original subject.

"Just explain the situation to the web guys," I said with a brittle smile. "They're from New Orleans. They know all about Mardi Gras. I'm sure they'll understand what we're up against."

Ox's eyebrows beetled over his deep-set eyes. "Approving the content for that page will take you fifteen minutes. Thirty, tops. It doesn't make sense to put it off when you could just do it now."

I dried my hands and returned to my workstation. "I already agreed to the initial launch of the bare-bones site on your timetable," I reminded him. "I need you to be content with that. Upgrading can come later. Right now, we have more important things to think about."

He gave me a look, which I ignored. "Such as?"

"I just found out that Ivanka Hedge and Richard Montgomery will be at the party tonight. I could use some help figuring out the best way to approach them and I'm behind here, as you can see. So instead of arguing with me, why don't you pull up a table and help? The sooner we fill all these orders, the sooner I can get to that page you're so worried about."

The sour look on Ox's face sweetened slightly. He wanted the Hedge-Montgomery wedding business as much as I did. "I have a wedding consult in fifteen minutes," he reminded me. "And I have to deliver the birthday party cake before six. Otherwise, I'd be glad to."

Which kind of proved my point. We were both too busy to be playing around with upgrades to the website. I breathed a silent sigh of relief, thinking that we'd put the website issue on the back burner for now. Allowing two hours with the future bride and groom, I guessed he'd finish the consult just in time to deliver the sculpted football helmet cake to a sports bar across town for a die-hard Saints fan's fiftieth birthday bash. That would put him back at Zydeco just in time to drive to the country club with a van full of King Cakes. That schedule left almost no time to bring up the website issue again until tomorrow.

But Ox wasn't finished yet. "Have you given the other matter any thought?"

My relief died a quick death, and that put a scowl on my face. Rather than snapping at Ox, I channeled my frustrations into rolling out one of the many balls of dough waiting for my attention into a long rope. "If you're asking about the blog, the answer's still no."

"Why am I not surprised? Just tell me one thing: Did you do what I suggested?"

I shook my head. "I haven't had time to read other blogs. Ask me again when Mardi Gras is over. We can revisit the idea then."

"Then will be too late," Ox said, leveling me with a look. "Have you read *any* of the e-mails I've sent you?"

"Of course." It was just a tiny white lie.

He perched on the edge of an unused table. "This is the hot season, Rita. We can only sell King Cakes for a few weeks every year, but we make seventy-five percent of our annual income during those weeks. With business down overall and the economy tanking, we need every advantage we can find."

I couldn't argue with that. "I understand,"

I began.

Ox went on before I could finish. "A bakery without an online storefront is practically obsolete in today's market. We should have launched the website when Zydeco opened."

I couldn't argue with that either. My almost-ex *had* been notoriously outdated. "That's why I agreed to launch the site to begin with," I pointed out. "I just didn't realize it was going to be so time-consuming. Can't we just push it off another six months? Get the site up and running when we're not so busy so that we're ready for next year?"

Ox shook his head. "That's not a good idea. Nobody looks for businesses in the phone directory anymore. Newspaper advertising is almost obsolete, and we're getting lost on the radio with all the other ads shouting over the top of us. If consumers want to find something these days, they go to the Internet. We need the site up and running now. This year. We can't afford to wait."

"But we *have* a page," I said. "It's working. Orders are coming in. Why can't we wait for the rest?"

His exasperation with me came out on a heavy sigh. "It's not enough to just put a static page on the Internet and hope for the best. We need updated content daily and a presence on the social networks driving traffic to the site. One of us should be tweeting and posting on Facebook every day."

He was passionate about the website, but lack of passion had never been an issue with Ox. Hoping he wasn't going to suggest that I be the one to start tweeting, I glanced toward the boxes stacked near the loading dock. "You really think we need more orders? Between our regular business and the King Cakes for Mardi Gras, we're barely keeping up as it is."

"Yes, I do." He sighed and rubbed his face with one hand. When he spoke again, his tone was a little less severe. "We're in danger of appearing way behind the times, especially since Gateaux just launched their new site. If we aren't competitive, we'll lose more market share than we already have."

He certainly knew which buttons to push. Dmitri Wolff, owner of Gateaux, a rival pastry shop, had been actively trying to put Zydeco out of business since we opened. He'd made a serious effort to buy out Miss Frankie, and he was still our biggest competitor.

I didn't want to make business decisions based on fear, but I could feel my resolve weakening. "Why can't we just make it up after Mardi Gras?" I said with a frown. "The quality of our specialty cakes should speak for itself."

Ox stood again and the corners of his mouth curved into a regretful smile. "I wish it did, but if we lose as much business as I think we will, it could take three or four years to recoup. We're not in a position to take a hit like that."

Logically I knew the drop in business after Philippe's murder wasn't my fault, but that didn't stop me from feeling responsible. My shoulders sagged and I gave in to the inevitable. "Fine," I said with a sigh. "I'll check out the content for the web page before I leave for the day. Will that make you happy?"

"Ecstatic," he said with a grin. "And the blog? You'll write one?"

I'd rather make a thousand buttercream roses using a sandwich bag, but the work was seriously starting to back up and I was the sticking point. "Fine. Okay? Just not *now*."

Triumph flashed in Ox's eyes. "Good."

Yeah. Whatever. He wasn't the one who had to come up with pithy, perky topics to write about several times a week. I made a face at him and shooed him away. "You only say that because you won. Now go. Get back to work. Do something creative and wonderful so I don't regret this moment of weakness."

He grinned. "Your wish is my command," he said as he turned to leave.

If only that were actually true.

THREE

I concentrated on rolling and braiding the rounds of dough that kept piling up in front of me. Within minutes, I was caught up in the rhythm of the work and some of my tension began to fade.

Working in the kitchen always helps me relax, and soon I'd destressed enough to enjoy the feel of dough under my fingers and the aromas of yeast and cinnamon that filled the air. After an hour or two, I was even feeling cautiously optimistic about my chances of being able to leave by six.

King Cakes aren't actually difficult to make and they're not especially time-consuming either — unless you're making several hundred at a time. Abe Cobb, Zydeco's baker, works during the wee hours of the morning while the rest of us sleep. He's not really a people person, so he likes it that way. Last night, while the cakes for our regular business orders baked and cooled, he had prepared enough dough to keep the rest of us busy all day. He'd spent hours scalding the milk, activating the yeast, mixing in cinnamon, nutmeg, vanilla, and lemon zest and then kneading and leaving the dough to rise in every available space until the rest of us arrived at daybreak.

Dwight, with his cap and beard mask, takes the next step in the process. When he's not sculpting a cake or working with fondant, he punches down the risen dough and kneads each ball until the dough is smooth and elastic. Then he sets it aside to rise a second time until it's doubled in size, a process that takes about ninety minutes.

And that's where I come in.

Between problem-solving and handling my other obligations, I divide each batch into three balls of equal size, then roll each one into a thin rope. I braid them together, forming each braid into a circle and pinching the ends to create a seal. Once I have a ring of braided dough, I insert the small plastic baby figurine, then place the cakes on baking sheets and slide them to the end of the table, where they rise for a third time, until the cakes are doubled in size. This time the wait is about thirty minutes. Once the cakes have risen, Estelle Jergens breaks away from her gum-paste work to transport each tray to the kitchen for baking. When they come out of the oven, she relays the baked cakes to the cooling racks.

Estelle is short and round, with a riot of red curls that escape every effort she makes to restrain them. At forty-something, she's also the oldest member of the staff. Carting all those cakes around has her moving in and out of the kitchen so quickly, I expect her to lose those forty pounds she's always complaining about by the time Mardi Gras is over.

Her third job is to carry the cooled cakes to Sparkle Starr's corner of the design center — a spot that somehow escapes the sun no matter what time of year it is. The location of Sparkle's workstation is no accident. I'm half convinced she'd turn to dust if the sunlight ever made direct contact. She's the daughter of aging hippie parents who raised their children in a commune long after the lifestyle went out of fashion. I'm still trying to figure out whether Sparkle's dour personality and her love of all things goth is natural or if she's in rebellion against a childhood of flower power and free love. Either way, the name doesn't fit the woman.

When I first met Sparkle, her pale complexion and pitch-black hair gave me the willies. But she was so cool and efficient on the job, not to mention extremely talented, I now hardly notice the piercings in her face or the dragon tattoo that appeared on her wrist two weeks ago.

This week she's spent most of her time creating dozens of carnations out of modeling chocolate for a wedding shower cake. In her spare time she drizzles glaze over each cooled King Cake, creating a decorative pattern unique to Zydeco and avoiding the puddles of glaze created by careless or hurried work. Any cake that doesn't meet her exacting standards is shuffled off for donation to one of the local soup kitchens or homeless shelters.

Once she's finished, Sparkle passes the cakes to Isabeau Pope for the final step in the production process. Isabeau's young, blond, and unfailingly perky. She's also Ox's girlfriend. In spite of predictions that they wouldn't last three months, their relationship is heading into its ninth month and seems to be flourishing. Which is fine with me, so long as it continues not to cause any ripples in the staff pool.

Isabeau has been hard at work making a garden of butterflies from sugar paste, royal icing, and sanding sugar for the tenth anniversary of a popular butterfly garden.

Every so often she breaks away to sprinkle purple, green, and gold-colored sugar over each King Cake in carefully measured stripes, then passes the cakes to a couple of the temporary workers I've hired to help out. The cakes are packed into colorfully decorated boxes along with a handful of plastic beads and cheap metal coins bearing the Zydeco logo. When the boxes are sealed, they're routed to stacks designated for shipping, local delivery, or walk-in clients.

It was a good system, established by Philippe when he first opened Zydeco. The work goes smoothly — as long as everyone does their part. Unfortunately, the interruptions that are so much a part of my day as boss often make me the weak link in the chain. I hate being the weak link, especially since I'm also still struggling to prove myself to the staff. Miss Frankie is always pushing me to step back from the actual hands-on work and spend my time supervising everyone else. But that's not why I went to pastry school, so I ignore her.

It was a little after two when Edie Bryce — another old pastry school classmate — came into the design center. Edie wasn't a success in the kitchen, but she's an organizational genius, which is why she's Zydeco's office manager. Her almond-shaped eyes •

were narrowed and she'd pulled the corner of her mouth between her teeth, two signs that she was worried about something.

But then, Edie worries almost as much as I do.

"Um . . . Rita? Got a minute?"

I pushed a baby into the cake in front of me. "Sure. What's up?"

She glanced over her shoulder toward the door she'd just come through. "I know you're busy, but there's somebody here to see you."

"Now?" I moved the finished cake out of my way and pulled an empty baking pan toward me. "I didn't see any consults on my calendar this morning," I said. "Did I miss something?" I knew full well I hadn't. Lately Edie's organized and color-coded schedule looked like someone had turned loose a kindergarten class with a year's supply of food coloring, but I checked and double-checked it so often, I knew I hadn't missed an appointment.

Edie shook her head and slid another worried glance at the door to her office. "You didn't miss anything. This isn't a client."

Zydeco isn't a traditional bakery with an open-door policy. Except for the King Cakes at Mardi Gras, our business is by appointment only, and Edie runs a very tight ship. Nobody gets past her, which made her request this afternoon highly unusual. I stopped rolling dough and looked at her. "You want me to talk to a walk-in?"

"Not exactly." She looked almost embarrassed.

Which made me nervous. "What's going on, Edie?"

"You have visitors. They're . . . family."

I made a face at her. "Very funny." Except for Miss Frankie, I have no family in New Orleans. My only blood relatives all live twelve hundred miles away in Albuquerque, New Mexico. Which meant my visitors had to be distant relatives of Miss Frankie's. But this wasn't the time or the place for an impromptu family reunion. "Just take care of whoever it is, okay? Explain that I'm busy."

"I don't think that's a good idea," Edie said, but that's as far as she got. The door behind her opened and a man with a stocky build and hair more salt than pepper stepped through. His skin was tough and wrinkled from years of worry and too much sun, and the corners of his mouth turned down in a scowl.

Uncle Nestor?

His eyes locked on mine and he boomed over the chaos, "What's all this, *mija*? Are you going to keep us waiting out there all day?"

My heart rose at the same time my stomach dropped. I was elated to see him. That went without saying. My uncle Nestor and aunt Yolanda had taken me in and raised me as their own after my parents died. But what was he doing in New Orleans? And why hadn't he told me he was coming?

FOUR

"Well, *mija?*" Uncle Nestor said again. "Are you going to stand there all day, staring at me?"

Hearing that familiar, gruff, lightly accented voice pulled me out of my stupor. My uncle is moody and opinionated, with a hair-trigger temper. He's also kind and compassionate — in his own stern way. Life with him is never boring, and I'd missed him horribly. It had been only a few months since I'd last seen my aunt and uncle, but it felt like years.

I abandoned my workstation and threw myself into his arms just as my aunt Yolanda appeared in the open doorway. Her chocolate brown hair was cut in a choppy style that made her look younger than ever, and her dark eyes were full of love — the kind I imagine a mother might feel for her daughter.

I'd talked with them at least once a week

since I moved to New Orleans, but seeing them again made me realize how worried I'd been that they were angry or disappointed with me for leaving New Mexico last summer and then staying in New Orleans for the Christmas holidays.

"I tried to convince him to wait out front for you," Aunt Yolanda said with a fond scowl in her husband's direction. "But you know how he is."

Did I ever. Uncle Nestor is strong-willed and stubborn and nobody can tell him anything, but at that moment I didn't care. I hugged them both tightly and stepped away to look them over again. "What are you doing here? Why didn't you call?"

"Call?" Uncle Nestor's voice was so gruff, a few of the staff members stopped working to look at us. "What? We can't spend a weekend with our favorite niece without an appointment?"

"Of course you can," I said quickly. But as the first flush of excitement over seeing them faded, the reality of my work schedule began to hit me. "It's not that. It's just . . . well . . . it's nearly Mardi Gras and we're swamped. I don't know how much time I'll be able to spend with you." I owed them both so much, I wouldn't have hurt their feelings for anything in the world. Plus, I

41

could count on one finger the number of times Uncle Nestor had left his restaurant in someone else's hands since he'd opened its doors — the fact that he'd obviously left it to come all this way was significant.

But they weren't staying long. He'd said *the weekend*, right? Surely I could squeeze in some quality time with them over the next couple of days.

"We didn't come here to be a bother," Aunt Yolanda assured me. "Do what you need to do. We'll see you when we can."

That should have made me feel better, but instead it raised the question for me of why they *had* come unannounced. Why this weekend? Why not for Mardi Gras itself?

Uncle Nestor waved a hand over his head to indicate that he agreed with her, but his attention had been captured by the work going on all around us. "I had no idea your operation was so big, *mija*."

Coming from anyone else, that might have been a compliment. Uncle Nestor managed to make it sound like an accusation. And that left me squirming inside with guilt. I hated feeling as if I needed to defend myself, so I tamped down the urge and said, "It's not usually like this."

Uncle Nestor pursed his lips and clasped his hands behind his back, walking between the tables like a general inspecting his troops. But that only made my irritation flare. He had a habit of taking over whenever he walked into a room, but these were *my* troops. Not his. I was still trying to establish my authority here. I didn't want anything to make me appear weak.

Uncle Nestor stopped at Isabeau's table, raising his eyebrows at the multicolored sugar that had fallen to the floor. After a moment he moved on, this time stopping in front of Dwight and running a look over his wrinkled shirt and threadbare jeans. "What's all this?" he asked, but I wasn't sure whether he was talking about the work or Dwight's appearance.

To my relief, Dwight didn't seem to notice his disapproval. "King Cakes," he said without looking up. "Big tradition in these parts."

"I know what a King Cake is," Uncle Nestor said. "But so many?"

I explained what Ox and I had discussed earlier about the bulk of our business coming from these flaky cakes, which earned a surprised grunt. "Right now we're making around two hundred a day," I explained. "We'll be making at least that many every day for the next week or so."

Aunt Yolanda moved closer and touched

43

my arm. "We've come at a bad time. I knew we should have called first."

I didn't want her to feel guilty, so I grinned, trying for a carefree effect. "It's fine. Really! I'm so glad to see you nothing else matters."

She grimaced. Hard. Which told me I'd gone a little over the top with that last bit.

Uncle Nestor completed his inspection and turned back toward me with his hands on his hips. "So, this is what you left us for."

I shifted a little under the weight of his stare and Aunt Yolanda's scowl and wished they'd chosen to show up on a day when the work proceeded in an orderly and controlled fashion. A day when I looked competent and organized and when dirty dishes weren't piled everywhere waiting for Estelle's nieces to come in after school and load the dishwashers.

"You know why I stayed here," I said. "Miss Frankie needed me." It was a cop-out. I knew it, and so did he. I squared my shoulders and took a more adult approach. "And it was a good chance to strike out on my own. All that money you spent on my education would have been wasted if I'd stayed in Albuquerque."

"Ha!" he said to Aunt Yolanda. "There we have it." Irritation settled like a storm cloud in his dark eyes. "If there was something wrong with working for me, I'd like to know what it was."

"There's nothing wrong with it," I assured him. "Agave is a wonderful restaurant. But if that's what you wanted for me, why did you send me to pastry school?"

"So you could use those skills in *my* kitchen."

"I worked at Agave for two years after Philippe and I separated. I was still doing prep work for other chefs when I left."

He waved off my argument with a flick of his wrist. "Patience, *mija*. Everything doesn't have to happen at once." As if he'd settled that, he put his hands in his pockets, rocked back on his heels, and changed the subject. "Where is Miss Frankie anyway? I'd like to say hello."

"She's at home," I told him, "but I'm sure she'll be thrilled to see you again." Relieved that we'd moved on, I gave him an affectionate nudge with one shoulder. "Come on. Admit it. You're impressed by what you see here."

Uncle Nestor snorted and turned away. "I suppose it's all right." Which in Uncle Nestor–speak is the equivalent of "It's fabulous!" from anyone else. "You're making a mistake to let your people leave so

45

much clutter lying around," he said. "Organization is the key to success."

"Nestor . . ." Aunt Yolanda warned. "You promised."

He growled, but when he spoke again, his voice was a little less brusque. "Your aunt missed you at Christmas. So did the boys."

Meaning my four burly cousins, all of whom were grown and could hardly be considered "boys."

"I missed you, too," I said, hoping he wouldn't rehash the arguments we'd had over my decision to stay in New Orleans with Miss Frankie.

"We could have done with a few more pictures."

"I'll be better about that from now on," I promised. "What are your plans for this evening? Are you free? There's a party I have to go to . . ." I wasn't sure that I wanted Uncle Nestor grumpy-facing it at the Captain's Court, but surely he'd snap out of his mood before then. Besides, not inviting them would be rude, and I liked the idea of having two more people I actually knew among the guests.

Uncle Nestor looked at me as if I'd lost my sense. "We're here to see you, *mija*. We're doing whatever you're doing."

Aunt Yolanda nodded. "We know you're

busy. Would you rather give us your key and let us take a cab to get settled in?"

My key?

It took a couple of seconds for her meaning to register. When it did, my stomach rolled over. Omigod, of course they planned to stay at my place. I'd told them all about my beautiful new home (which I'd inherited from Philippe), and had thrown out the invitation for them to come and stay with me anytime — never really imagining they'd take me up on it. At least not without notice.

A mental image of the mound of dirty laundry on my bedroom floor raced through my head, along with the breakfast dishes piled in the sink. And the empty take-out containers from the Thai restaurant next door sitting on the table from last night's dinner. What can I say? Lately I was home just long enough to make a mess, not long enough to clean it up.

And now I had houseguests, one of whom would have a field day pointing out everything I was doing wrong. I spent a few seconds pondering my options. Stay and work like a responsible adult, or scurry home and hide my mess before Uncle Nestor spotted it. There really wasn't any question. I'd rather face half a dozen angry pastry chefs than disappoint my uncle.

As I unbuttoned my chef's jacket, I sensed Dwight tensing with disapproval, but I ignored him and tossed my jacket over an empty chair. I delegated the most pressing jobs and promised to be back as soon as humanly possible, then rushed out the back door to make sure the car was clean before Uncle Nestor got into it.

I almost wondered what else could go wrong today, but I stopped myself just in time. I was afraid I'd get an answer.

FIVE

As soon as we arrived at the house, I hustled Aunt Yolanda and Uncle Nestor into my second-floor guest room, and while they unpacked their suitcases, I stuffed dishes into the dishwasher and carted trash outside to the bin. I used the Swiffer on the kitchen floor, put fresh towels in the guest bath, and hid dirty clothes in my closet.

The rest of the clutter was almost tolerable, but I still couldn't relax as I showed them through the place. It really is a magnificent house, and I was surprised by how much I wanted them to approve, even as I waited for Uncle Nestor to notice a dust bunny or spot a cobweb. Along with the house, I'd inherited Philippe's substantial bank account and the Mercedes parked on the street. I was slowly getting used to my new lifestyle, but I worried that Uncle Nestor would think it all too ostentatious.

Aunt Yolanda gushed over everything, but

Uncle Nestor grumbled about the stairs he had to climb, the view from the guest bedroom, and the fact that the heater turned on twice while we were there. He'd forgotten batteries for the portable cassette player that lulled him to sleep at night, and apparently New Orleans didn't have a radio station that would satisfy him. His earphones weren't working properly, and the hangers in my closet would leave creases in his pants.

Once I'd left them getting settled and was driving back to Zydeco, I found myself wondering whether time and distance had dulled my memory, or if Uncle Nestor really was grumpier than he used to be. Not that it mattered. Whatever had brought on this foul mood of his was beside the point. I reminded myself that I could tolerate anything for a weekend, and tried to feel optimistic about taking him to the party. Everything would be fine.

Back at Zydeco, I put my family concerns on the back burner and spent the rest of the afternoon trying to work hard enough to make up for my absence. Ox got stuck in traffic trying to reach the birthday venue, so at least I didn't have to take any grief from him. I felt so guilty about abandoning the staff, I changed my mind about closing up early, which went a long way toward gaining me points with them, even if it set us back further on orders. But Dwight was all sharp edges and disapproving looks until the minute we loaded the King Cakes into the van and sent him to the country club, locking the bakery doors behind us.

I was feeling extra prickly myself, trying hard to *laissez les bons temps rouler* but coming up short. It's hard to let the good times roll when you know for certain you'll be paying the price tomorrow for the choices you've made today. I was also nervous about meeting Ivanka Hedge and planning what I'd say when I did. I mentally ran over the outfit I planned to wear, second-guessing the halter neckline, the pleated bodice, and the beaded design at the waist. Were they as flattering as I'd imagined when I bought the dress?

Not that I could do anything about it. I had nothing else even remotely suitable in my closet, and no time to shop. But that didn't stop me from fussing over my choices.

By seven o'clock, as I climbed the sweeping front steps of The Shores with my aunt and uncle, my nerves were stretched taut and ready to snap. I'd been here with Miss Frankie a couple of times, but never for such a large-scale event. Definitely not for an event people might later connect with me and, by extension, Zydeco. I could score in a big way for the bakery if everything went well tonight, but what were the chances of that? I was exhausted, and my new strappy black sandals were already making my feet hurt. I'm not used to wearing heels.

I took a deep breath and let it out slowly to steady my nerves. For months I'd been looking forward to showing off my new life to Uncle Nestor and Aunt Yolanda, but now that they were here, I wondered what they'd think of it. Would they enjoy themselves at the party or would they be miserable all evening? Should I have come earlier to help set up the serving station? And what if Ivanka Hedge didn't show up after all? Would I get another chance to land the all-important contract?

Aunt Yolanda, looking elegant in a pair of black silk pants and a beaded top I'd loaned her, stared at the clubhouse as if she'd never seen anything like it. She probably hadn't. The clubhouse at The Shores is a three-story building that could have been ripped off the set of *Gone with the Wind*. Fronted by a circular drive of crushed oyster shells and backed by acres of lush green lawn, tennis courts, and an Olympic-sized swimming pool with views of the club's world-class golf course, it was way out of our league. The whole area whispers money, history, and long-standing tradition. Though I'm getting more comfortable here, I still sometimes struggle with a sense of inadequacy. I suspected Uncle Nestor was having the same reaction.

While a uniformed valet disappeared with the car, Uncle Nestor climbed the stairs behind us, his hands in his pockets, his shoulders hunched, scowling at everything we passed. The air was cool and dry, lightly perfumed by the flowers blooming on nearby azalea bushes. It was a nearly perfect evening, but Uncle Nestor couldn't even let himself enjoy it.

When I was a girl, we never went a month without worrying how all the utilities and the rent would be paid. Even if we met those basic needs, we were never sure there'd be enough left over for groceries. Uncle Nestor and Aunt Yolanda had worked long hours to make ends meet, leaving my cousins and me alone a lot as we grew older. My aunt and uncle had never once hinted that I was a burden, but I'd secretly suspected that the extra person to feed and clothe — a girl, no less, who couldn't even wear their sons' hand-me-downs — had been the tipping point in their budget.

Aunt Yolanda had taken our circumstances in stride, praising God for blessings she hadn't yet received and urging us to do the same. But Uncle Nestor had gone down a different path. He'd taken those early hardships as a sign of failure, believing that his circumstances were a punishment for some sin he never talked about. Even now, with Agave a success, he walked through life as uncomfortable with his current good fortune as he was in the suit I'd pulled for him from the spare closet where I'd put Philippe's clothes. My poor uncle spent his days just waiting for God to throw the next big roadblock in his path.

I'd fallen somewhere in the middle, unable to rise to Aunt Yolanda's level of faith but not as negative as Uncle Nestor either. I'd found joy in the kitchen as the boys and I scraped together creative meals from the meager contents of our cupboards. Those early days had sparked my love of cooking. Which was actually a little miracle, I guess. It could so easily have gone the other way.

"I didn't realize Miss Frankie was so well off," Aunt Yolanda whispered, pulling me back to the moment.

"She has money," I said, "but it hasn't gone to her head. She's as down-to-earth as they come."

Uncle Nestor eyed the club's broad veran-dah with suspicion. "Family money?"

"Some of it," I said. "I'm not entirely sure where it all comes from."

He gave me a raised-brow look. "You haven't asked? Or she won't tell?"

"I haven't asked."

He huffed and turned away, and my nerve endings tingled. I wasn't imagining it. He really did seem more caustic than he used to be, but why was that? Was he that angry at me for moving to New Orleans?

There was nothing I could do about it now, so I ignored him and took up the conversation with Aunt Yolanda. "You remember how Miss Frankie was at the wedding, don't you?"

"Utterly charming," Aunt Yolanda agreed.

"And completely genuine," I assured her. "I know you'll like her when you get to know her better."

Aunt Yolanda smiled. "Don't worry so much, Rita. I'm sure we'll like your new friends."

"She's not worried about us liking them," Uncle Nestor groused from behind us. "She's worried they won't like us."

That was so unfair! I turned toward him with a scowl. "That's not true. The people coming tonight aren't exactly friends of mine. Their opinions don't matter." I hesitated on the threshold, taking in the long central corridor lined with glass trophy cases and an impressive library. I could hear the muted sounds of activity coming from somewhere in the back, but the hushed silence that greeted us told me we were one of the first to arrive. That ought to make Miss Frankie happy.

I swallowed my feelings of inadequacy and kept talking to Uncle Nestor as if I weren't battling a giant case of nerves. "Other than the staff at Zydeco, I've probably only met a handful of these people for about thirty seconds at Philippe's funeral. I have no idea what I'll talk about with any of them. I'm a little nervous about that, but there's also a chance that I can make a good impression on some important potential clients tonight. If I'm distracted and edgy, that's why. It has nothing to do with you."

Aunt Yolanda gave me an encouraging hug. "You're an intelligent woman and you have a great sense of humor. You can talk to them about absolutely anything. Don't you dare let anyone make you feel inferior."

I smiled and hugged her back. "Thanks, *Tía*. You always know just what to say. I don't expect you and Uncle Nestor to hang around here all night. If you get tired or bored, just say the word. I'll call a cab so you can go back to my place."

With a soft snort, Uncle Nestor said, "You stay, I stay."

Great. I wasn't worried about Aunt Yolanda. She could hold her own in any social situation, but I wondered if Uncle Nestor would have trouble finding common ground with the other guests in his current mood. He seemed determined to be offended.

I didn't have time to dwell on my concerns, because at that moment Miss Frankie swept into the foyer, greeting us all with her warm, honey-coated smile. She's several inches taller than I am and thin as a rail. Even thinner since Philippe's death. Her chestnut hair had been teased, styled, and sprayed, and the sequins and beads adorning her outfit gleamed in the glow of the crystal chandeliers overhead.

She hugged me briefly, then tugged me inside. "Thank the good Lord you're here. I was beginning to get worried." Without missing a beat, she turned her smile on Aunt Yolanda and Uncle Nestor. "And how nice to have the two of you here! Isn't this wonderful? I was thrilled when Rita called to let me know you'd be joining us."

That was exactly the reaction I'd been

counting on from her.

Miss Frankie snagged Uncle Nestor's arm and led him down the marble-floored corridor toward the staircase that led to the second-floor ballroom. "Rita tells me you surprised her this afternoon. Isn't that fun? I just love surprises, don't you?"

Uncle Nestor has never liked being on the receiving end of a surprise, but he went along without argument and even managed a smile of sorts, which I took as a good sign. Aunt Yolanda and I climbed the stairs behind them and followed them through an archway created by two massive gold-sequined saxophones into the club's ballroom, where dozens of round tables had been covered in crisp white tablecloths and positioned facing the long rectangular table where the krewe's highest-ranking officials would sit. Feathered and sequined carnival masks, strings of beads, and Mardi Gras–themed confetti spilled down the center of each table. Huge vases of cut flowers, each decorated with a different musical instrument, stood between support posts swathed in yards of shimmering white satin and twinkling white lights.

Uncle Nestor gave a little gasp of surprise.

Which Miss Frankie mistook for approval. "Don't you love it? The krewe's theme this year is 'Jazz Hot.' Just wait until the band starts playing. This place will really come to life then."

I was pretty sure Uncle Nestor didn't *love* it, but I was distracted by the mouthwatering aromas that filled the air, reminding me that I'd skipped lunch . . . again. I often get so wrapped up in my work that I forget to eat. My stomach rumbled and I thought about the menu Miss Frankie and I had spent days planning. I could look forward to bacon-wrapped jalapeños stuffed with cheese, crab cakes fried golden brown and served with a creamy lemon-dill sauce, hot and spicy jambalaya, garlic cheese grits, mounds of fresh shrimp accompanied by spicy cocktail and remoulade sauces, loaves of crusty French bread and beignets, and an assortment of desserts, the highlight of which would be the King Cakes that Dwight should have delivered by now.

I made a mental note to check on the cakes after my aunt and uncle were settled. At Ox's urging, I'd delegated the tasks of cutting and serving the cake tonight, and now I was really glad I'd listened to him. Putting Isabeau and Sparkle in charge of the cake service would give me one less thing to think about, especially with Aunt Yolanda and Uncle Nestor here, but I still wanted to make sure the cakes had arrived safely and that someone was on top of the setup.

I was so caught up in my thoughts that I almost plowed into Uncle Nestor's back before I realized that he'd stopped walking. He paused just inside the archway to look around, and the smile on his face faded bit by bit.

"Nice digs," he said when he realized we were all looking at him. "But it's a little out of our league. Wouldn't you say, Yolanda?"

Aunt Yolanda laughed, smoothing over his comments with her customary grace. "It's beautiful. And looks like so much fun. Have you been a member of the club long?"

"All my life," Miss Frankie said. "My mother's people have been part of The Shores for as long as this building has been standing."

"How lovely," Aunt Yolanda said. "Roots are so important. I hope it's all right for us to join you and your friends this evening. Rita assured us we wouldn't be in the way."

"In the way?" Miss Frankie looked astonished at the very idea. "You're family. How could you be in the way?"

Uncle Nestor tugged at the knot in his tie. "Thanks for having us," he said in a flat voice, "but we don't belong here."

60

"Neither do half the people on the guest list," Miss Frankie said with a laugh. "This is just an informal little get-together for the krewe's board members, the people who've run the committees all year and their spouses. A chance to blow off steam before the work begins in earnest and to honor those who've been so busy behind the scenes. I'm thrilled as can be that you're here, and everyone else will be, too."

Aunt Yolanda ran a glance over the elaborate decorations, the long table laden with dishes for the buffet at the far end of the room, a small four-person jazz band tuning up in one corner, and half a dozen waiters milling about near the kitchen. "This is informal?"

Miss Frankie followed her gaze and laughed again. "We like to do things up big here in the South. It all looks more impressive than it is. Now, why don't the two of you have a seat? I'll have someone bring you some drinks while Rita and I run over a few last-minute details."

"Good idea," I said. "I'd like to talk to you about Ivanka Hedge before she gets here."

"We'll get to that in a minute," Miss Frankie said. She led Aunt Yolanda to a seat near the captain's table and motioned for

Uncle Nestor to sit by his wife. He hesitated for a moment before taking a seat, probably looking for the plastic cover to keep stains away.

He finally planted himself on a chair and Miss Frankie motioned for me to follow her as she went in search of a waiter. She has more energy than most women half her age. I had to quick-step to keep up with her, and that wasn't easy in my new sandals. She tossed off instructions as we walked. "I'll try to stick with you as much as possible in the beginning, but don't worry if I slip away. You'll be just fine. Everyone will love you."

"I'm not worried about that," I said, trying not to breathe hard. "I'd like to get your take on the best way to approach Ivanka when she gets here."

Miss Frankie stopped a waiter and sent him to check on Aunt Yolanda and Uncle Nestor before responding to me. "You're just meeting the woman, sugar. You're not cinching a deal. Be personable. Be charming. Be approachable. And don't talk business. With anyone. You promised, remember?"

"I remember," I said, and I *would* try, although I had no intention of forgetting my responsibilities completely. But Miss Frankie didn't need to know that. I'd slip away occasionally to make sure things were running smoothly and she'd be none the wiser.

I must have seemed sincere, because she patted my cheek affectionately and swept an arm to encompass the massive room and all the decorations. "Now, what do you think? How does it look?"

We passed a bank of windows that looked out over the expansive grounds and terraced gardens, where thousands of tiny white lights gave the place an almost magical appearance. "Everything looks great and smells even better. You've done an incredible job."

"Thank you, sugar." Miss Frankie beamed with pride. "That's music to my ears."

"I don't know why you keep insisting that I should pretend to be the hostess tonight. You've done all the work. You should get the credit."

She laughed and started walking again. "That's nonsense. It's your party. I was just happy to help, especially now that your uncle and aunt are here. This will be a great chance for them to see you shine."

I wondered whether Uncle Nestor would appreciate any shining I might do, but before either of us could say more, we heard footsteps and chatter, warning us that new arrivals were heading our way. Miss Frankie clapped her hands with excitement and signaled the band to start the music as she pressed me into duty. "Your guests are arriving, sugar. Shoulders back. Head high. Put a smile on your face. And remember to relax. Tonight's all about having fun. Don't you waste a minute being concerned about your aunt and uncle. I'll make sure they're taken care of."

Relax. Right. I lifted my chin and put a smile on my face, but leaving worry behind was a whole lot easier to say than do.

SIX

I spent the next two hours watching for Ivanka Hedge's arrival and experiencing a little dip of disappointment every time someone who wasn't Ivanka came through the sparkling saxophones. I met the guest of honor, Musterion's captain, and his wife, along with the krewe's first and second lieutenants and more of Philippe's friends than I could possibly count. I struggled to connect names and faces with the brief histories Miss Frankie had been sharing with me for the past few weeks, and did my best to remember who'd served on which committee, especially those who'd worked on the Social Committee with Philippe.

I heard countless stories about Philippe's life before we met and more about his life after we separated. Some were charming and amusing. Some made me nostalgic for the early days of our relationship, and some made me wonder how well I'd really known him.

Little by little, most of the staff from Zydeco drifted into the party. Dwight came in first, wearing what passes for formal wear with him — a clean pair of threadbare black pants and a white shirt that looked as if it had been wadded in the bottom of a laundry basket for a month. I saw raised eyebrows as he came through the archway, but he'd knotted a tie — so wide and old-fashioned it must have come from Goodwill — around his neck, and I guess that was enough to put him on the right side of the club's rigid dress code for one night.

He was followed quickly by Sparkle and Estelle. Sparkle wore a dark purple gown with a tight-fitted corset and black ribbon lacing, which she'd paired with lace-up high-heeled boots. Estelle had also cleaned up nicely. In fact, she looked amazing in a silk turquoise sheath and loose-fitting silk jacket. I was pretty sure the outfits had put a hefty dent in both their budgets, which just proved how important Mardi Gras was to the people around here.

Wearing an expression that clearly said, "Don't talk to me," Sparkle settled at a corner table with a glass of champagne, while Estelle drifted from group to group, greeting people she knew. Ox and Isabeau showed up next. After spending the afternoon stuck in traffic, he made a beeline for the alcohol. She headed straight for my aunt and uncle, earning major brownie points and my undying gratitude in the process. Only Abe was missing, but that didn't surprise me. A party like this would have been hell for him.

By nine o'clock, my mind was a blur of details and my feet were killing me — and there was still no sign of Ivanka Hedge. Aunt Yolanda seemed to be making new friends, which didn't surprise me. Slightly more surprising was the realization that after a second (or maybe a third) beer, Uncle Nestor had actually stopped baring his teeth at people. Maybe things were actually looking up.

After the first hour Miss Frankie started drifting away, leaving me on my own for long stretches at a time. When she wasn't at my side, she floated from one group of guests to another, greeting old friends with exuberant hugs and kisses and looking interested in what everyone had to say. I tried to follow her lead — minus the physical displays of affection — but I was so far out of my comfort zone, my head felt as if someone had put it in a vise.

Wishing for some ibuprofen, I snagged a fruity Riesling from a passing waiter and sipped gratefully. The wine danced across my tongue and the burst of flavor I experienced as I swallowed made me want more. I drained the glass quickly and contemplated the wisdom of a second. Many of the guests were showing obvious signs of inebriation, and the noise level created by all that music, conversation, and laughter confined in one room had risen to deafening levels as a result. I didn't want to go overboard with the wine, but a pleasant buzz might ease the ache in my head and even help me relax.

And that *was* the goal, right?

I left my empty glass on a tray and joined the line of guests waiting to place their drink orders. To my relief, the bartenders were fast, and less than ten minutes later I turned back toward the crowd, running a quick glance over the King Cake service station as I did. I hadn't had a chance to thoroughly check out the setup, but with Miss Frankie otherwise occupied and a free moment of my own, this seemed like the perfect opportunity.

Miss Frankie's warning to relax rang in my ears as I wound my way through the crowd toward two long tables draped in white and covered with confetti. The largest King Cake we'd made sat on the table amid the decorations, waiting for Musterion's captain to perform the ritual cake cutting at the stroke of midnight. At the far end of the table, rows of silverware waited beside stacks of napkins that had been arranged in an artistic twist. The rest of the cakes should be in the kitchen, where the kitchen staff would cut and plate them so the waitstaff could deliver them at the appropriate time.

Reassured that everything was in order, I started to turn away. But as my eyes glanced off the stacks of napkins for the second time, I realized that something was wrong. I moved in for a closer look, telling myself the missing Zydeco logo was probably just a trick of the dim lighting. But even when I stood directly over the stack of napkins, I couldn't make that cartoon alligator standing next to the outline of a wedding cake appear.

I didn't know whether to be worried or irritated over the omission. I'd spent a substantial chunk of money on those napkins, figuring they'd work as a subtle form of advertising, and Estelle had assured me that she'd talked with the club's kitchen manager about using them tonight. I knew the box had been in the van with Dwight when he pulled away from Zydeco, so why weren't they on the table?

I glanced around for Estelle or Dwight, hoping one of them could tell me what had gone wrong. I couldn't find either in the crowd, so I decided to check with the kitchen manager myself.

I know, I know. I'd promised Miss Frankie that I wouldn't work, but I couldn't just ignore the problem. And anyway, how long could it take to swap out the napkins? Five minutes? Ten? Even Miss Frankie couldn't complain about that.

After checking to make sure she wasn't watching me, I slipped through the crowd and pushed through the doors I'd seen the waitstaff using all evening. Behind the scenes, the corridors were brightly lit and bustling with the activity that made me feel at home in a way the high-society crowd in the ballroom couldn't.

I followed a line of waiters bearing empty trays along a short corridor and rode the service elevator to the ground floor, drawing up in front of the kitchen just as a heavyset man backed through a set of swinging doors pulling a cart loaded with silver serving trays full of food for the buffet. He was watching his load so intently he almost flattened me in the process.

I jumped back and put out a hand to keep him from plowing right over me. "Hey! Watch out!"

He shot a look over his shoulder that was steely enough to sharpen knives. He looked harried and irritated, and ready to bite my head off. It was an expression I knew well. One I'd seen on Uncle Nestor's face many times when he was working. I'm pretty sure others had seen the same look on my face. When he realized that I wasn't one of his coworkers, he made a visible effort to rein in his temper and even managed a thin smile. "Sorry, ma'am, but you shouldn't be here. This area is for staff only."

I smiled back to show there were no hard feelings. "I understand, and I hate interrupting when you're obviously busy, but there's a problem with the King Cake serving station. Could you tell me where to find the kitchen manager?"

He released his grip on the cart and straightened slowly. "What kind of problem?"

"The napkins are wrong."

He looked confused. "Excuse me?"

"The napkins," I said again. "Someone has put the wrong ones out."

The irritation he'd wiped away just seconds earlier came back with a vengeance,

71

along with a look that said he considered himself several rungs higher up the ladder than me. "I personally checked that service station earlier. Everything was fine."

I tried not to squirm under the weight of his superior expression. I wasn't that frightened little Hispanic girl from the wrong side of town anymore, and I refused to let him make me feel that I was. "I'm not trying to make more work for you," I said, still determined to play nice. "And I don't want to hold you up when it's obvious you're busy. If you could just tell me where to find the kitchen manager, I'll take care of it myself."

He held out a hand, fingers splayed, as if he was trying to avoid touching something nasty. "I *am* the kitchen manager."

Peachy.

I gripped his cool, limp hand and gave it a firm shake. "Well, then, I guess you're the man I'm looking for. I'm Rita Lucero, the hostess for tonight's party. Could you tell me where to find the box of napkins I had delivered this afternoon? They're embossed with Zydeco's logo."

With a put-upon sigh, the manager started pushing the cart toward the service elevator. "I'm sure they were delivered, but the staff set up that serving station using the

72

club's napkins. That's our usual practice. You understand. It's club policy."

I'm pretty sure my mouth fell open. "Seriously? You have a napkin policy?"

He gave me a tight-lipped smile. "My hands are tied. I'm sure you can use your napkins for some other event."

Maybe, but that wasn't the point. I was 95 percent sure he was lying to me because he didn't want to be bothered, and that just made me angry. Perhaps I should have just let it go, but there was a principle involved. And some pride.

"Obviously there's been a misunderstanding," I said, "but I'm sure you and I can clear it up easily."

The elevator bell dinged softly and the manager gave his cart a nudge, positioning it so I'd have a hard time getting on the elevator. "Not if it means you interfere with the work my staff has done." The doors swished open and he maneuvered the cart inside. "Look, Ms. . . . Whatever. If the napkins you're so worried about were delivered, I'm sure they're here somewhere. I'll make sure they're returned to you when the evening is over. There's no need for you to worry. Just relax and enjoy the party." With that he pulled the cart into the elevator behind him, still blocking the door. An instant later, the doors swished closed, leaving me staring at my very angry reflection in the shiny metal.

SEVEN

I counted to ten as the elevator carrying the kitchen manager climbed to the upper floors. I didn't want to make waves and put Zydeco in a bad light, but the man's condescending attitude and his refusal to honor our agreement had my blood boiling.

Counting to ten didn't help, but it never had. The time for negotiating was over. I was determined to find those napkins and deliver them to the King Cake station as originally planned. Still seething, I tried every door in that long corridor in case someone had tossed the napkins into a storage room. When that failed to yield results, I stopped a passing waiter and asked directions to the club's service entrance, reasoning that Dwight had probably put the box back in the van when that annoying manager refused delivery.

When the waiter directed me to a narrow hallway on the far side of the kitchen, my irritation jumped a few degrees higher. The club had a policy for napkins, but not for security? I was more convinced than ever that the kitchen manager had lied to me — and I *hate* being lied to.

A few minutes later, I let myself out the back door and headed toward Zydeco's van, parked beneath a solitary streetlamp on the far side of the employee lot. The night was surprisingly chilly, but it felt so good to step away from the craziness inside and breathe the cool, fresh air that I took my time walking toward the van. By the time I reached it, I'd calmed down enough to register that I didn't have my keys.

Terrific.

On the off chance that Dwight had left me a way in, I checked every door on the van, but I was out of luck. Dwight had locked up securely.

A less irritated woman might have given up at that point, but the stubborn streak I'd inherited from my mother kept me going. Cupping my hands around my eyes to block the light, I scoured the inside of the van. Sure enough, the box was there, nestled behind the driver's seat. I swore under my breath and made another circuit, as if I thought one of the doors might have unlocked itself by magic.

All my life I'd struggled with a sense of inadequacy. It had taken years to get it under control, and I hated how quickly it could rise up to haunt me. The kitchen manager's patronizing attitude had infused those napkins with special meaning. Come hell or high water, I was going to get them on the table before midnight.

I hurried back across the parking lot, calculating how much time it would take me to find my keys, retrieve the box, and replace the napkins. Distracted, I tugged on the door I'd come out of a few minutes earlier, but my hand slid off the handle and the door stayed shut. Paying closer attention, I tried again but the door still didn't open. I tried again. And again. Eventually pulling so hard I broke two fingernails, but the door didn't budge an inch.

"You have *got* to be joking," I muttered to myself, stepping off the pavement into a flowerbed so I could see through a window. That narrow corridor stretched away toward the kitchen, but the waiters and kitchen staff who'd been rushing around a few minutes ago had disappeared completely. Reasoning that they couldn't have gone far, I banged on the door a couple of times.

Nothing.

I shouted for help.

Nada.

With my mood deteriorating rapidly, I finally conceded that I wasn't going to get back inside through that door and set off in search of another way inside.

The grounds were brightly lit on the other side of the building, the side where members and their guests were coming and going, but the employees didn't fare so well. Shrubs and bushes that had appeared lush and green in the daylight now cast deep shadows across the sidewalk and lawn, and only a couple of security lamps in the parking lot helped to chase away the gloom.

The cool air that had seemed so inviting before had grown uncomfortably cold and I shivered as I walked, cursing the kitchen manager for the locked door and my lack of a sweater or jacket. Logical? No. But by that time I was ready to blame him for just about everything that had gone wrong.

My feet cramped in the strappy little sandals and the hem of my skirt grew damp from brushing the grass. After what felt like hours, I hobbled around a curve on the path and found a small clearing in the trees just large enough for a lopsided park bench and a trash can.

Almost weeping with relief, I limped over to the bench and tugged off my sandals, barely resisting the urge to toss them into the trash can at my side.

I could see the members' entrance of the club from there, but it was still at least fifty yards away. A cluster of uniformed valets lounged on the front steps, enjoying their free time until the guests started leaving. Between here and there, the sidewalk I'd been following turned into a pathway that wound in and out of the trees, probably tripling the distance I'd have to walk.

I don't know how long I stayed there, rubbing my sore, tired feet and listening to the sounds of the night. I'd already been gone from the party longer than I'd expected to be and I had no doubt that Miss Frankie had noticed by now that I'd slipped away. I'd have some explaining to do when I got back inside and, frankly, I wasn't in any hurry to have that confrontation.

Bits of conversation and laughter carried on the breeze kept me from feeling isolated, and I closed my eyes for a minute to decompress. That was a mistake. Exhaustion washed over me like a wave at high tide. The next thing I remember was the sound of a door opening and closing somewhere nearby. I sat bolt upright, heart pounding as I tried to shake the cobwebs from my groggy head. I was barely capable of thought, but I was coherent enough to know that if there was a way back into the club that didn't require another fifty-yard hike, I was all over it.

I got to my feet and reached for my shoes, but the sound of voices coming from the bushes stopped me short of actually picking them up.

"There you are," a woman said. "I've been looking everywhere for you. What are you doing out here?"

I heard a soft sound that might have been feet scuffing on pavement followed by a man's voice drawling, "I'm fortifying myself with a drop of liquid courage. Care to join me?"

Apparently, I wasn't the only person who'd bailed on the party. I left my shoes on the bench and followed the walking trail into the bushes, hoping to spot the door they'd used and figure out a way in for myself. I'd only gone a few feet when I rounded a sharp curve and glimpsed a couple standing on a small patch of concrete in front of a door that had been propped open with a piece of cinder block.

I guessed the woman to be in her mid-forties, a striking brunette with a Victoria Beckham haircut. The man was a few years younger. Tall. Handsome. Privileged. His light-colored hair was tousled, as if he'd been running his fingers through it, and he held a silver flask in one hand. But it was the look on his face, a mixture of contempt and pain — obvious even from a distance — that made me pull back into the shadows to avoid being seen.

The woman let out a deep sigh that almost got lost in the sounds of the night and waved a hand toward the flask. "Is that really necessary? There's plenty of alcohol inside."

He studied the flask for a moment before he answered her. "That's true, Mellie dear, but the company out here is infinitely more interesting."

A cold gust of wind blew through the trees and she wrapped her arms around herself for warmth. "That's because nobody else indulges you the way you do yourself."

"Some call it indulgence," the man replied. "I call it survival."

Mellie rolled her eyes. "It's hardly that," she said. "Now please, come back inside. Bradley's going to be looking for you, and you don't want to disappoint him."

The man took a long pull on the flask and carefully capped it. "Don't you think it's a little late to be worried about that?"

A flicker of conscience told me I shouldn't

be listening, but sore feet and curiosity kept me rooted to the spot. I couldn't remember meeting either of them, which only added to my interest. Plus, I didn't want to make a noise and give myself away. They'd think I was spying on them . . . and I was. I knew for certain that both Miss Frankie and Aunt Yolanda would object to that.

Mellie let out an exasperated sigh. "So you'll just hand Susannah a reason to complain about you? I thought you were smarter than that."

The man laughed. "She doesn't need any help from me. That woman makes a career out of complaining. I don't know how my brother puts up with her or . . . or why."

Mellie grinned slyly. "Oh, I think you do."

"Sadly," he agreed. "It's downright pitiful what that brother of mine will do for sex. No offense intended. He made the biggest mistake of his life when he left you, Mellie."

"Water under the bridge," she said. "You need to learn how to put the past aside, Judd."

"Ah, but that's the tricky part about the past," the man countered. "It won't go away. Believe me, I've tried to make it disappear. Repeatedly."

"You're trying the wrong methods. Alcohol won't change anything."

"Perhaps not," he agreed with a lift of an eyebrow, "but it helps me forget those things I cannot change." Ignoring Mellie's disapproving frown, he held up the flask to offer a toast. "I give thanks every day to the good Lord for creating such a useful tool."

Mellie held out a hand as if she thought he might willingly give up the flask. "Just listen to you," she scolded. "Your mother would roll over in her grave if she could hear the way you talk. Now come back inside and pretend to care about your brother's big night for an hour. After that, I don't care what you do."

The man stared at her outstretched hand for a moment, then shook his head and laughed. "I have a better idea, sister dear. Why don't you run back inside and care about tonight for me? That ought to make him happy."

She smiled sadly and put her hand on the younger man's cheek. "It's not him I'm concerned about, Judd. I thought you knew that."

He patted her hand gently and stepped away. "I know that you've always been decent to me. More decent than any of the others, though God only knows why you should be."

"You're much harder on yourself than

anyone else is," Mellie told him. "I wish you could figure that out."

Her words didn't appear to have an impact. Judd just stuffed his hands in his pockets and turned from her. "Go on in," he said as he took a step away from the door. "I'll be in shortly."

A look of weary exasperation crossed her face, but she didn't try to stop him. "I'm going to hold you to that," she warned. He kept walking, and a moment later he disappeared into the trees. With another regretful sigh, Mellie slipped back into the building and I let out the breath I'd been holding.

I stood there just until the sound of his footsteps died away, then hurried back up the path to the bench where I'd left my shoes. Mellie hadn't moved the cinder block when she went back inside, and I was anxious to use the door myself before I lost my chance.

It only took a moment to retrace my steps. I rounded the curve in the trail and the bench came into view, but my shoes weren't where I'd left them. Slightly winded, I stopped walking and stared at the empty park bench in confusion.

Something at my side rustled and Judd stepped out from the shadow of a huge magnolia tree, my sandals dangling from the fingers of one hand. "Evenin', ma'am. If I'm not mistaken, I believe these belong to you."

He must have known I'd been eavesdropping. I could feel the heat rushing into my face, but I hoped he wouldn't notice in the darkness. "Yes, I — I —" Brilliant. I reached for the shoes. "Thank you."

He moved his hand just out of my reach. "Did I startle you?"

"A little," I admitted. "I wasn't expecting to run into anyone out here. I came out through the service entrance and somehow managed to lock myself out. I've been looking for a way back inside." I realized I was babbling and cut myself off before I could embarrass myself further.

He regarded me for a long moment then dipped his head slightly. "You're in luck, then. I know this place like the proverbial back of my hand. But are you sure you want to go back inside? If you ask me, it's much more pleasant out here."

It was lovely. And quiet. But I shook my head regretfully. "I'm afraid I don't have a choice. I'm needed at the party."

He tipped the flask and took a drink, eyeing me with curiosity as he did. "Duty. She's a tough master, that's for certain." He held the flask in my direction. "Care to imbibe before you go back in? I have in my possession some of the finest scotch my family's money can buy."

I waved away the offer. Whatever he was drinking must have been powerful stuff, though, because I could smell the fumes from where I stood. "Thanks, but I shouldn't. I need to keep my head on straight for the next few hours."

With a shrug, he slipped the flask into his pocket. "If that's the way you want it. So you're looking for a way in, are you? What brings you out here all by yourself in the first place?"

"I needed something from the van," I said. "I'm with Zydeco bakery. We provided the King Cakes for tonight's party."

His lips curved into a sly grin. "Oh, I know who *you* are, sweetheart. You've been the object of much discussion around here. People have been waitin' for tonight with bated breath. They've been speculatin' for months about whether you'd try changin' things."

That didn't surprise me. I'd suspected as much. "And the verdict?"

Judd sketched a mock salute. "Even your detractors have conceded. You've done well . . . for an outsider."

I laughed then shivered a little as a cool

breeze blew across the grounds. "I'd ask who my detractors are, but I really don't want to know."

"I couldn't tell you anyway," Judd said in a flat voice. "If I did, they'd have to kill me." He peeled off his jacket and held it out to me.

I accepted it gratefully and slipped it on. "I'm Rita, by the way," I said as I held out a hand. "Lucero."

Instead of shaking, he touched my fingertips and bowed low over my hand. Charming, even if he was pickled. "As I said, I know who you are."

"Ah, but I don't know *you*," I reminded him. "Or did we meet inside and I've forgotten?"

When he lifted his head again, a smile curved his lips. "Fear not, my dear. Your memory hasn't let you down. We haven't met until this moment."

"So then you are . . ."

"A source of never-ending disappointment to my family." He waved me back toward the sidewalk. "If you'll come with me, I'll show you the quickest way to get inside out of the cold."

He led me a few feet to the right then slipped into a copse of trees where a path had been worn into the grass — which explained how he'd beat me to the clearing.

"You have a secret entryway?" I joked as I stepped around an exposed tree root. "I take it that means you've spent some time here."

He grinned over his shoulder. "I've been coming here since I was a boy. My parents were always busy with something, so I spent a lot of time exploring." He came to a stop in front of the door and held it open for me. "There you go, m'dear. You'll find the stairs to the lobby just beyond the weight room." He handed over my sandals and backed a step away.

"You're not coming?"

He shook his head. "Later, perhaps."

Beneath the gallant smile, there lurked a deep sadness. I wondered what his story was. But I couldn't stand out here talking to him all night. Miss Frankie would have my hide if I did.

"Thank you," I said. "You've saved my life — or at least my feet."

"Then I am a happy man."

I would have bet everything I owned that was the biggest lie I'd heard all night.

EIGHT

It wasn't until Judd had disappeared through the trees again that I realized I was still wearing his jacket. I thought about going after him, but he'd made it pretty clear he wasn't in the mood for company. Plus, I really needed to get back to the party. And I still hadn't resolved the napkin issue.

And besides, the prospect of meeting up with Judd again later wasn't altogether unappealing.

I forced my feet back into my sandals and climbed the stairs, trying not to wince as I walked through the saxophone arch into the party. The band was playing a slow song that sounded vaguely familiar, and several couples had moved onto the dance floor. I folded Judd's jacket and tucked it under the tables at the King Cake serving station, then looked around to see if Uncle Nestor and Aunt Yolanda had gotten into the spirit. Miss Frankie descended on me before I could spot them.

"Where in the world have you been?" she demanded. Her eyes spit fire, but the smile on her face was faultless.

"Outside," I said, hoping to avoid a long explanation. "I'm sorry. I didn't mean to be gone so long."

"People have been asking where you were."

"Well, I'm back now," I pointed out, then tried to divert her. "Has Ivanka Hedge arrived yet?"

"No, and you're lucky she hasn't. I swear —"

I cut her off as politely as I could. "Can it wait until later? I need to find Estelle. Have you seen her?"

The smile on Miss Frankie's face slipped ever-so-slightly. "Sugar, have you been working?"

"Not exactly." I craned to see over the heads of people standing close by, but that was a waste of effort. The sea of partying humanity had grown in the time I'd been gone. Just as I was ready to give up, I spotted a flash of turquoise near the bandstand. "I'll be back in a minute," I assured my mother-in-law. "I just have to ask her one little question."

Miss Frankie grabbed my hand as if she

intended to stop me. I'll never know whether she would have succeeded, because at that precise moment a hush fell over the crowd closest to us and people turned toward the archway wearing expressions filled with such anticipation I wondered if Ivanka had finally arrived and I stopped myself from leaving.

"Who is it?" I asked Miss Frankie.

"I can't tell," she said with a slight scowl. "Let's go see, shall we?"

We made our way through a wall of people who let us through with expressions ranging from impatience to outright irritation. And all for nothing. Instead of the cool willowy blonde I was hoping to find, a large man with dark hair, close-set eyes, and a broad smile surged into the room. He wore a ten-gallon cowboy hat and greeted the people around him like a politician on the campaign trail.

I recognized him immediately as Big Daddy Boudreaux, a minor celebrity in New Orleans — owner of half a dozen car dealerships and a string of other small businesses. As far as I could tell, he spent the majority of his time blowing up storage sheds and jumping out of airplanes to prove that his cars were the best and his prices the lowest around — and of course, he did it all on camera for his commercials.

Biting back disappointment that he wasn't Ivanka, I turned away again and glimpsed Miss Frankie's expression. It was gone in a blink, but I knew I hadn't imagined the slight curl of her lip or the coolness in her eyes.

Intrigued by her reaction, I grabbed another glass of wine and moved closer to her. I spoke softly, hoping my voice wouldn't carry. "I take it you're not a fan?"

"Of Bradley's?"

For some reason it struck me as odd that Big Daddy Boudreaux had an actual first name. "Bradley?"

Miss Frankie gave me a smile that was all wide-eyed innocence. "Only a handful of us can get away with calling him that. And why wouldn't I be a fan? He's the life of the party."

"Then why the sour look on your face?"

She shrugged. "Indigestion."

I didn't believe that for a moment, but I didn't get a chance to pursue it.

Big Daddy — with that big-ass hat and look-at-me grin, I couldn't think of him any other way — spotted Miss Frankie and advanced on her with wide-spread arms. "There she is. How are you, darlin'?"

She surrendered to a quick hug, but

another pained look flickered over her face, convincing me that her "indigestion" was a figment of her imagination. "Well, Bradley, I was beginning to think you weren't coming. It's been such a long time since I saw you. I hope you've been well."

He let out a hearty laugh. "Are you kidding? I wouldn't miss the Captain's Court for anything, especially not when I knew it was in your hands."

"How you do go on," Miss Frankie said, smiling at him as if she'd just found a long-lost friend. I knew I hadn't imagined the look on her face, but I also knew that she'd rather die than let an unwelcome guest sense her true feelings. "I'm flattered. I wasn't sure you'd remember who I was."

Her soft-edged response hit its target. He shrugged and glanced at the people around him, playing his audience with a smile that was both haughty and sheepish. He probably practiced it in front of a mirror in his spare time. "I know. I know. I could just kick myself. I meant to call when Philippe passed, but things got the better of me."

Miss Frankie's expression didn't change as she beckoned me closer. "Rita? Come here, sugar. I want you to meet an old family friend. Bradley Boudreaux, this is my daughter-in-law, Rita."

I went eagerly, curious to find out more about their relationship. Big Daddy's smile faltered as I moved closer, and I glimpsed what might have been genuine sorrow in his eyes. "You're Phil's wife?"

Phil? Even I had never called him that.

I told myself not to overreact to the "wife" thing. After seven months in New Orleans, I should be used to hearing myself referred to that way, but it still tweaks my conscience. I've given up trying to explain, though. Our relationship was too complicated at the end, making explanations too convoluted.

I nodded and offered him a hand to shake and a little white lie to swallow. "It's a pleasure to meet you."

Big Daddy bypassed the hand and pulled me in for a hug so enthusiastic it took my breath away — and not in a good way. He smelled of bourbon and cigars, both of which made my gag reflex kick in. "No wonder Phil abandoned us for so long," he said to Miss Frankie over my shoulder. "Just look at her! She's gorgeous."

Double gag. I extricated myself from the hug and smiled, saying the only thing I could think of: "You're an old family friend?"

"Sure am. Phil was my little brother Judd's closest friend when they were kids."

Hearing that name brought my head up sharply. *This* was the brother Judd had talked about with Mellie? I wondered why Philippe had never mentioned his old friend Judd when we were married. I wondered why Miss Frankie had never mentioned the Boudreauxes' absence at the funeral. Or why she'd never once mentioned knowing Big Daddy when we saw one of his obnoxious commercials on TV.

"The two of them used to drive me crazy," Big Daddy said. "Tagging along after me, wanting to do things with me and my friends." He turned the wattage up on his smile and aimed it at Miss Frankie again. "Those were some good times, weren't they?"

Pain flickered in her eyes, so I tried to edge away from those boyhood memories. "I've seen you on TV, but I had no idea you were a friend of Miss Frankie's. I can't imagine why we haven't met before."

Big Daddy's broad smile turned into a deep frown. "It's a damn shame, isn't it? I wasn't at the funeral. It wasn't right, and I hated myself for missing it," he said again. "But the wife and I were on a cruise. I didn't even hear about it until we got back, and by then it was too late."

And he hadn't found a minute to call on

Miss Frankie since then? Busy man.

Up close and personal, he was much taller than he looked on TV, and he managed to slip an arm around my shoulders as he talked. My skin crawled, but I didn't completely understand why. I only knew that I didn't like the guy. I made an effort to move away from him, but he tightened his hold, sticking to me like icing on warm cake.

"Judd should have been at the funeral, though. No excuses. But that's my little brother. He's a good kid and he means well, but . . ." His voice trailed off and he shook his head slowly.

I wondered why excuses were okay for Big Daddy but not for his little brother.

"Speaking of Judd," Big Daddy said, craning to see over our heads, "is he here tonight?"

I didn't answer but Miss Frankie nodded. "He came in about an hour ago."

The scents of food, alcohol, and Big Daddy were making my head pound. I rubbed my forehead — at least I tried to. Big Daddy had my arms crushed against my side, giving me very little room to move.

I was getting a little claustrophobic crushed up against him like that, so I finally shrugged him off as politely as I could. That's when I spotted the young woman standing behind him, arms folded across her chest and face pinched in anger. She was probably mid-thirties, close to my own age, with sleek brown hair and a heart-shaped face. She glared at me, her eyes narrowed behind a pair of glasses with rectangular black plastic frames.

I had no idea what her problem was, but I put a little more distance between the big guy and myself to show her that I meant no harm.

Miss Frankie greeted the woman with her customary warmth. "Violet, dear, it's lovely to see you, too." She turned to me and said, "Rita, you must meet Violet Shepherd. She's Bradley's right arm. I don't know what he'd do without her."

Not his wife, then. Lucky girl. Violet sent me a pained smile and I sent her one back. Luckily I was spared the need to make small talk, because just then a tall man with mocha-colored skin and a deep frown on his face strode up to Big Daddy and jabbed him in the shoulder. "We need to talk, Boudreaux. Outside. Now."

Big Daddy's hot, smelly breath blew over my shoulders and down my back as he turned to face the new arrival, who looked enough like Denzel Washington to make me do a double take.

"Now, Percy, that's no way to act," Big Daddy scolded. "We're at a party, and you're likely to upset the ladies. Whatever it is can wait until tomorrow or the next day."

Percy swept a contrite glance over the three of us. I didn't know about the other two, but I was in no imminent danger of emotional upset.

"I'm sorry, Miss Frankie," Percy said. "But this is important." He looked from one of us to the other and smiled apologetically. "I'm sure y'all understand."

Miss Frankie and I mumbled that we did, but Violet looked at him over the rims of her glasses. "I don't think this is the time or the place —"

Big Daddy gave her a look that stopped her cold, then turned to Percy. "God Almighty," he said half under his breath. "I said *not now*. Talk to me later. Or tomorrow."

Percy held his ground and the frown on his face deepened. "Now," he warned.

Big Daddy gave him a flat-eyed look. "I'm not going to let you stir up a ruckus and ruin the night. Whatever it is that has your boxers in a bunch will keep. Violet, set up an appointment or something. Percy, have yourself a drink and calm down."

Percy looked as if he wanted to argue

further, but Violet turned her Vulcan Death Stare on him and ordered, "Call the office on Monday, Mr. Ponter. I'll set up an appointment for you."

"Monday will be too late," Percy said, but he cut a glance at Miss Frankie and me and relented slightly. "My apologies, ladies. I didn't mean to cause a scene." He started to turn away, firing one last shot at Big Daddy before he left. "Don't think this is the end of it, Boudreaux. We'll settle this tonight, one way or another."

Miss Frankie noticed a couple of guests listening to the exchange. Wearing her trademark smile, she took them by the arms and led them away, chatting easily about the music. An uncomfortable silence rang between the rest of us for about two seconds before Big Daddy's plus-one took charge. Turning her death glare into a smile, she tucked one lock of dark hair behind an ear and put a hand on Big Daddy's beefy arm. "Is there anything you want me to do?"

Big Daddy waved her away. "Don't worry so much, Violet. You're my assistant, not my mother. Why don't you go amuse yourself? I'll catch up with you later."

Even though she'd been trying to kill me with her eyes, I felt kind of bad for Violet. Apparently, Big Daddy's on-camera schtick was no act. He really was a jerk.

Violet's face burned, but she pivoted away without another word . . . and plowed straight into a tall young woman with pale blond hair. Ivanka Hedge stumbled backward into her fiancé, Richard Montgomery III, with a cry of alarm. Violet growled something that might have been an apology but probably wasn't, and kept going.

Luckily, Richard, an elegant but plain-faced man of around thirty and slightly balding, kept Ivanka from falling, but the look on her face made it clear that she wasn't happy.

Then again, neither was I. I started toward her, an apology on my lips, but she sailed past me with a little moue of distaste.

My heart sank like a stone. There went my chances of making a good first impression.

If I'd disliked Big Daddy Boudreaux before, I positively loathed him now.

I craned to see where Ivanka had gone, but I'd already lost sight of her.

"You lookin' for the ice princess?" Big Daddy asked in my ear.

I scowled over my shoulder and moved a step away. "If you mean Ivanka Hedge, then yes. Did you see where she went?"

Big Daddy looked out over the crowd and

jerked his chin toward a set of doors leading onto the balcony. "Over there with my wife. You want to talk to her?"

"Yes. Thanks. If you'll excuse me —"

He raised one hand over his head and slipped the other around my waist. "Hey, Ivanka! Over here!"

I gaped at him in horror and extricated myself from his grasp. "That's not necessary," I said as nicely as I could. I smoothed my dress, readjusted the parts that had gotten skewed, and looked up to see both Ivanka and a shorter, softly rounded woman with a pale complexion and burgundy hair in a wedge cut, pointedly ignoring Big Daddy's summons. That must be the Susannah I'd overheard Judd and Mellie talking about.

Interesting that neither woman paid attention to him.

"Thanks for nothing," I muttered.

Big Daddy waved that beefy hand through the air, dismissing me, my concerns, and Ivanka all at once. "Listen, darlin', she's not worth getting yourself all worked up over."

Said the man with the bulging bank accounts.

I had a sour taste in my mouth, but I spooned a little more syrup into my smile for Miss Frankie's sake. "I'll keep that in mind."

"I'm serious. She's a friend of my wife's. I know what she's really like. You wouldn't like her."

"Well, hard to say if I never meet her," I said. "Now if you'll excuse me —"

He grabbed my hand and pulled me around to face him. "Listen, darlin', let me give you a word of advice. You can make yourself crazy chasin' after people who don't give two hoots about you. Don't do it. Just be yourself. That's what I do."

That wasn't exactly a selling point. At that moment, Big Daddy Boudreaux was the last person I wanted advice from.

I heard his big booming laugh following me as I walked away, and I made a silent pledge to avoid him for the rest of the night. I had a feeling that Big Daddy was going to be a problem. I just wish I'd known then how much trouble he was going to cause.

.

NINE

Finally free of Big Daddy, I hurried after Ivanka and Richard, still hoping to wrangle an introduction. I got held up a couple of times, first by Isabeau, who wanted to check on a couple of details related to serving the King Cake at midnight, and next by Estelle, who wanted to show me the pictures Ox had asked her to take for the blog.

By the time I'd asked Estelle to check on the napkins and placated her by slipping her memory card into my evening bag, I'd lost sight of the happy couple again. Luckily, Mrs. Big Daddy hadn't moved, so I decided to take my chances with her.

I made my way through the crowd and stopped in front of her wearing my friendliest smile. "Mrs. Boudreaux?"

She ran a squished-bug glance over me. "Yes?"

"I'm Rita Lucero, I'm the hostess —"

She cut me off before I could finish. "Yes,

yes, yes. I saw you over there with my husband. Is there something you need?"

At least I didn't have to wonder what made the Boudreauxes' marriage tick. They were perfect for each other. "Your husband mentioned that you're a friend of Ivanka Hedge. I'd really love to meet her before the night is over."

She darted a glance at a dark-haired man wearing tortoiseshell glasses who stood a little to one side. Until that moment, I hadn't realized they were together. She shared a little smirk with him and tossed, "Wouldn't everyone?" over her shoulder as they walked away.

Stung by her dismissal, I made two circuits of the ballroom, checked the balcony, scoured the grounds with their twinkling lights, surveyed the tables scattered across the terraced lawn, then made another brief tour inside before acknowledging that Ivanka and Richard must have already left. I'd lost my chance, thanks to Big Daddy.

Big Dud was more like it.

Everywhere I went I heard his booming voice or thunderous laugh. The longer the night went on, the more space he seemed to take up. Like dough left to rise, he seemed to double in size, which may help to explain what happened next.

It was a little after ten and I was locked in conversation with a vague young woman with thin straight hair and winsome eyes. Boredom wrapped itself around my head and squeezed. Visions of my nice, quiet bedroom in my nice, quiet house danced in front of my eyes. While she prattled on about vintage seeds and soil types, I stifled yawn after yawn and looked around for someone — anyone — who might save me.

After several minutes, I saw Uncle Nestor standing near the stairs wearing a look of irritation. An instant later, I saw what had put it there.

Big Daddy had boxed him in beside the staircase, a glass of whiskey in one hand, a cigar in the other. He was talking nonstop, gesturing broadly and leaving a trail of smoke behind with every word.

Uncle Nestor watched him with a caged-tiger look that made me nervous. That was all the excuse I needed to cut my conversation short. I muttered an excuse and started to move away from the young woman, whose name I'd already forgotten.

Apparently, she wasn't listening. "You'd be amazed by the gardens," she said, trailing behind me. I guess she thought I found the subject of chemical fertilizers as fascinating as she did. "So many people think that if a little does a lot of good, a lot will be even better. They couldn't be more wrong."

"I'm sure that's a problem," I said, forcing a smile. "I hope you can find a solution. Now, if you'll excuse me —"

"You have *no* idea. People call me all the time wanting help with some plant they've killed." She droned on, sounding a little like the teacher in the Charlie Brown cartoons. *"Wah wah-wah. Wah wah wah."*

Across the room, Big Daddy threw back his head and laughed at something, and the scowl on Uncle Nestor's face deepened. Even from a distance, I could see color flooding his face.

". . . and of course, aphids can be *such* a problem . . ."

Never again, I promised myself. Never ever again. If Miss Frankie wanted to host a party, she could do it without me.

Uncle Nestor jabbed a finger at Big Daddy and said something I couldn't hear. But I didn't need to hear what he said to know that the situation was deteriorating fast. I glanced around for Aunt Yolanda, hoping she'd noticed what was going on with her husband. I spotted her near the balcony doors, laughing with Miss Frankie and her neighbor, Bernice. I doubted she even knew where Uncle Nestor was.

". . . and you have to dig that into the soil, which can be time-consuming . . ."

Smirking, Big Daddy waved Uncle Nestor's hand away. Cigar smoke billowed between them, but I didn't have to see my uncle's face to know that was going to be a problem. Under normal circumstances, I wouldn't have been as worried, but I was pretty sure Uncle Nestor had been drinking for the past couple of hours, and I still didn't know why he was in such a foul mood to begin with.

I walked away from my gardening friend in the middle of an observation about tree sap just as Big Daddy belted out a rafter-shaking laugh at Uncle Nestor's expense. I slipped past a couple of women and ducked between two men and a waiter carrying a huge tray of hors d'oeuvres. Just a few more feet. Just a handful of people to get past.

But I might as well have been miles away. While I looked on in stunned disbelief, Uncle Nestor blasted Big Daddy with a right hook that would have made George Foreman proud.

Big Daddy rocked under the force of the assault. If I'd been more nimble, I would have vaulted over the furniture to get between them. As it was, I had to skirt tables, chairs, and tipsy guests, and that slowed me down.

I hurried out through the glittering archway as Big Daddy shoved his drink and cigar onto a nearby table and grabbed Uncle Nestor by the lapels of his jacket, slamming him into the wall. A couple of nearby pictures slid off-center from the impact, and I heard the sound of breaking glass just behind me.

It seemed to take forever to push through, but I finally got there and grabbed Big Daddy's arm, trying to pull him off my uncle. "Let go!" I shouted. "I mean it, Big Daddy. Let him go *now*!" He was way too big for me, but I created enough of a distraction for Uncle Nestor to slip out of his grip.

Before I could catch my breath, Big Daddy took his eyes off Uncle Nestor for a split second and my scrappy little uncle launched himself at Big Daddy for the second time. This time he landed a solid blow to Big Daddy's chin, and with it he punched a big fat hole in my bubble of optimism. What was going on? The Uncle Nestor who raised me would never get into a fistfight like this.

I glanced around for help, assuming that everyone had heard the shouting, but the music and laughter must have drowned out the sound. Only a handful of people seemed aware of the scuffle, and I saw Edie trying to distract the few guests who'd noticed.

Thank God for small favors.

Making a mental note to thank her later, I set out to calm both men down before Aunt Yolanda and Miss Frankie got wind of their argument. I waded in a little deeper and tried to get between them, counting on Uncle Nestor to back off rather than hit me. "Stop it!" I ordered. "Both of you. Right now."

Big Daddy wiped a spot of blood from the corner of his mouth and gestured toward Uncle Nestor. "The old man attacked me." He looked around at the small crowd for backup. "You all saw it. Son of a bitch came at me like a crazy man."

Uncle Nestor let fly with some Spanish. I only understood a few words, but every one of them was on the list my cousins and I hadn't been allowed to say when we were younger.

Big Daddy twitched a bit, readjusting his shirt after the tussle. He jerked his head toward Uncle Nestor. "Is this guy for real?"

He had some nerve. Uncle Nestor might be emotional, but even in his current mood I had a hard time accepting that he'd turned into someone who'd start a fight unprovoked. Uncle Nestor didn't start trouble, but he knew how to end it. Big Daddy must have said something to set him off.

But I didn't want to ruin the evening for Miss Frankie by prolonging the confrontation. I forced myself to say, "I'm so sorry," though I had a hard time getting the words out around the big old lump of resentment in my throat.

"Don't you dare apologize for me, *mija*. He's the one who should be sorry." Uncle Nestor shook a finger in Big Daddy's big, ugly face. "You're lucky that's all you got, *pendejo*."

To my immense relief, Big Daddy shrugged him off, but he turned to me with a scowl. "*You're* lucky I'm in a good mood. Otherwise, I might just call the police and tell them to lock the guy up. He's nuts."

That stopped me cold. "He's not crazy. What did you say to him?"

One thick eyebrow rose in surprise. "Excuse me?"

"What did you say to him?" I asked again, deliberately overenunciating.

Big Daddy ignored the question and dug another cigar out of his breast pocket. "This guy's a friend of yours?"

"Yeah. He is."

"Well, then, take my advice and get him some professional help before he hurts somebody." He strode away before I could come up with a good response, which was probably a good thing. I turned away and took a couple of calming breaths before dragging my uncle into a small, unused meeting room.

I locked the door and glared at Uncle Nestor, who was still red-faced and angry. "What was that all about, *Tío*? Why did you hit him?"

Uncle Nestor brushed at his shirt and jacket as if Big Daddy had left traces of something unsavory behind. "Nothing for you to worry about, little girl."

When I was younger, I'd liked it when he called me that. But with my thirty-fifth birthday looming in a couple of months, it had been a long time since I qualified as a child. "I'm not a little girl," I said automatically. "And it sure is something for me to worry about. This is my party, remember? Technically, Big Daddy is my guest."

"Then you ought to be more careful about who you associate with."

"And you ought to be more careful about who you take a swing at," I snapped. "That guy might be a jerk, but he's a local celebrity and a lot of people like him. Your little stunt could give Miss Frankie, Zydeco, and me a big fat black eye in the press."

Uncle Nestor's scowl grew more sullen.

"That's all you're worried about? This new life of yours? This new family you've picked out?"

For a moment, I could only gape at him in disbelief. "You have got to be kidding me," I said when I could form words again. "You're jealous?"

He shot a look at me from the corner of his eye. "Don't be absurd."

"What's absurd about it?" I demanded. "You've been taking shots at me, at the bakery, and at Miss Frankie since the minute you arrived."

He shrugged and focused on tucking his shirt into his waistband. "I would never do anything to hurt you, *mija*. You know that."

"You have a funny way of showing it," I said under my breath, but I never could stay mad at him and I didn't want to prolong the drama. I hugged him quickly. "Just steer clear of Big Daddy for the rest of the night, okay? No more trouble."

He gave another shrug. "Of course."

"I mean it," I warned. "And would it kill you to smile?"

He flashed a grin that wasn't entirely genuine, but I'd take what I could get. I stepped away from the door and he walked through it to rejoin the party. After closing my eyes and counting to ten, I did the same.

And I reminded myself that I only had to get through the next couple of hours. After that, I could take Uncle Nestor home. Everything would be better tomorrow. I was sure of it.

TEN

We served the King Cake promptly at midnight.

Estelle had worked her magic, slipping the Zydeco napkins into place when nobody was looking. I told myself not to gloat over this minor victory, but it did reenergize me. And I needed that, since I was anxious about the reception the cakes would receive. Other than the controversial addition of filling in some of the cakes, I'd remained true to Philippe's recipe. I thought they'd turned out well, but these folks were connoisseurs. Most of them had been eating King Cake since they were babies, and the perfectionist in me needed the cakes to score a hit.

I hovered while Musterion's captain made a short speech and introduced the officers for the coming year, a roster that included Big Daddy Boudreaux as captain and Percy Ponter as treasurer, a little detail I found interesting. Several hours had passed since he'd confronted Big Daddy, but Percy didn't look any happier than before. He glared at Big Daddy throughout the ceremony, and several times I thought he was actually going to interrupt. He didn't, though, and Big Daddy seemed oblivious to any negative undercurrents. He beamed and thanked people for their votes and made lavish promises about the upcoming year.

I tuned him out and worried about the King Cakes. Were they still fresh? Would the ceremonial cake hold its shape when the captain made the first cut? Would the guests like the flavor? Would they accept the fillings?

While I hovered, holding my breath in anticipation, I saw Judd lurking at the back of the crowd. So he'd come inside to support his brother after all. I hoped Mellie had seen him and then wondered why it should matter to me. I'd liked him instinctively, and maybe I'd felt some kinship. I'd lived in the shadows of my bigger-than-life ex-husband and cousins, so I had an idea how Judd must have felt having Big Daddy for a brother.

To my relief, the speeches finally ended and the captain pronounced the King Cake excellent. The club's waitstaff surged into the room carrying trays of plated cake, and everything else flew out of my head. Ox and I circulated among the guests, accepting compliments and encouraging anyone who expressed an interest in our cakes to make an appointment with Edie. I lost sight of Judd and didn't think about him again until the party began to break up around 1 a.m.

Miss Frankie and I stood near the glittering saxophones kissing cheeks, accepting hugs, and saying good-bye to the guests in true Southern style. By one-thirty, even my lucky staff had cleared out and what few guests remained had migrated indoors. I could have counted on two hands the number of die-hard guests who were hanging around, and I hoped they would all leave soon. Miss Frankie would stay until the very end, and she'd expect me to do the same.

After a while, the club's staff began clearing away dishes and glasses, removing the tablecloths, and packing away decorations. I checked to see how many lingerers there were and spotted Mellie across the room deep in conversation with Susannah Boudreaux. Susannah looked upset. Or maybe she was drunk. Or both. It was hard to tell.

I retrieved Judd's jacket from under the serving station and draped it over my arm, then decided against interrupting Mellie and Susannah and instead joined Miss

Frankie and Aunt Yolanda, who were sitting on a couple of stray chairs near the head table.

Miss Frankie held a glass of champagne in one hand, but her head was tilted back against the chair and her eyes were closed. Aunt Yolanda sat with her bare feet stretched out in front of her, her shoes abandoned on the floor nearby.

Relieved to have the party behind me, I sank onto a folding chair beside Aunt Yolanda and kicked off the sandals that had all but crippled me. I wriggled my toes, wishing I could curl up and go to sleep right there. If I hurried home, I could maybe catch three hours of sleep before I had to leave for work. I had the feeling it was going to be a very long day.

Miss Frankie opened one eye and smiled at me. "The party was a huge success, sugar. I know it wasn't easy after a full day at the bakery, but all of Philippe's friends were taken with you. You charmed everyone."

Not the important ones. My failure to make contact with the Hedge-Montgomery wedding party was my biggest disappointment. A close second was the amount of time I'd had to spend making sure that Big Daddy's off-color jokes and generally irritating personality didn't offend anyone.

Now that I thought about him, I realized that I hadn't noticed when he'd left. I wouldn't have imagined him leaving without drawing attention to himself but, frankly, I appreciated the silence. I was through with him, that's all that mattered.

I yawned. Stretched. And tried to focus on the positives. "So who got the official baby in the cake this year?"

"Esther McIntosh," Miss Frankie said. "She's the art gallery owner and her husband is an attorney. I introduced you to them, remember?"

I ran through the names and faces I'd tried to mentally catalog in the past few hours. "Tall woman? Thin? Wearing an African-print caftan?"

Miss Frankie nodded. "Her husband looks like he should be coaching the Saints, not teaching tax law."

I was pleased with myself for remembering. "They ought to do a good job with next year's party," I said to be polite. I didn't really care who got the job next year as long as it wasn't me. I stole a glance at my watch and grimaced at how quickly my sleep time was ticking past.

Aunt Yolanda glanced around the ballroom, still littered with plates, glasses, napkins, and silverware. The musicians had packed up their instruments, and the relative silence after a night of rousing jazz numbers made my ears ring.

"I should figure out where Nestor has gone," Aunt Yolanda said. "I haven't seen him in a while."

I hadn't either, I realized with a pang of guilt. After that fight with Big Daddy, I'd vowed to keep an eye on him but I'd been distracted by other things. "Maybe he's slipped away somewhere to get some rest." And by "get some rest" I meant "sleep off all the booze he'd swallowed during the evening." Why else would he have started the fight with Big Daddy? If he was "resting" somewhere, waking him would be like poking a tiger with a sharp stick, but I'd have to risk it. He'd be even angrier if I left him to sleep it off at The Shores.

I stood and realized that I still had Judd's jacket. Yawning, I tried to decide whether to leave it with a member of the staff or give it to Mellie. She obviously knew him well. The one minor problem: She and I hadn't actually met. Which made explaining how I knew to give her Judd's suit coat a little tricky.

Counting on Miss Frankie to help with that, I nodded discreetly toward the two women on the other side of the room. "I don't remember meeting the woman standing with Susannah Boudreaux. Who is she?"

Miss Frankie sat up and took a look. "You didn't meet Mellie? How did I let that happen?"

"It's not your fault," I assured her quickly. "There were so many people here. It would have been impossible to meet each one personally. Is she a friend of yours?"

Miss Frankie nodded. "I've known Mellie since she was a girl. Susannah is relatively new to these parts. Her people come from Charleston, I believe."

That didn't tell me much. "I saw her talking to a guy earlier," I said. "Tall. Blond. Kind of good-looking, I guess." I held up the suit coat. "He loaned this to me, but I never saw him again. She called him Judd. Am I right in assuming he's Big Daddy's brother?"

Miss Frankie brightened. "I'm sure it probably was. He was here earlier."

"So Mellie is his ex-sister-in-law?"

"That's right. Mellie was married to Bradley several years ago. They've been divorced for a while, more's the pity. She was the best thing that ever happened to him." She scowled thoughtfully and lowered her voice a notch. "Susannah is his current wife. The third one. There was one in between, but she didn't last long. Bless her heart, Susannah there tries hard, but she's no match for Bradley."

I glanced again at the two women from the corner of my eye and wondered if the wife/ex-wife thing explained the tension I sensed between them or if there was something else going on. I tried to picture either woman married to Big Daddy. Neither one seemed like his type, but maybe I had a slightly biased idea of what his type was. I'd have bet on platinum blond, dumb as a rock, and 95 percent plastic.

Neither Mellie nor Susannah fit that mold. Neither had Violet, come to think of it, who seemed to be vying for a spot as Wife No. 4. In fact, all three women could have been triplets, separated at birth by a decade or so.

I decided not to interrupt them. I'd hang on to Judd's jacket for a little while longer. Seeing him again to return it would be no hardship. "Why don't we gather our things," I suggested, "and then we can look for Uncle Nestor. Are there any private rooms around here where he might be lying down?"

Miss Frankie got to her feet, but it seemed to take some effort. "Several," she said. "I'll help you look." She smiled at me so fondly, my earlier doubts about the party dimmed. Now that it was over, I could admit that I hadn't really minded playing hostess for the evening. I just didn't want to make a habit of it.

"I have a better idea." Aunt Yolanda reached into the purse at her feet for her cell phone. She pressed a couple of buttons and almost immediately we heard the sound of Uncle Nestor's ringtone coming in through the open doors to the balcony.

"Now, wasn't that easier?" She shut her phone with a snap and crossed the room, calling out as she walked, "Nestor? What are you doing out there? We're ready to go."

He didn't answer, but that didn't surprise me. I still fully expected to find him sleeping it off somewhere. I trailed after her so I could help rouse him if my suspicions proved correct. "Maybe he fell asleep in one of the deck chairs."

"You underestimate your uncle," she said. "He's probably tidying up."

I thought *she* was underestimating the amount he'd had to drink, but I didn't say so aloud. Besides, my uncle isn't the type to "tidy." He cleans the way he does everything else: all out. If he were cleaning up after Miss Frankie's party, he'd be sweeping everything in sight into garbage bags.

Aunt Yolanda waited for me to catch up with her, and put an arm around my shoulders when I did. "You're happy here, aren't you, Rita?"

The question surprised me and so did her timing, but I nodded. "Yes, I am."

"Are you sure? You seem a little . . . jumpy."

"That's because I'm still adjusting. And this" — I gestured toward the party mess — "isn't really my thing. I love Zydeco. I have a great staff and I love the work I'm doing. And you've seen my house. It's incredible. I'm happy with my decision. I'm just not sure that you and Uncle Nestor are happy for me."

"I'm thrilled for you," she said, giving me another squeeze of reassurance. "And Nestor is fine with it, too."

I laughed at her careful phrasing. "Fine with it? I wish I could believe you. He seems hurt. Maybe even a little resentful toward Miss Frankie."

"He's also adjusting, *mija*. If he does feel any resentment, it's only temporary. He's worried about you and he misses you. Just be patient with him. He'll get there."

Guilt tweaked at me again. "You know it was never my intention to hurt either of you. I didn't stay here because I care more about Miss Frankie than the two of you."

"Of course we know that." She turned to face me, resting both hands on my shoulders. "There's *nothing* in the world Nestor and I want more than your happiness. If this is the life you choose, we're in your corner. I hope you know that."

I hugged her tightly, grateful for her steadiness and soft-spoken approval. "Thank you. I don't know what I'd do without you."

She smiled as I stepped away, but I glimpsed something that looked almost melancholy beneath her expression. I had to ask, "Is everything okay with the two of you, *Tía?*"

She pulled back, eyes wide. "With us? Of course. Why?"

"It's just a feeling I get. The two of you showing up here without warning. Uncle Nestor leaving Agave in somebody else's hands. He called three times before we even got here to make sure things were running smoothly. Something's . . . different."

She laughed, but it sounded more brittle than amused. "Such an imagination you have. We're fine. We wanted to see how you're doing, that's all."

Again, I tried to believe her, but I couldn't ignore the anger I'd seen in Uncle Nestor.

While I tried to figure out what to say about that, Aunt Yolanda turned away and looked out through the doors, staring into the night, her back stiff, her chin high, but that only made me more convinced that she was hiding something. But we'd been going nonstop since the minute they arrived, so she could have just been tired. I'd ask again tomorrow, when we were both rested.

I held back, thinking I should give her a moment alone, but she called out to me only a heartbeat later.

"*Rita?* Oh my God. Rita! Come here. Quickly!" She sounded frantic. Frightened, even.

"What is it?" I asked, hurrying toward her. "What's wrong?"

With trembling hands — so unlike my unflappable aunt — she pointed at something on the ground below us. "There's someone in the pool. I think he's in trouble." Before I could reach her, she darted across the balcony and started down the steps to the ground level.

"Who is it?" I called after her, but she was already gone.

It seemed to take forever to reach the other end of that long balcony, and by the time I got there, she was racing down the stone steps toward the swimming pool.

It took only one glance to figure out what had upset her. Someone was floating in the pool, facedown and unmoving. With my heart in my throat, I bolted down the steps. Even in the dim lighting from the tiki torches and twinkling white lights, I recognized who it was:

Big Daddy Boudreaux.

"Call nine-one-one!" Aunt Yolanda shouted as she knelt down beside the water. "I think he's dead."

The gentle hum of the pool's filtration system and the soft lap of water against the sides of the pool were deceptively soothing sounds, especially since my pulse was racing frantically as the reality of the situation sank in.

Ignoring the logic that told me that nobody could breathe in that position, I stepped around a small statue that lay near the pool and plunged down the concrete steps into the water. It was only waist deep, but it dragged heavily on me as I made my way toward him.

Big Daddy bobbed gently on the waves I created. He didn't stir, but in spite of a massive, bloody wound on the back of his head, I held on to the frantic hope that he might only be injured. "I need your help," I called to Aunt Yolanda. "We need to turn him over."

She stayed right where she was, shaking her head sadly. "It's too late, *mija*."

"You don't know that." My voice came out high-pitched and sharp-edged. "We need to turn him over and check for a pulse."

"Rita —"

"Please, Aunt Yolanda. We have to at least check."

Reluctantly, she followed me into the water and together we rolled Big Daddy onto his back. But as his swollen and bruised face emerged from the water, I realized that Aunt Yolanda was right.

Just a little while ago he'd been larger than life. Now Big Daddy Boudreaux stared sightlessly up at the sky, his mouth slightly open and his eyes bulging. In horror, I backed a step away, creating a wave that rolled over him and submerged his face again. An angry wound marred his forehead, probably where he hit his head as he fell in. I didn't need to check for a pulse. I could tell just by looking.

He was dead.

ELEVEN

"Okay, Rita. Let's go over this again. What time did Mr. Boudreaux arrive at the party?"

Two long hours had gone by since I'd placed the 911 call, and I'd told my story in detail at least three times. Half an hour ago, I'd been deposited in one corner of the ballroom and told to wait. Now I was sitting across the table from Detective Liam Sullivan, who apparently wanted me to tell the story again.

Sullivan and I had met last summer, during the investigation into Philippe's murder. He's tall, dark-haired, and yes, handsome. I'd fallen a little bit in love with him when he saved my life, though I'd never confessed that to anyone.

I didn't mind answering his questions, but I wished I could have changed clothes first. My dress was still damp from going into the pool and the wet fabric clung to me like a second skin, chilling me to the bone. I huddled a little deeper into the light blanket Sullivan had asked one of the staff to bring me, and dug around in my fog-filled head for an answer. "I think it was around nine, but I can't swear to it. And no, I don't *know* how he ended up in the pool. He was just there."

I knew I sounded testy, but who wouldn't under the circumstances? There was a dead body in the swimming pool, and my uncle was missing. My aunt and mother-in-law were being interrogated in other parts of the club, as were the handful of guests and the staff who'd still been there when we sounded the alarm. I was worried about how Aunt Yolanda and Miss Frankie were holding up and starting to feel very concerned about Uncle Nestor, who seemed to have disappeared completely.

On top of all that, I'd been running nonstop for almost twenty-four hours and I'd had a few glasses of wine at the party. Exhaustion and alcohol were seriously impairing my ability to cope.

Sullivan glanced at his notes and ran a look over me. "You told Officer Matos that Mr. Boudreaux was drunk."

Usually Sullivan's eyes are a shade of blue so light they're almost disconcerting. Tonight they were dark and gray, like storm clouds rolling in off the Gulf of Mexico. Plus, he was using his stern-cop voice, which, in spite of the charming Southern drawl, was probably sharp enough to cut diamonds.

"I said that I *thought* he was drunk," I clarified. "And that it's possible he stumbled into the pool on his own."

Sullivan lowered his notebook to the table. "And you believed that?"

I shrugged with my face. "It's possible."

"You saw the body," he said. "That explanation might account for one wound, but Mr. Boudreaux has lacerations on his face, bruising on his temple, swelling on his cheeks, and a serious contusion on the back of his head."

Just thinking about that awful head wound threatened to activate my gag reflex. "He could have hit his head when he fell in."

"But he didn't," Sullivan said. "I know that just from looking at him, and I'm guessin' you know it, too."

"I don't know anything," I said stubbornly. I didn't believe Big Daddy's death was an accident any more than Sullivan did, but I resented the implication that I might know more than I was telling him. "You don't know what happened either. Don't you need a coroner's report or something?"

Sullivan fixed me with a hard gray stare. "Yeah. Technically. But it's hard to imagine Mr. Boudreaux going into the pool and hitting both the back of his head and his face on the way down. I'm bettin' he didn't get the wound on the back of his head from bouncing off the side of the pool."

"So what are you saying?"

"I'm saying he had help gettin' that way."

I pulled the blanket a little tighter and let out a resigned sigh. I thought about the statue at the side of the pool and wondered if someone had used it to send Big Daddy to his reward. I sure didn't want the man's death to be deliberate. Neither Miss Frankie nor Zydeco needed to be involved in another murder. Neither did I, and I hated to think of Aunt Yolanda and Uncle Nestor wasting their whole visit talking to the police. "I guess I shouldn't be surprised that somebody killed him," I said. "He wasn't exactly the nicest guy in the world."

One of Sullivan's eyebrows shot up. "What does that mean? Did you have some kind of trouble with him?"

"Me?" I shrugged. "Not really. I only met him for the first time a few hours ago." It was the perfect time to tell him about Uncle Nestor popping Big Daddy a couple of times, but he hadn't asked about anyone else having "trouble" with Big Daddy. Someone was sure to tell Sullivan about the fight, but I just couldn't get the words out. I wasn't ready to throw Uncle Nestor under the bus. I knew it was irrational, but I hoped they'd find the killer so quickly I wouldn't have to rat him out.

Sullivan shifted his weight and propped both arms on the table. "Why don't you define 'not really' for me?"

Another chill shook my body and I huddled deeper into the blanket. "He was loud and obnoxious and grabby. A bit too friendly, if you know what I mean."

"Are you sayin' he made a pass at you?"

"I guess you could call it that. I'm not sure his heart was in it. It seemed almost like a habit. He saw a woman and he made a grab."

"And —"

"And nothing. I handled it. He went away and bothered other people. No big deal."

Sullivan studied my expression for a moment before asking his next question. "Did he bother anyone else in particular?"

I carefully sidestepped the Uncle Nestor factor one more time and stayed focused on the female guests. "Not that I know of. He made the rounds and talked to a lot of people. So you think somebody hit him, and then pushed him into the pool?"

Sullivan didn't so much as blink. "Something like that. I'm told you found the body. Is that right?"

I gave him a thin-lipped nod and linked my hands on the table. "My aunt Yolanda and I found him."

"Tell me about that."

"We were looking for my uncle. The party was over and we were comparing notes about how we felt it had gone — you know how you do . . ."

He nodded, but didn't say a word. I took that as a cue to keep talking. "Anyway, we realized that neither of us had seen Uncle Nestor for a while, so we decided to look for him."

"You went outside to do that? Why not search the clubhouse?"

If it had just been me, I might've left out the detail about the cell phone — actually, I'd neglected to even mention it to the first cops, it seemed so unimportant. But then I thought about how Aunt Yolanda was a stickler for the truth and realized that she'd probably spilled her guts to the cop interrogating her. After all, she believed that the truth would set her free. And if my story didn't match, we could end up in big trouble.

"We were going to," I explained. "But Aunt Yolanda called his cell phone and heard it ringing outside. She went out onto the balcony and that's when she spotted Big Daddy in the pool."

Sullivan's eyebrow arched high over one slate-colored eye. "I didn't see any of that in the notes Officer Crump gave me."

"That's because I forgot to tell him. I didn't even think about it. And don't give me that look. Nestor's my uncle. He didn't have anything to do with Big Daddy's death."

"Do you have any idea who might have wanted Big Daddy dead?"

"Besides every woman he ever met? Not really."

"I assume you have a guest list," he said, refusing to even crack a smile. "I'll need a copy."

"Miss Frankie has all of that information. Most of the guests were members of the Krewe of Musterion. This was some sort of a bash for the bigwigs. Apparently, Big Daddy was just elected as captain for the coming year." Thinking about all of that made me sit up a little straighter. "You know who you should talk to? This guy named

Percy something. Ponter, I think they said. He's one of the officers for next year and he was upset with Big Daddy earlier in the evening."

Sullivan made a note. "Any idea why?"

I shook my head. "Big Daddy told him to make an appointment for next week, that's all I know. Big Daddy's assistant might know, though. She was there. Her name is Violet." I dug around in my memory and came up with the rest. "Shepherd."

Sullivan wrote that down, too. "Anything else?"

I ignored my nagging conscience and shook my head again. "No, that's it." I'd tell Sullivan about the fight once we found Uncle Nestor and I heard his side of the story. Surely he'd be more forthcoming now.

"When you went outside after the party, did you notice anything out of place in the backyard? Anything unusual? Anything that didn't belong?"

The quick change of subject caught me off guard, and exhaustion, worry, and fear made it hard to catch up. Disjointed images flashed through my head. Aunt Yolanda hurrying toward the pool. Me following. The twinkling white lights on the shrubbery and trees. A few tiki torches still burning. A few burned out. Chairs askew. That statue on the cement and glasses scattered about. Most of it telltale signs of a big party, but not especially unusual. Certainly nothing sinister.

"There was a statue," I said after I'd sifted through the details. "On the cement by the pool. Other than that, nothing. I wish I could be more help. It's all too hazy."

One corner of Sullivan's mouth lifted in what passes for a smile when he's working. "It's all right," he said. "I know it's tough. If you remember anything later, give me a holler."

I nodded to show how agreeable I could be.

He seemed satisfied and moved on again. "Tell me again about finding Mr. Boudreaux in the pool."

"Like I said, Aunt Yolanda saw him first. She called for me."

"Did either of you actually *see* Mr. Boudreaux fall in?"

"No. If we had, we would have helped him."

I got another eyeball, this one directed at my damp clothing. "Looks like maybe you tried to help him anyway."

"I thought maybe he was still alive. He wasn't." I glanced at the clock on the wall, realized how long we'd been sitting here, and felt my empty stomach turn over. "Could you check with your guys to see if anyone has heard from Uncle Nestor? He's been gone a long time."

Sullivan shook his head. "If anyone had heard from him, I'd know it. Let's just get through the rest of the questions and then I'll see what I can find myself." Tough cop faded for a moment and my friend made a brief appearance. "It'll be okay, Rita."

I appreciated the gesture, but we both knew he couldn't make that kind of promise. "And what if it's not? What if something happened to him? What if —" The words got stuck in my throat and tears burned my eyes. I'd been holding it together so far, but the fear of losing Uncle Nestor made it hard to breathe. I tried to remember the last time I'd actually seen him at the party, but those details were lost, too. "He and Aunt Yolanda are all I have, Liam. He *has* to be all right."

Sullivan got up from his seat and came around the table. I wish I could tell you that he gathered me in his arms and comforted all my fears, but he's not that kind of guy. He put a hand on my shoulder and murmured something I couldn't quite make out. Not nearly enough, but I guess better than nothing.

While I sobbed into my hands, Sullivan

crossed the room and plucked a couple of Zydeco napkins from the table. He shoved them at me, and I spent a minute or two mopping up so we could move on again.

When I'd dried the tears and blown my nose, I took a couple of deep breaths, trying to get the air all the way to my core, where the panic had taken up residence. It was making images of Uncle Nestor going after Big Daddy flash through my head, and they were images I did not want to remember.

Not that I thought Uncle Nestor was responsible for Big Daddy's untimely demise. But the realization that others might speculate about my uncle made everything inside me hurt.

I wadded the soggy napkins in my hand and glanced at the sequined saxophone archway. "Is it really necessary to drag my aunt off and interrogate her like a common criminal? She doesn't know anything either. And Miss Frankie shouldn't be alone at a time like this."

Sullivan linked his hands together on the table and locked his eyes on mine. "They're fine, Rita. Your aunt is being treated with respect, and Miss Frankie is a lot tougher than you give her credit for. The sooner you answer my questions, the sooner you can check on both of them. I assure you my people aren't roughing them up or shoving bamboo shoots under their fingernails. Now, if you're ready . . ."

I sat back in my chair and made an effort to look calm and collected. "Fine. What else do you want to know?"

"How about telling me when you last saw Mr. Boudreaux alive?"

"Maybe an hour before we found him in the pool," I said.

"Where was he? And what was he doing?"

"He was here, in the ballroom. Near the bandstand, I think. Talking to people."

"Any idea who he was talking to?"

I shook my head. "Like I said before, I didn't pay that much attention to him." At least, I hadn't after the fight. That had been a couple of hours earlier. He'd had time to annoy a dozen other people since then. "He talked to just about everyone in the room and he seemed to know them all, and of course, everyone knew who he was." I rubbed my forehead and looked at him from the corner of my eye. "There's going to be press, isn't there?"

"I'd count on it. Mr. Boudreaux was well known in these parts. And that's going to create pressure from the top to solve this quickly. Why? Are you worried about Zydeco?"

139

That was as good an explanation as any. I nodded and said, "We don't need any more negative publicity. We're barely climbing out of the ditch we fell into after Philippe died." But the truth was that Zydeco was nowhere near the top of the list of things I worried about. Uncle Nestor, Aunt Yolanda, and Miss Frankie took the top spots.

"We'll try to solve this quickly," Sullivan assured me. "If we can do that, you and Zydeco may not even hit the radar this time around."

I could only hope.

"It's too bad you don't remember who he was talking to," Sullivan said. "In addition to the wound that probably killed him, there's some bruising on Boudreaux's chin and cheek. Looks like maybe he was in a fight recently — like within the last few hours. I don't suppose any of you can shed any light on that?"

I argued with myself for another few seconds, vacillating between telling the truth and protecting Uncle Nestor. But again, I reasoned that somebody would mention the fight to the police, if not tonight, then soon. So I opted for the truth, even though just the thought of bringing Uncle Nestor into this made my stomach hurt.

Folding my arms across my chest, I said,

"It was nothing."

Sullivan's eyes lingered on my defensive posture a moment too long. "What was nothing?"

"The fight. It didn't mean anything. Just a couple of guys who had too much to drink, that's all."

"So you do know."

"It was over in a minute or two. And it happened hours before Big Daddy died."

"Details, Rita. Who are you talking about, and what happened?"

"You have to keep in mind how obnoxious Big Daddy was," I said, trying to smooth out the pavement before I shoved Uncle Nestor under the bus. He already thought I'd betrayed him by staying in New Orleans. He'd never forgive me for ratting him out to the police. "He was loud and abrasive and —"

"I got that part," Sullivan interrupted. "Who are you talking about?"

Hating that I had to choose between truth and loyalty, I ran my tongue across my lips again. I opened my mouth to speak, but the sound of angry shouting cut me off before I could get a word out. Sullivan and I scrambled to our feet and bolted across the ballroom. I had to struggle out of the blanket first, which put him a few steps ahead of me. He paused briefly on the threshold to growl, "Stay here," before pushing the door open and charging out onto the balcony.

Naturally, I ignored him.

I made it outside in time to see him start down the steps toward the pool, where Susannah Boudreaux was leaning heavily on a uniformed officer. She lifted one trembling hand and pointed at something — or someone — hidden from my view by a large flowering shrub. "That's him!" she shouted. "Right there."

Sullivan reached the bottom of the stairs and I craned to see who she was pointing at. I caught a glimpse of Aunt Yolanda and Miss Frankie emerging from separate doors onto the patio and a handful of crime scene techs milling about, all of whom stopped working to see who she was talking about.

"That's him," the woman shrieked again. "That's the man who attacked my husband!"

Everyone in the yard turned to stare — at Uncle Nestor.

TWELVE

Silence rang in the night air for roughly two seconds before all hell broke loose. Susannah Boudreaux screeched and pointed and demanded that my uncle be arrested, tried, and executed on the spot. Half a dozen officers drew their weapons and trained them on Uncle Nestor, all shouting at him to get down on the ground and put his hands behind his head.

Uncle Nestor was a child of the 1960s, and his distrust of "the man" was legendary in our family. I didn't know whether to be more frightened that he'd do something stupid, or angry with the police for putting him in a position that might bring out the worst in him.

And I didn't have time to figure it out. With a cry of distress, Aunt Yolanda started down the steps on the other side of the yard, heading straight for her husband. I understood why she wanted to get to him, but running into the middle of all those armed and angry cops seemed like a really bad idea.

I started down the other set of stairs, struggling to keep my balance on the slick stone. "Aunt Yolanda," I shouted. "Wait! Stop!"

She kept going. I wasn't sure if it was because she couldn't hear me over the rest of the shouting, or because she was ignoring me. Panicked, I gathered my still-damp skirt above my knees so I could make better time. "Aunt Yolanda! No!"

She reached the lower terrace and sprinted toward the pool, where Uncle Nestor was, thank God, obeying instructions. Red-faced and angry, he was down on his knees, hands linked behind his head. There'd be hell to pay when we finally got out of here, but at least he was alive to rant about it.

While one scrawny officer patted Uncle Nestor down, two others kept their weapons trained on him. I guess I understood why. He looked capable of almost anything. Relieved that, at least for the moment, he was cooperating, I whipped around to find Aunt Yolanda and spotted her at the far edge of the pool, corralled by a burly officer with a bulldog face.

She didn't look much happier than Uncle

Nestor, but I didn't care. They were both safe. That's all that mattered.

I stopped running and paused for a moment to catch my breath. The cool, damp lawn on my bare feet made me wish I'd brought the blanket with me. I shivered and started walking toward Aunt Yolanda, but a uniformed officer with a grim expression and a name tag that read *Kilpatrick* blocked my path.

"Stop right there," he barked. He was tall and thickly muscled, and it was obvious to me that he took his job seriously.

"That's my aunt," I panted. "I just want to make sure she's okay."

"She's fine. I need you to stop right where you are." I might have argued, but Kilpatrick's hand was resting on the butt of his gun and his expression said he had no qualms about shooting me where I stood.

I didn't *think* he would, but I decided not to take unnecessary chances. Nervous energy and impatience made it hard to just stand there, and the sound of Uncle Nestor's voice, gruff and raised in anger, made it even harder. I couldn't make out what he was saying, but the fact that he was saying anything at all made me nervous.

"You're making a mistake," I said to Kilpatrick. "He didn't do anything wrong."

145

Kilpatrick gave me a heavy-lidded look, but he didn't say a word. He just left me standing there, waiting, watching, and wondering, until Sullivan strode across the lawn toward me.

His eyes had turned ice cold. "You want to tell me about it?"

I wasn't completely sure what he was asking about, so I went with an innocent, "About what?"

"The fight. And don't pretend like you don't know which fight I'm talking about."

I swallowed. Shifted from foot to foot, and then came clean. "Big Daddy and Uncle Nestor?"

"Bingo."

Sullivan wasn't happy. But then, I wasn't either. I could hear someone coming up behind me, but I didn't look to see who it was. "They had a disagreement earlier. I was just about to tell you about it when Uncle Nestor showed up."

The person behind me gasped, and I knew without looking that it was Aunt Yolanda. I couldn't let myself look at her, though. Sullivan was giving me the death glare.

"And you didn't mention it before because . . ."

"Because it had nothing to do with Big Daddy's accident."

146

"Why didn't you tell *me* about this, *mija?*" Aunt Yolanda demanded.

I slid a guilty glance over my shoulder. "Because it was over in a few minutes, Aunt Yolanda. It was nothing." I tried a reassuring smile, but my lips felt frozen and lifeless. "I didn't want you to worry."

Sullivan gave me a look. "So again, you didn't mention any of this to the police because —"

"Because they're not connected," I said again.

"You mean, you don't *want* them to be connected."

"I mean that I'm *sure* they aren't connected," I said. "Big Daddy said something inappropriate. Uncle Nestor lost his cool. They exchanged a couple of punches and then they went their separate ways."

"It had to have been a minor scuffle," Miss Frankie said helpfully. "I didn't know a thing about it."

"Nestor would never hurt someone else on purpose," Aunt Yolanda agreed. "That woman is blowing the whole thing out of proportion."

"You may be right," Sullivan said gently. "But since neither you nor Miss Frankie actually witnessed the argument, you'll forgive me for keeping an open mind." He turned his attention back to me. "You know for a fact that they went their separate ways?"

Everything inside me wanted to say yes, but I couldn't make myself tell an outright lie. "No. But Uncle Nestor sort of disappeared and I thought maybe he was lying down somewhere. Parties really aren't his thing."

Sullivan let out a heavy sigh. "Okay, tell me now. And tell me everything. No holding back. What did they fight about?"

"I have no idea. I couldn't hear them."

"You didn't ask?"

"Of course I asked. Uncle Nestor wouldn't tell me."

"And you didn't think that was odd?"

I shook my head. "Uncle Nestor keeps to himself when something's wrong. It can be frustrating, but it didn't raise any red flags for me tonight."

"Big Daddy didn't say anything either?"

"He ducked the question," I said. "Frankly, I was glad to steer clear."

"Which was the best thing you could have done," Miss Frankie said. "You know how men are, Detective."

He smiled a little. "I believe I do, ma'am. Anything else you're not telling me, Rita?"

I shook my head. "Not that I can think of."

Sullivan stuffed his notebook into his breast pocket, and then he put a hand on my shoulder and gave it a reassuring squeeze. Which is one of the things I like best about him. "Why don't you take your aunt home? We'll bring your uncle over when we're finished talking to him."

I found the idea that he didn't plan to lock Uncle Nestor up overnight reassuring, but Aunt Yolanda didn't seem to appreciate that subtle distinction. She crossed her arms over her chest and lifted her chin the way I'd seen her do a thousand times when I was growing up. "I'm not going anywhere without my husband."

"It's nearly four in the morning —" Sullivan started to say.

Aunt Yolanda skewered him with a look before he could finish. "I'm not going anywhere without my husband," she repeated.

Sullivan slid a glance at me, but I wasn't about to step in. Aunt Yolanda was already upset with me for not telling her about the argument. I wasn't going to take his side against her and make things worse.

I took Aunt Yolanda's arm and turned toward the clubhouse. "We'll wait inside."

I had no idea how I'd get through another hard day at work tomorrow. Even if we went home right now, I'd barely get any sleep, which probably wouldn't help at all. But those worries fell way below convincing Sullivan that Uncle Nestor wasn't responsible for whacking Big Daddy over the head and then pushing him into the pool to drown.

THIRTEEN

The seven o'clock alarm jolted me out of a deep sleep long before I was ready. With a groan, I reached for the clock and punched the snooze button. It was barely two hours since I'd closed my eyes. Even though sunlight was already streaming in through my bedroom windows and we had a busy Saturday scheduled at Zydeco, I might have let myself slip back to sleep if reality hadn't punched me in the face with memories of last night's tragedy.

Big Daddy Boudreaux. My devastated aunt. My stubborn uncle, who had flatly refused to answer any of Sullivan's questions. Miss Frankie, who'd been showing definite signs of wear when I drove away. In the end, Sullivan had let us go home around four-thirty in the morning, but only because he had no direct evidence against Uncle Nestor and because I'd crossed my heart and hoped to die if I failed to deliver Uncle

Nestor to the police station this morning.

Sullivan's warning echoed in my head as I lay there trying to squash the sick feeling in my stomach. "I need your uncle to tell me what happened between the two of them," he'd said. "Convince him to start talking by morning or my hands will be tied. I'll have to detain him for questioning."

I'd tried all the way home to get Uncle Nestor to confide in me, but all I'd gotten for my trouble was stony silence and a reminder from Aunt Yolanda that the good Lord expects us to honor the people who raised us. Neither of them was speaking to me by the time they climbed the stairs to the guest room.

I didn't for one minute believe that Uncle Nestor had killed Big Daddy Boudreaux, but the circumstantial evidence against him was mounting. Surely Uncle Nestor could understand that, so why wasn't he doing everything he could to clear away suspicion?

Wide awake now, I pulled on my robe and hurried downstairs to the kitchen. Usually Aunt Yolanda got up with the sun, but this morning the house was still quiet. So quiet that if the patent leather pumps she'd worn last night hadn't been lying just inside the front door, I might have wondered if I'd only dreamed their visit.

Determined to start off on the right foot this morning, I pulled a canister of French roast from the pantry and put on a pot. First things first. Aunt Yolanda and Uncle Nestor would need a good breakfast when they got up. Besides, working in the kitchen always helped me think. After breakfast we'd give our statements to the police and then I'd head to Zydeco, where I could at least pretend that it was just another day.

I'd just started the coffee brewing when my cell phone rang, sounding unnaturally cheerful and far too loud in that quiet house. I fumbled with the phone, trying to silence it before it woke up my aunt and uncle.

"Rita? Thank God I caught you," Edie said when I answered. "Where are you?"

"Still at home," I said around a yawn. "I was just about to call you. What's going on? Is something wrong?"

"Wrong?" Edie snorted a laugh. "Besides Big Daddy Boudreaux dying at The Shores, you mean? Isn't that enough?"

My spirits drooped. "You've heard?"

"Um . . . yeah. It's all over the news. I heard it on the radio when I was coming to work this morning, and Good Day New Orleans is all over it. We have the TV on in the back so we can watch the reports. I take

153

it you haven't been watching?"

"I just got up," I admitted. "Didn't get to bed until almost five." I was going to pay for that later. "So what are they saying?"

"Just that Big Daddy Boudreaux is dead under suspicious circumstances. No real details yet except that it happened at the Musterion party."

I was realistic enough to know the news wouldn't stay buried, especially since Big Daddy had been a bigwig in the business community and all, but I'd been hoping for a *little* more time. "So what else are they saying?"

"They're talking a lot about his work, his contributions to the community, and his connections within Musterion. Of course, they're all over the fact that he was elected as captain for next year, and practically naming him a saint for some big-deal charity fund-raiser he was in charge of last fall."

"I'm pretty sure he was no saint," I mumbled. I wondered how Judd was taking the news that his brother had been killed, and what Mellie was feeling.

"So . . . suspicious circumstances. That's code for murder, right?" Edie asked, cutting into my thoughts. "Do the police have any idea who did it?"

"Not that they're sharing with me. I don't

think they have any solid leads yet. It's still too early in the investigation. But I have to take my aunt and uncle down to the station this morning so we can give our official statements. I don't know how long that will take, but I'll get there as soon as I can."

"Of course. Sure. We'll be okay for a while."

"I hope it doesn't take long," I said. "Big Daddy's wife practically accused Uncle Nestor of murder last night. I'm pretty sure it was just the booze talking, but it may take a little while to get that all straightened out."

"The police don't think he did it, do they?"

"Of course not," I said sharply. "My uncle didn't have anything to do with Big Daddy's death."

"I never said he did," Edie said quickly. "But if the police want statements from all of you, you're already connected to the murder in their minds."

"Only because Aunt Yolanda and I found the body. That makes us material witnesses or something."

"That's kind of the point, Rita," she said. After a slight hesitation, she continued, "Don't worry about us. If you need to take a day or two with your aunt and uncle, that's okay."

I blurted a disbelieving laugh. "Considering how much work we have to do? Absolutely not. I'll be in as soon as we're finished at the police station. I'm hoping it won't be later than noon."

Again a beat or two passed before Edie responded. "At least take the day off," she said. "Your aunt and uncle are probably pretty upset. They'll need you around."

Yeah. Maybe. But I was getting a strange vibe from her. "What's going on, Edie? Why do I get the feeling this isn't really about me and my family?"

She sighed heavily, and when she spoke again, her voice was softer, as if she didn't want to be overheard. "It's nothing personal, Rita. It's just that there are already reporters outside. Thanks to the staff at the country club, they've made the connection between last night's party and Zydeco."

The country club staff? My money was on that unpleasant kitchen manager.

"You were the hostess," Edie went on. "So they're going to be looking for a statement from you. Ox and I both think it might be a good idea for you to lay low for a few days — you know, until the police have a real suspect."

She didn't have to say the rest, but I didn't like hearing that she and Ox had been making decisions for the bakery behind my back. I was already tired and cranky, so her argument rubbed me the wrong way. "Listen, Edie, I refuse to cower and hide just because Big Daddy Boudreaux had the misfortune to die at that stupid party. And maybe you should remember that I'm the one in charge at Zydeco, not Ox. He needs to quit trying to take over."

"He's not trying to take over," she snapped back. "He's concerned about the bakery, that's all. If Zydeco goes under, we all lose."

"Zydeco is *not* going under," I insisted. "Instead of anticipating the worst, why don't we do something constructive?"

"Such as?"

I floundered for a moment, trying to come up with something. "Put something on the website maybe. A statement about how sorry we all are over the unfortunate passing of such a beloved public figure."

"We could do that," she said slowly. "Are you going to write it?"

"Ask Ox to do it. If he works fast, he can text it to me for approval and have it uploaded before I even leave the police station. Just please work with me and not against me. My aunt and uncle aren't speaking to me, and I don't need you and Ox throwing up roadblocks and making things worse."

"We're not trying to make things worse," she said. "We're just trying to look out for Zydeco while your attention is splintered." She took a deep breath and let it out slowly, as if I was trying her patience. "Look, Rita, you can't take care of everything all the time, and right now you have your hands full. Nobody's trying to take your job or push you out. Let us help you."

I hesitated, but only for a heartbeat. Accepting help doesn't come easily to me, but she had a point and I'd be foolish not to acknowledge it. Besides, tired as I was, I needed help remembering my own name. I rubbed my temples with my fingertips, as if that might relieve the stress headache I could feel starting. I sat down at the kitchen table. "I wish I knew what Uncle Nestor's argument with Big Daddy was about last night. If I knew that, maybe I could convince him to talk to me about it."

She laughed at that. "Their *argument*? Is that what you're calling it?"

I stopped rubbing and leaned my head against the back of the chair. "Fine. Their fight." A memory of last night wormed its way through the fog of exhaustion and I sat up again quickly. "Hey! You were there. Did you hear what they were talking about before the fight?"

Edie didn't say anything for a few seconds, but I could hear her breathing so I knew we hadn't been disconnected. "I was there," she said after a while, "but I didn't actually hear much. And most of what your uncle said was in Spanish."

"So nothing?"

Another pause. "I don't think it's a good idea for you to get involved, Rita. Just let the police do their job."

"I'm not trying to get involved," I said impatiently. "Sullivan asked me to get Uncle Nestor to talk. I'm just trying to cooperate with the police. If you know anything about that fight, please tell me."

Edie sighed heavily. "All right. But I'm only doing this under protest. I hope you know that."

"Duly noted. What did you hear?"

"Not much, like I said before, but I'm pretty sure your uncle said something about his family's honor. That's it, though. I swear."

Everything inside me turned icy cold. Nothing means more to Uncle Nestor than family. He's not a cold-blooded killer, but if anything was going to push him over the edge, insulting or hurting someone in his family would be what did it. "That must mean Big Daddy said something about Aunt Yolanda," I said, feeling miserable.

"Or you."

"Or me," I agreed reluctantly. Considering what a creep Big Daddy was and the fact that Uncle Nestor doesn't go around punching people indiscriminately, it must have been something completely inappropriate. No wonder he was closed up tighter than a clam. He must know that if he told the police what they fought over, the police would be convinced he had a motive for murder.

FOURTEEN

Standing in the middle of the kitchen and sipping French roast as if it would save my life, I spent the next few minutes hashing out the day's work schedule with Edie. She tried again to convince me to steer clear, but I still thought she underestimated me. I was perfectly capable of giving the press a brief statement without embarrassing Zydeco. And once the police cleared things up with Uncle Nestor, there would be nothing to worry about on that score.

I made a batch of biscuit dough using ice-cold water and butter straight out of the fridge. When the biscuits were cut out and ready for baking, I pulled an onion, eggs, shredded white cheddar, and bacon from the refrigerator and took out my frustrations and confusion at the cutting board.

Cooking has always been soothing to me, and as I chopped and sautéed, the scents and repetitive motions helped clear my

161

mind and lift my spirits. After a few minutes, I felt good enough to begin my mental to-do list. In addition to the work at the bakery, I needed to call Miss Frankie to make sure she was holding up all right. Even if she and Big Daddy weren't close, they'd clearly known each other for a long time. Finding an old friend dead was bound to have a negative impact on anyone's day. I also wanted to pay a condolence call on Judd Boudreaux. It seemed like the right thing to do, and it would give me a chance to return his suit jacket.

And, of course, I needed to take care of my houseguests.

I crisped bacon and crumbled it, then spread it and the sautéed onions over the biscuits. After whisking together heavy cream and sour cream, I mixed in the cheese and eggs, then poured the whole thing over the onion-and-bacon-covered biscuits. By the time I slid the baking dish into the oven, my mouth was watering in anticipation.

I turned on the TV so I could hear the news for myself. After a few minutes, the sports report gave way to a series of commercials, one of which featured Big Daddy Boudreaux skeet shooting and blasting clay pigeons to smithereens. Each one was painted with a number to represent the price of a used car on his lot, and each one exploded after a blast of his shotgun, showing his adoring public how Big Daddy was slashing prices just for them.

"This van has got to go!" he announced with a cheerful grin. "It's so spotless and the mileage is so low, we could get away with selling it to you for sticker price, but we aren't like that here at Big Daddy's. Come in today and I'll sell it to you. Not for twenty thousand." *Kablam!* "Not for eighteen." *Kaboom!* "Not even for seventeen-five." *Kapowie!* "No siree. Come to Big Daddy's today and you'll walk out the door for seventeen three thirty-nine. That price is so low I ought to check myself in for a psych evaluation."

He brayed a laugh that made my skin crawl. It was eerie watching him preen for the cameras.

While the morning team covered the world news, I sat down with my coffee mug just as Aunt Yolanda shuffled into the kitchen wearing a pink silk nightgown and matching robe. Her dark hair was tousled and her eyes were puffy. From sleep? Or had she been crying?

I watched closely as she poured herself coffee and carried it to the table. I was

163

searching for signs that would help me gauge her mood. She wasn't one to hold grudges, but we were all walking in uncharted territory and I wasn't sure what to expect from her this morning.

Cradling the cup in both hands, she closed her eyes and inhaled deeply. "This coffee smells like heaven," she said when she opened her eyes again. "I really need it this morning."

She sounded normal enough. I smiled with relief. "You and me both. I'm sorry your first night in town was so —"

"Eventful?" She finished the sentence for me and smiled softly. "It certainly wasn't your fault. We'll go see the police first thing and then we can put this whole nightmare behind us."

"It shouldn't take long," I agreed. "What do you and Uncle Nestor have on the agenda after we visit the police station? I wish I could show you around the city, but I have to get to work. Still, that shouldn't keep the two of you from doing some sightseeing."

Aunt Yolanda put her cup on the table and stood. "We haven't talked about that yet. I guess we'll figure it out when we get there. Now, what shall I fix for breakfast?"

"You're not fixing anything," I said. "I've

already got a breakfast casserole in the oven, and I was planning to make a tropical fruit salad to go along with it." The salad was a recipe I'd picked up in Chicago. One of my favorites.

Aunt Yolanda sat back down and her shoulders sagged. From this angle I could see shadows under her eyes and lines around her mouth I'd never noticed before. I knew with a certainty I couldn't explain that none of them had appeared overnight. The realization that she was aging made me unspeakably sad. I said the only thing I could force out of my mouth: "If you don't want the fruit salad, I can throw together something else."

"I'm sure it will be delicious." She straightened her shoulders and lifted her chin. As if she willed it, the light shifted and the shadows under her eyes faded. "You don't need to take care of us, *mija*. We'll be fine."

"Are you kidding? You're guests in my home. If I let you fend for yourselves, my aunt would skin me alive. Sit. Enjoy your coffee."

She sank back, looking a little lost. That was another thing I'd never seen before.

I carried my cup back into the kitchen and gathered mango, papaya, pineapple, kiwi, and mandarin oranges. "We'll be down near the French Quarter," I said, trying to keep the tone light. "Maybe you could spend some time there. There's a parade scheduled for later, so it'll be crowded, but you could take one of the walking tours of the Quarter and Jackson Square. Maybe even wander down to the river."

Aunt Yolanda held up a hand to stop me before I could finish. "You're wearing me out already. We didn't come to see the city, Rita. We came to see you. Nestor has been worried about you."

I pulled a fresh mango onto the cutting board. "He doesn't have to be. I just wish we could have a little fun before you leave. Last night's party was work for me, but between now and Mardi Gras there's something going on almost all the time. Is there any chance you could stick around for a few more days?"

She shook her head. "We have tickets on a ten-fifteen flight on Monday morning. We just wanted to see where you've chosen to call home."

I wasn't sure whether I was more disappointed or relieved, but I held out my arms like a game-show model. "Well, here it is. What do you think?"

"It's a lovely home, Rita. Truly beautiful.

But that's not what I meant. You know how protective Nestor is of our family, and you have a special place in his heart. You're his only sister's only child. The only girl in our family. He's been worried sick about you here, alone —"

"I was alone in Chicago," I reminded her.

"You were at pastry school, and then you were married. You weren't alone for long."

"So you're here to check up on me." A pebble of bitterness found its way into my heart. I had four strapping cousins, each of whom had disappointed his parents in some creative way — Santos by marrying the wrong woman, Aaron by dropping out of college, Manny by dodging the family business to become a musician, and Julio by fathering a baby out of wedlock. He'd married the mother eventually, but for a while it had filled Aunt Yolanda with a deep and abiding shame. But *I* was the one they'd come to check up on?

Was it just because I was "the girl"? Or because I was my mother's daughter? I knew that my mother had disappointed her older brother with some of her choices. Sometimes it seemed as if he was biding his time, just waiting for me to follow in her footsteps.

I sliced off one side of the mango and

made angry gashes in the pale orange flesh, scoring it with a little too much gusto and slicing through the skin. "I'm doing fine," I said again. "But he doesn't believe that, does he?"

Aunt Yolanda scowled at me over the rim of her coffee mug. "He's concerned. He loves you. Is that so bad?"

I stopped slicing and put the knife aside. "He thinks I made a mistake by staying here."

"He wants to be sure you didn't," Aunt Yolanda said. Her smile was gentle, and I thought about all the times she'd interceded between Uncle Nestor and me when I was younger.

I held out my arms again to encompass the magnificent kitchen in the heart of my magnificent home. "I've managed not to go wild with all of this for months. You'd think he'd realize that I'm not going to lose my head now. And yeah, I'm happy. How could I not be?"

"It takes more than things to make a person happy," Aunt Yolanda chided me.

The grin slid from my face. "I'm talking about more than things, *Tía*. I'm doing what I always wanted to do. The bakery is amazing. The staff is great. And New Orleans is —"

"A long way from home," my aunt said before I could finish. "Your uncle and I miss you."

The look on her face made me uncomfortable. There are few things I hate more than making Aunt Yolanda sad. "I miss you, too," I said. "But don't you want me to make my own way in the world?"

"Yes, of course."

"So here I am. Making my way. I'm not gone, you know. I'm just not underfoot all the time."

Aunt Yolanda scowled at me. "You were never underfoot, Rita. You must know that."

"I do," I assured her, although there was that lingering doubt. "You and Uncle Nestor saved my life when you took me in. I love you both more than I can say."

"And yet you're happy to live so far away."

I expected guilt trips from Uncle Nestor, but Aunt Yolanda was usually more understanding. Coming from her, this conversation left me tilting on my axis like an off-center cake. "I lived further away than this when Philippe and I were married," I reminded her. "It didn't seem to bother you then."

Aunt Yolanda touched my cheek with her fingertips. "That was different."

"Because I had a husband?" I stared at

169

her in disbelief. "I could almost expect something that archaic to come out of Uncle Nestor's mouth, but not yours."

Aunt Yolanda gave me a look, reached for her mug, and sipped. "That's not what I meant, Rita. Please don't put words in my mouth. Your uncle will talk to you when the time is right."

"When the time is right?" I stared at her, unable to speak for a long moment. "I hope you won't take that attitude when it comes to the police."

"Your uncle knows what's best."

"I'm not so sure," I said. "Look, he's not the king of the castle here. He's one guy on a list of suspects in a murder investigation. He doesn't get to call the shots."

The shadows in her eyes appeared again and her lips formed a thin, disapproving line. "He is not a murder suspect."

"The dead man's wife seems to think he is," I said. "And the police can't clear him if he doesn't tell them what they want to know. I love the fact that you're so supportive of him, *Tía*," I said, putting my hands over hers, "but throwing up roadblocks to protect him isn't doing him any favors. If you really want to help him, convince him to talk to the police when we get to the station."

Her gaze flashed to my face. "He's not ready."

"He *has* to be ready," I insisted. "It's not up to him."

She shook her head again. "He has a hard head, your uncle. You know that."

I did, but frustration made the headache I'd been fighting all morning spike sharply. "Did he at least tell *you* what happened between him and Big Daddy?"

"Me? No."

"Did you meet Big Daddy last night? Did you hear anything that went on between the two of them?"

Aunt Yolanda nodded. "I met him for a moment. We barely spoke." She turned her hands over and laced her fingers through mine. "Don't worry, *mija*. Your uncle did not kill that man."

"I know he didn't," I said. "Now we just have to make sure the police believe it, too."

Aunt Yolanda smiled softly. "Your uncle will do the right thing," she said firmly. She glanced around, her expression curious. "Where is he anyway?"

I was halfway to my feet, but her question stopped me cold. "What do you mean, where is he? I thought he was in the guest room with you."

"With me? No." A frown furrowed Aunt

171

Yolanda's brow. "He was gone when I woke up. Are you saying you haven't seen him this morning?"

My heart slammed in my chest and all sorts of diabolical possibilities raced through my head as I punched his number into my cell phone. When I heard the phone ringing upstairs, I disconnected and hurried to the front door, cursing myself for not checking earlier. I never should have trusted Uncle Nestor to behave for a couple of hours. Sure enough, the deadbolt had been unlocked and so had the regular door lock.

Sullivan had warned me to keep an eye on Uncle Nestor, but I'd let him stroll right out the front door while I slept.

Epic fail.

FIFTEEN

Heart thudding, I raced up the stairs to my bedroom. My head shuffled through questions the whole way. Where had Uncle Nestor gone? And why hadn't I heard him leave? Not that I expected answers. I still didn't know where he'd disappeared to last night. Why was he being so secretive? Was he trying to protect Aunt Yolanda or me? If so, what had Big Daddy said that made him think we needed protecting?

I tugged on a pair of jeans and a Phoenix Suns T-shirt so faded I could barely see the logo anymore. Back on the first floor, I stepped into flip-flops just as Aunt Yolanda appeared at the top of the stairs, also fully dressed, and looking worried in spite of her assurances that everything would turn out okay.

"Finding that man's body in the pool has made me jittery, I guess," she said. "Nestor's probably gone for a walk to clear his head.

173

I'm sure he is just fine."

There were two big problems with that theory. First, Uncle Nestor doesn't *take* walks. The idea of him willingly going anywhere on foot was as foreign to me as the idea of putting powdered sugar in an omelet. And second, Uncle Nestor hates mornings. Even if he woke up with a brand-new personality and decided to take a stroll, he wouldn't have done it with the sunrise.

"You're probably right," I said, "but he's not familiar with the area and he doesn't have his phone with him. He can't even call if he gets disoriented." I smiled, trying to hide my own worry and keep hers under control. Somehow, I kept my voice sounding normal when I said, "I'll feel better knowing that he's all right, that's all."

"You don't think something's happened to him, do you?" Her bottom lip trembled slightly. She looked away, trying to hide it from me, but she was too late. It was a little thing, but completely out of character for my aunt. She's a warm and loving person, but she's not a crier. My worry level ramped up another notch.

"Are you sure he didn't say anything to you about going out?"

Aunt Yolanda shook her head and sank into a chair near the window. "No. I didn't even hear him get up."

"That's not surprising," I said, still trying to sound reassuring. "I'm sure you were exhausted after traveling all day and then staying up until almost sunrise. Not to mention all the adrenaline of last night. The surprising thing is that he dragged himself out of bed so early." He must have had a compelling reason.

She glanced out the window, took a deep breath, and closed her eyes as she exhaled. When she opened them again, she treated me to a shaky smile. "You don't have to pretend with me, Rita. It's not becoming."

"I didn't mean to sound condescending," I said. "I just don't want you to worry. But I'm having a hard time imagining Uncle Nestor getting up with the dawn and heading out into a strange city for his morning constitutional. That's just not something he does."

"It is now."

I could only stare at her.

"Times change," she said, but her voice sounded strangely quiet. "People change."

I paused with my hand on the doorknob and looked at her more closely. "I've only been living here for six months."

"Seven."

"Okay. Seven. And in that time Uncle

Nestor has started going for walks? On purpose? What's going on? What aren't you telling me?"

"He's not getting any younger, *mija*. Neither of us is. He's been burning the candle at both ends for most of his life. It's time to slow down a little, that's all."

I didn't have time to figure out whether or not I believed that explanation because just then I heard footsteps coming up the front walk and everything else evaporated out of my head. Almost weak with relief, I opened the door.

Lights flashed in my face and a middle-aged man with a hawk nose and graying hair stuck a microphone in my face. I covered my eyes so I could see and registered Uncle Nestor standing beside the reporter, his leathery face creased with irritation.

"Miss Lucero," the reporter said, "could I ask you a few questions about last night's event at The Shores?"

I'd assured Edie that I could handle this, but not here, on my front step, without my hair and makeup done. And not before I'd had a chance to get Uncle Nestor's side of the story. "I'll be happy to talk with you later —" I began.

The reporter cut me off. "You were the hostess for last night's Musterion party, is that right? Were you a friend of Big Daddy's?"

"I met him for the first time last night," I said. "Now if you'll excuse me . . ."

The reporter turned away from me and focused on Uncle Nestor. Not exactly what I had in mind.

"Is it true that you attacked Mr. Boudreaux last night?"

"Where did you hear that?" I demanded before Uncle Nestor could answer.

The reporter gave a little shrug. "I have my sources."

"*What* sources?"

He ignored my question and lobbed another one of his own. "My contacts tell me that the police were very interested in what Susannah Boudreaux had to say when they questioned her. What's your connection to her?"

"There isn't one," I snapped, wondering which big-mouthed police officer had given her my uncle's name. I grabbed Uncle Nestor's arm and jerked him toward the open door. "Get inside," I ordered. "Don't say a word."

He went as stiff as a board and dug in his heels. Which made my anger spike. I needed a little cooperation, not for him to be even more difficult. Putting myself between the camera and Uncle Nestor, I tried hard not to look flustered and nervous. "If you have questions about Mr. Boudreaux's unfortunate death," I said, "please take them to the police."

"I'm told the police haven't ruled out foul play." The reporter made it sound like an accusation. I finally placed him as a reporter with NLTV, a small local station that ranked fairly low in the market share. Behind him, a youthful cameraman in jeans and a T-shirt captured every expression. Viewers of the station would judge our guilt or innocence by what they thought they saw on our faces. I knew they would, because that's what I'd do. It's human nature.

"You'll have to ask the police about that," I suggested sweetly as I gave Uncle Nestor a push toward the door, muttering, "I'm serious, Uncle Nestor. In the house. *Now!*"

He finally started moving, and I trailed behind him. Five feet and one door, and we'd be safe — at least until the next time we opened the door. Four feet. Three . . .

"NLTV has received other tips from concerned citizens about the altercation between the two of you," the reporter said. "I've been told that it happened just a few hours before Big Daddy was found dead. What do you have to say about that?"

"Nothing," I tossed over my shoulder. "No comment." I gave Uncle Nestor one last shove and he was finally inside. I grabbed the door and started to shut it just as Mr. NLTV asked, "What are you trying to hide, Miss Lucero?"

I slammed the door in his face and leaned against it heavily. My heart was thundering like a timpani drum and my breath came in short, raspy gasps. We'd escaped — at least for now — but I had a bone to pick with Sullivan when I saw him.

As my breathing began to even out again, I realized that maybe it wasn't the police who'd connected the dots between the fight and Uncle Nestor for the reporter. Uncle Nestor was a stranger in town, but he'd probably been introduced to more than a hundred people last night. I had no idea how many of them were aware of the fight. I could have sworn that only a few people had known about it. Apparently someone had told Susannah Boudreaux about it, and she'd probably picked up Uncle Nestor's name from the police. If she liked to complain like Judd claimed, she could be venting to anyone who'd listen.

And if Susannah Boudreaux was throwing Uncle Nestor to the wolves, we could be in big trouble.

Not good. Not good at all.

SIXTEEN

After a few moments, the voice on the other side of the door faded and my heartbeat stopped banging in my ear. As my head cleared, I began to notice details that had escaped me outside, like the fact that Uncle Nestor was wearing jogging shorts and a gray sweatshirt, and that his sweatshirt had several damp patches that hinted at physical exertion.

Aunt Yolanda hurried toward him, her face creased with worry. "What was that?"

"A reporter." He pulled off the sweatshirt and wadded it in his hands. "Asking about last night."

Aunt Yolanda's eyes clouded. "A reporter? Here? Why?"

"He was looking for Uncle Nestor," I said. "Susannah Boudreaux told him about the fight Uncle Nestor had with Big Daddy."

Anger flickered across my aunt's face. "Why would she do such a thing?"

181

"Apparently, she thinks Uncle Nestor whacked her husband on the head and pushed him into the pool," I said. "Or maybe she just wants the police to think that. She was talking to Big Daddy's ex-wife at the end of the party, and I thought she seemed upset at the time. Maybe she already knew that her husband was dead." It was a stretch, but I was desperate enough to clutch at any straw I could find.

Uncle Nestor grunted. "She's a foolish woman."

"She'd have to be, to marry Big Daddy Boudreaux," I agreed.

As if that had solved all of his problems, Uncle Nestor kissed Aunt Yolanda on the cheek and started walking toward the stairs.

But I wasn't finished with him yet. "Hey! Wait a second," I said. "We need to talk. Where have you been?"

"Out," he said, and kept walking.

Oh no. No, no, no. Outside, he wouldn't move to save my life. Now, he wouldn't stand still for even a second? My frustration level rose a few degrees. I hurried past him and blocked the stairs. "Out where? And don't tell me it's none of my business. You have some explaining to do, *Tío*."

He scowled so hard his neck almost disappeared, and he wiped sweat from his forehead with a sleeve. "I felt like getting some air. Is there a law against that?"

"There ought to be, especially when you're a person of interest in a murder case and there's a reporter camped on the front steps. How did you get past that guy when you left anyway?"

He shrugged and looked at me as if I'd asked a silly question. "I didn't have to get past him. He wasn't there when I left."

That surprised me. "He wasn't? What time did you leave?"

"It was early. I didn't look at the clock."

I didn't believe that for an instant. Uncle Nestor is almost fanatical about the time, and being late for anything makes him edgy. But I realized that he was steering me off-track, so I zeroed back in on what I really wanted to know. "Where did you go?"

Aunt Yolanda put a hand on my shoulder and said, "Let's talk about this later. Nestor only walked through the door a minute ago."

Uncle Nestor waved her off with a flick of his wrist. "It's all right, Yolanda." Turning back to me, he said, "I told you already. I wanted some air. I walked around a block or two, and came back. And now I want a shower."

He started to walk past me, but I held my ground. "Uh-uh. Not yet. I need some

183

answers. I know you both think I'm being pushy, but Detective Sullivan *asked* me to talk with you, and we have to meet him at the station in an hour. Promise me you'll tell him everything."

He looked at me as if I'd said a word he didn't understand. "Everything?"

"Yeah. Everything. What you and Big Daddy fought about last night. Where you were when he died. Why Susannah Boudreaux is trying to make you look guilty. You know . . . the facts."

The frown on Uncle Nestor's face deepened. "How would I know what that crazy woman is thinking?"

"She must have some reason for trying to make you look guilty. Did you even meet her last night? Was she there when you and Big Daddy fought? I don't remember seeing her, but maybe I missed her."

Uncle Nestor's irritation level went from zero to sixty in a heartbeat. "This is ridiculous. You're forgetting who you're talking to, Rita. I don't have to answer to you."

His sudden flash of anger surprised me. "I'm not the one being ridiculous," I said. "I'm not the one who's refusing to explain why I punched a man in the nose who just happened to end up dead a couple of hours later. I'm not the one refusing to say where

I was when Big Daddy was being murdered. And I'm not the one sneaking out of the house at daybreak and then acting like it's no big deal. What's going on with you? Why are you acting like this?"

Uncle Nestor's gaze shot briefly to Aunt Yolanda, but whatever he was looking for on her face, I sure didn't see it. She leaned against the wall, arms crossed, eyes narrowed at me as if I'd crossed the line.

Yeah, sure, I was the one being unreasonable. "Come on," I said, pleading with her to help me. "You can't seriously think he's being smart about this. He's in big trouble. Help me convince him of that."

"Everything will be fine," she said. "It's in the Lord's hands."

I plowed my fingers through my hair and growled in frustration. "I'm all for trusting in God," I said, clenching my teeth to keep myself from shouting at her. "But Uncle Nestor can't just sit here, refusing to talk, and expect God to pull his butt out of the fire. It doesn't work that way."

Aunt Yolanda gasped and put her hand over her heart. Uncle Nestor got in my face. "Seems to me, somebody's forgotten the way she was raised. *And* who raised her. Don't you ever speak to your aunt that way again."

185

"Then talk to me! Give me something I can tell Liam when we get to the station so he can cross you off the list of suspects!"

Something unpleasant flashed through Nestor's dark eyes. "Is this *Liam* a special friend of yours? Is *he* why you turned your back on your family?"

My uncle can be intimidating, and he was working up a heavy head of steam, but we have the same blood flowing through our veins. I felt my temper snap like a toothpick. "Don't you dare try to change the subject."

"Don't you dare try to evade my question. Is that what this is about, Rita? Some man?"

For half a heartbeat I felt about fifteen again. Young. Defenseless. And yes, even a little frightened. But I wasn't a kid anymore. I owned this house. Nobody could send me away because I'd made them unhappy.

I straightened my spine and looked him in the eye. "You're so busy trying to pin the blame for my decision on someone or something," I shouted. "Why can't you just accept the fact that I left New Mexico because I wanted to?"

"Why? Didn't we give you enough? Didn't we do enough for you? You needed this fancy house and that Mercedes?"

I was dimly aware of Aunt Yolanda saying

something and trying to wedge herself between us, but I was too angry to stop now. "You gave me plenty," I shouted at the man who'd been like a father to me. "You did everything I could have asked for, and I love you for it. So don't you dare try to make me out to be some ungrateful stray you took in so you can feel better about yourself!"

"That's what you think I'm doing?"

"Isn't it?"

He tossed his wadded sweatshirt onto the stairs and used both hands to punctuate his conversation. "That's the trouble with you, Rita. You've got tunnel vision. All you can see is one thing. You're just like your mother."

I wasn't sure what "one thing" he was talking about, but the last part scored a direct hit. "That's the nicest thing you've said to me in years," I snarled.

"Always chasing the dream," he said. "Always looking for something better." His flying hands came close to my face. I knew he wasn't trying to hit me, but I moved up a step to make sure he didn't accidentally connect.

"So? What's wrong with that? What's wrong with trying to improve my life? And maybe I do have tunnel vision, but that's not a bad thing either. Right now, I seem to be the only one in the family who can see what's going on here."

Aunt Yolanda managed to squeeze in between us. "Stop it, you two! Stop right now."

Uncle Nestor stopped waving his hands and clenched them at his sides instead. "What's wrong with that," he ground out between teeth clenched as tightly as my own, "is that you only see what you want to see. If you had some problem working with me, you should have talked to me."

"I tried, but you wouldn't listen. You were smothering me. You put me in the kitchen and gave me entry-level jobs that were far below my skill level, and you expected me to keep my mouth shut and be happy about it. I'm a trained pastry chef, not a short-order cook."

He shook a finger in my face, but he had to reach over Aunt Yolanda's shoulder to do it. "You're forgetting yourself, little girl."

"I'm not a little girl," I snapped. "That's what you don't seem to remember. If you want to know why I decided to move here, take a look in the mirror."

I wanted to take the words back the instant they left my mouth. Uncle Nestor's expression, filled with a mixture of fury and hurt feelings, made me want to crawl into a hole and hide. He pushed past me again, grabbing his sweatshirt as he pounded up the stairs.

This time I didn't even try to stop him.

Aunt Yolanda started after him, angrier than I'd ever seen her. She stopped halfway up the stairs and turned back to me. "That was a thoughtless thing to say, Rita."

"I know. I'm sorry. He just makes me so mad sometimes."

"Well, obviously, the feeling is mutual. But I won't let you upset him like that again. He's not a well man, so don't say anything you can't take back. He needs rest and quiet, not arguing and accusations."

I heard myself gasp. "What do you mean? What's wrong with him?"

"We'll talk about it later," she said, and headed upstairs to check on Uncle Nestor.

Later. That's all I'd heard since they got here. I had so many questions that needed answers, I could only hope that "later" didn't come too late.

SEVENTEEN

To my relief, the NLTV news truck had disappeared by the time we stepped outside again, but even that didn't ease the tension between the three of us. We made the drive to the police station in stony silence, but not because I wanted it that way. In fact, nothing had really gone my way since yesterday. Big Daddy's murder had thrown my whole life off-kilter, and I wanted it back on track. I wanted to clear Uncle Nestor and find out that he wasn't really sick after all. Not necessarily in that order.

The bright sunlight and clear blue skies overhead mocked the shadows Aunt Yolanda had planted in my heart while we were standing on the staircase. My imagination was working overtime, considering and cataloging every horrible disease it was possible for Uncle Nestor to have contracted. Searching his face in the rearview mirror for clues. Wondering how many possibilities

I'd missed.

My mood fluctuated as I drove, alternating between irritation, guilt, and sheer terror at the thought of losing Uncle Nestor. He'd been my rock since my parents died, when I was twelve. I couldn't imagine a world without him in it. What's more, I didn't want to imagine it.

As we drew closer to the French Quarter, traffic slowed to a crawl and people lined the sidewalks, claiming spots for that night's parade. Some were in costume, some in street clothes, but they all seemed in the mood to do what the people in New Orleans do best — they were ready to party.

Under other circumstances, I might have pointed out places of interest on our way, but I wasn't in the mood to play travel guide, and I was pretty sure neither of the grim-faced people riding with me had any interest in the scenery.

We managed to avoid any reporters on our way to the front doors of the station, where Detective Sullivan met us. In spite of my protests, Aunt Yolanda and I were shuffled off with Officer Crump to read and sign our printed statements while Sullivan led Uncle Nestor down a long corridor for more questioning.

I didn't want to leave Uncle Nestor's side.

Logically, I knew it was unlikely that Uncle Nestor would keel over while he was with Sullivan, but I wasn't exactly firing on all cylinders. I'd learned at an early age that bad things happened when I let loved ones out of my sight.

But Uncle Nestor strode away as if nothing unusual were happening, and I took my cues from Aunt Yolanda. She appeared calm, so I tried to look the same.

When we were finished, Officer Crump escorted us to a long row of plastic chairs in a hallway lined with doors, and told us to wait there.

It was the first time we'd been alone since Aunt Yolanda had delivered her bombshell. The first chance we'd had to talk about Uncle Nestor. I waited for her to say something first for as long as I could stand it, which ended up being about five and a half seconds.

"You can't just leave me hanging like that," I said, shifting in my seat so I could look at her. "What's wrong with him?"

Aunt Yolanda slid a glance in my direction. "I'm sorry, *mija*. I should have told you sooner, I know."

"So tell me now."

She sighed softly, but it carried a heavy load of worry and heartache. "It's his heart."

My own heart dropped out of my chest in dismay at the same time it filled with relief that the word *cancer* hadn't come out of her mouth. "What's wrong with it?"

"He had a minor heart attack a few weeks ago, *mija*. He was at work when the pains started. Santos called the paramedics, thank God. Nestor insisted it was just heartburn."

I swear the ground shifted beneath my feet, but I managed to calm myself with the realization that he'd obviously made it to the hospital in time. I made a mental note to thank my cousin for making that call. "Why didn't you tell me?"

"I didn't want to worry you. You're so far away. How would it have helped for you to know? It would only have made you upset. You'd have worked yourself up over things you couldn't help with or change."

Usually I find her unruffled calm soothing. At the moment, it made me want to hit something.

I got to my feet, too agitated to sit still. "I assume the boys all knew about this."

Aunt Yolanda scowled. "Don't go there, Rita."

"I think we're already there, don't you? You told the boys, but you didn't tell me." Whether that was because I wasn't actually one of their children or because of the miles between us, I'd probably never know. It hurt me to think about that, so I tried to focus on the future. "How is he now?"

"Doing better. Well enough to travel, which is a big thing. But his doctor wants him to avoid stress. And you know how he is at the restaurant."

I barked a laugh. So much for avoiding stress on their vacation. Besides, Uncle Nestor thrives on stress. He isn't truly happy unless he's worried about something. "So you came here and left Santos in charge at the restaurant?" Santos has been working at Agave since the day Uncle Nestor opened the restaurant's doors. He's talented and competent, organized and well respected among the staff. He's also one of the big reasons I'd never have risen too far up the ranks if I'd stayed at Agave. He was the oldest son. The heir apparent. "How's Uncle Nestor dealing with that?"

"He's fine with it." Aunt Yolanda slid another glance at me and her lips curved ever so slightly. "For the most part."

I smiled and shook my head. "He hates it, doesn't he?"

"He's struggling," she agreed.

I sobered and thought back over the things I'd seen and heard since they came to town. "So the jogging? That's for real?"

"He's under doctor's orders to get some exercise, to change his diet. To change his life, really."

I sat beside her again, leaning forward so that my arms rested on my thighs. "No wonder he's been in such a foul mood."

She nodded sadly. "It's hard on him, but he's trying. He hates what the doctor has told him to do, but he wants to stay alive for the boys and the grandkids." She touched my arm briefly, "And for you. He loves you like a daughter, Rita. We both do."

Tears welled in my eyes. I brushed them away with the back of my hand, refusing to dwell on the negative and desperate to find something positive to cling to. "So what's the prognosis?"

"If he makes the changes he's supposed to make? It's good. He could live another forty years, get old and crotchety, and make us all miserable."

I laughed and felt a knot of tension loosen between my shoulder blades. "That's the best news I've had in two days. So you didn't come here just so I could see him one last time?"

Aunt Yolanda looked stricken. "No! We came so he could get some peace and quiet."

With a sour grin, I glanced around us. A couple of uniformed officers led a handcuffed young man with dreadlocks into an interrogation room. I could see another cop talking with a businessman in a rumpled suit and two others chatting outside an open doorway over coffee in paper cups. Voices rose and fell. Phones rang and computer keyboards click-clacked, all creating an odd sort of music. "Good choice."

Aunt Yolanda followed my gaze. "Well, of course, neither of us expected to land in the middle of a murder investigation."

I was still worried, but not frantic anymore. Knowing about Uncle Nestor's health problems just made me more determined to clear him of suspicion so he could go home on Monday and get the rest and quiet he needed. Obviously, he wasn't going to get it here.

While I tried to figure out what to do next, a door just down the hall opened and Mellie Boudreaux emerged, followed by one of the officers who'd been at the country club last night. I guessed from the way Aunt Yolanda watched Mellie that she recognized her, too.

Mellie paused just outside the door to shake the officer's hand. "You'll let me know if there's anything else you need from me?"

"Absolutely." He handed over a business card, which she promptly tucked into the

Coach bag on her shoulder. "And if you remember anything else, give me a call. Thanks again for coming in, Ms. Boudreaux. You've been a big help."

I caught Aunt Yolanda's gaze and saw curiosity flickering in her eyes. "Is that the ex-wife?" she whispered.

I nodded, pretty sure we were both thinking the same thing. Her being here was no coincidence. She'd obviously just given the police her statement. With Susannah busy pointing the finger at Uncle Nestor, I was desperate to know what Mellie had told the police.

She walked a few feet down the hall and disappeared into the ladies' room. I waited, biding my time, until the police officer went back into the room, then whispered to Aunt Yolanda, "I'll be right back."

"Where are you going?"

"Where else? The ladies' room."

"You're going to talk to her? Do you think that's wise?"

I stood and tried to look shocked by the question. "I'm going to freshen up. There's no law against that, is there?" And then I hurried away before she could give me an answer.

EIGHTEEN

Mellie was already standing at the bank of sinks when I came through the door of the ladies' room. Up close, I could see that she was a beautiful woman, with eyes the deep, rich color of fudge brownies. She gave me a quick noncommittal smile and started to look away, but then her eyes shot back to the mirror. This time she studied me a little closer. "You're Philippe Renier's widow, right? You hosted the party last night?"

I nodded in answer to her first question and gave a little shrug for the second. "It's Rita, please," I said, bypassing the party thing entirely. "I don't think we got a chance to meet last night, but you're Mellie Boudreaux, aren't you?"

She turned away from the mirror, tweaking the collar of a white linen shirt that was unbuttoned far enough to reveal an impressive amount of cleavage. "That's right. I have the dubious honor of being Big Daddy

Boudreaux's first ex-wife." She turned on a smile so open and friendly it was hard not to like her. "I just hope that crazy-ass Boudreaux blood is diluted enough to let our children have normal lives, God bless 'em."

I smiled and moved farther into the tile-covered room. Remembering how hard Philippe's death had hit me despite our separation, I said, "I'm sorry for your loss."

Mellie's expression sobered and she reached for a towel from the dispenser at her side. "Thanks, but I lost Bradley a long time ago. I did my mourning then."

Maybe so, but I was pretty sure I detected some regret in those dark eyes. I didn't want her to know that I'd chased her into the ladies' room, so I moved to the bank of sinks and waved my hands around to get the water started, then pumped soap from the dispenser. "So you're here to give the police your statement?"

She nodded and dug in her bag for lipstick. "Not that it's much of one. I only saw Bradley last night for a few minutes. I guess you're here for the same reason?"

I nodded. "It's such a senseless tragedy. Why would anyone want to kill him?"

Mellie slanted a glance at me. "Oh, honey, if you knew Bradley like I knew Bradley,

199

you wouldn't be asking that. You'd be asking who *didn't* want him dead."

She certainly knew how to get a person's attention. I didn't want to look too eager for information, so I rinsed the soap from my hands and tried for a casual expression. "What makes you say that?"

"Let's just say that it looks like the hens have come home to roost. Bradley hurt a lot of people in his lifetime. Somebody obviously decided to hurt him back."

"Any idea who?"

Mellie shook her head and applied her lipstick — a fuchsia/wine infusion mix that looked great on her but that I could never pull off. "Like I said, honey, it's a mighty long list. Bradley looked out for himself his whole life. If someone got in his way . . ." She broke off with a shrug, leaving me to fill in the blanks.

"Is that what you told the police?" I asked.

She dabbed at the corners of her mouth with her little finger and leaned back to inspect her reflection. "I have no reason to lie, if that's what you're asking."

"That's not it at all," I assured her. "I'm just trying to figure out what the police are thinking."

Mellie dropped her lipstick back into her purse and zipped it closed. "That's kind of hard to tell, isn't it? They're not sharing much with the rest of us."

"You were there when his body was found, weren't you? I thought I saw you talking to Susannah just a few minutes before that."

She sighed heavily. "You probably did. She's a silly little thing, but I have a soft spot for her. Being married to Bradley Boudreaux isn't easy."

"So you're friendly?"

She laughed again. "Does that surprise you?"

"A little, maybe," I said with a shrug. "You never know how two women who've been married to the same man will get along."

"Well, we get along fine, mostly because I'm so damn happy *she's* the one married to him now." She grinned, but the smile slid from her face after a moment and she turned a sober look on me. "Why do you want to know?"

"She tried to get my uncle arrested last night, and she talked to a television reporter about him this morning. I'm trying to figure out why."

"Susannah's an emotional little thing," Mellie said. "She thinks with her heart, not with her head. But your uncle *did* attack Bradley, did he not?"

Everything inside urged me to sugarcoat

their argument, but what good would that do? "How did you know about that?"

"I was looking for Bradley and happened to overhear some of what went on."

Apparently, more people had been aware of the fight than I'd first thought. "It wasn't a big deal," I said. "My uncle didn't kill Big Daddy."

Mellie plucked at a lock of hair and sent me a pitying smile. "Well, good luck convincing the police of that, honey. I wish I could help, but I may have made things worse for him."

My breath caught. "How?"

"Well, darlin', I have nothin' against your uncle, but I had to tell the police what I saw."

"Are you talking about the fight they had? Because that only lasted for a couple of minutes and it was over hours before the murder."

"Well, yes, I told them about the fight. Bradley really shouldn't have said what he said, but your uncle shouldn't have reacted the way he did. But I also had to tell them about what happened later."

I almost didn't hear the last part of what she said because my attention was riveted on the first part. "You heard what Big Daddy said to Uncle Nestor? What was it?"

Mellie studied me thoughtfully for a moment, probably trying to decide whether to tell me or not. Finally, she let out a resigned sigh and glanced toward the door to make sure we were alone. "I probably shouldn't say anything. The police wouldn't like us talking about the murder."

"We're not talking about the murder," I said. "We're talking about the fight my uncle had with your ex-husband. All I want to know is what Big Daddy said to Uncle Nestor that set him off like that."

"Why don't you just ask your uncle?"

"I have," I assured her. "More than once. He doesn't want to talk about it. He doesn't want to talk about anything, really. I don't know what's gotten into him." When she still didn't say anything, I tried a different tack. "Please? I'm desperate."

"All right," Mellie said, her voice low, "I guess I really don't think your uncle killed Bradley — though God knows I'd understand it if he did." Her lips quirked slightly. "You see, Bradley had a thing for women and cars. Always did. He traded in his cars every year so he could have the latest model. I found out a little too late that he did the same thing with women."

I mumbled something about being sorry, but I wasn't one bit surprised.

Mellie waved off my apology. "He cheated on me our whole marriage, but it took me a long time to realize what was happening and even longer to put my foot down and tell him it had to stop. Of course, he couldn't stop and that's when he left me for his second wife. She only lasted a couple of years, poor thing. Moved up north to Chicago and remarried, I heard. Anyway, it was like a sickness with him. He was like a moth, and beautiful women were the flame."

"It must have been hard to be married to a man like that."

Mellie nodded. "You don't know the half of it."

I let that settle between us for a few seconds, then followed up. "So what did he say?"

She glanced at the door again and dropped her voice a little more. "He made a couple of comments about what a beautiful woman your aunt is and then told your uncle to let him know if he ever got tired of her."

No wonder Uncle Nestor went ballistic. "And that's why Uncle Nestor hit him?"

"Not exactly." Mellie returned the lipstick to her purse and tucked the bag under her arm. "Your uncle hit him after Bradley said what a treat it would be to get you and your aunt together."

Knowing that Big Daddy had said something so rude, let alone had thought it, made me sick. Imagining Uncle Nestor's reaction made me nervous. I leaned against the cool tile and tried to focus my thoughts again. "Are you sure that's what he said?"

Mellie shrugged. "What can I say? He was a disgusting pig."

I wasn't sure I wanted the answer to the next question, but I had to ask, "So what happened later?"

"Are you sure you want to know?"

"I have to know." I squared my shoulders and lifted my chin, steeling myself. "It's okay. I need the truth."

In spite of my reassurance, Mellie seemed reluctant to go on. "They got into it again an hour or so later," she said after a pause. "I didn't hear what they were saying that time, but I assumed it had something to do with their first brawl."

It seemed like a reasonable assumption, so I nodded for her to go on.

"I was looking for Judd — that's Bradley's younger brother. I don't know if you met him . . ."

I nodded. "We met for a minute."

"I wanted to make sure he was doing all right. Alcohol and Judd do not mix." She flicked a glance at me and said, "Or maybe

I should say that alcohol and Judd mix too well. Anyway, I wanted to make sure he was holding up okay. Somebody told me he was out by the pool, so I went down there. Your uncle and Bradley were there, and they were literally at each other's throats."

I thought I'd prepared myself for whatever she had to say, but I hadn't. My knees felt rubbery and my spirits tanked. "They fought again?"

"They sure did."

"What time was that?"

"Around one maybe? I'm not sure. I really wasn't paying attention to the details . . . until I realized what was going on."

"And you didn't hear anything they said?"

"A few words. Not many I could under-stand. And I think we're about to cross the line here. I probably shouldn't say too much more."

"But you did hear something," I said, nudging her again.

She flicked a lock of hair off her forehead and backed a step toward the door. "I only heard one thing, really," she said, clearly eager to finish the conversation. "I heard your uncle threaten to kill Bradley."

NINETEEN

With Mellie Boudreaux's claim echoing through my head, I rejoined Aunt Yolanda on the chairs and made small talk. Maybe I should have told her what Mellie said, but I didn't want to worry her. She had enough on her mind, what with Uncle Nestor's bad heart and all.

Besides, no matter what Mellie might have overheard, I knew my uncle. He might have a short fuse and an explosive temper, but he's not a murderer.

After a while, Sullivan reappeared with a still-sullen and silent Uncle Nestor and told us we were free to go — for now. I wondered if the police were taking Mellie Boudreaux's story seriously, but I didn't want to ask in front of Aunt Yolanda, so I swallowed my questions and promised myself I'd ask Sullivan later.

We dodged reporters on the way back to the car and settled in for the drive home,

Uncle Nestor in the front seat with me, Aunt Yolanda in the back. I tried asking Uncle Nestor about his interview with Sullivan, but he still wasn't talking, so we drove back to the house in silence broken only by an occasional observation from Aunt Yolanda about things we passed.

She seemed fascinated by the Mardi Gras decorations and crowds gathering at such an early hour everywhere, but I suspected she was just trying to distract me so I wouldn't upset Uncle Nestor. To a casual observer, I'm sure she looked cool, calm, and collected, but I picked up on subtle clues that revealed how agitated she was. This was tough on everybody.

The minute we got to the house, Uncle Nestor climbed the stairs to the guest room and Aunt Yolanda followed a minute later, saying that she needed to lie down for a while.

Alone for the first time in several hours, I checked my cell phone and noticed that a message had come in since the last time I looked. It was from Miss Frankie, letting me know she was having lunch at The Shores with her neighbor, Bernice, and the police were still gathering evidence from the crime scene. I wondered what she had up her sleeve, but my call to her house phone went through to voice mail and Miss Frankie doesn't carry a cell phone.

I puttered around the house for a few minutes, listening for footsteps coming from upstairs. I needed to get to work. Yeah, I know. Edie had advised me to stay away. But I'm no good at taking advice. Besides, working always helps me think — and I desperately needed to sort through the jumble of questions rolling around in my head.

I waited until I was convinced that Uncle Nestor and Aunt Yolanda were settled in for a while, then changed into a pair of jeans and a T-shirt and scribbled a hasty note explaining that I'd gone to the shop. The bright noon sunlight filtered through the trees as I drove the back streets to the Garden District, and the city began to work its magic on me. Stately antebellum homes surrounded by well-trimmed lawns and ornate gardens filled with flowers stand side-by-side with boutiques and restaurants. It's a trendy, upscale neighborhood with lots of old-world charm. Technically, it was still winter, but it felt like the springs I'd known in New Mexico.

I parked in Zydeco's employee lot and walked inside, where I breathed in the delicious scents of yeast and cinnamon and felt my nerves begin to settle.

"What are you doing here?" Edie snapped when she saw me. "I thought I told you to stay away."

My mood curdled like sour milk. I didn't need attitude on top of everything else.

"I know what you told me," I growled back. "I came anyway."

"So I see." Edie was wearing striped leggings under a lime green tunic and a pair of soft-soled shoes, the toes of which sported intricately embroidered lotus flowers. With her porcelain doll face, the whole outfit made her look young and sweet. Very misleading.

I tried to look calm and in control, completely at ease with my decision to come to work, but I was second-guessing myself like mad. We were standing in the room that had originally served as the home's front parlor and now did duty as the bakery's reception area. It's Edie's domain, and she runs it from behind a wide U-shaped desk lined with stacking trays that are labeled and color-coded. In direct contrast to the organization she prefers, her desk was cluttered with the buildup of paperwork from orders we'd filled since carnival season began. Receipts and invoices teetered in stacks, waiting for her to update Zydeco's books on the computer.

A half-eaten shrimp po'boy sandwich from the corner grocery sat between her computer keyboard and a massive insulated cup, no doubt filled with her favorite, Diet Coke, making me realize that I should have stopped for lunch on my way. I'd never have time to get away for something to eat now.

"How are things going?" I asked, still trying to give the appearance of control. "Are we on schedule?"

Edie slipped behind her desk and dropped into her chair. "Everything is fine. I told you that already. There's no reason for you to be here."

"And yet I am, so it's a moot point," I said and turned toward my office. I unlocked the door and tossed my bag onto the floor beside my desk — also heaped with paperwork and piles of mail. "Where's Ox?"

"Filling in for you in the design room," Edie called back. Her voice was muffled, as if she'd gone back to work on the sandwich. "And he's none too happy about it either. Just so you know."

I ran a quick glance over the heap of work waiting for me, decided that none of it was urgent, and headed for the employee lunchroom. "Is there coffee?" I tossed the question at Edie as I passed her desk.

"I made some an hour ago."

Not fresh, but hopefully not bitter yet. I followed the aroma toward the sunny room that overlooked the street. "Anything to eat in there?"

"Estelle brought bagels and lox from Surrey's this morning. There might be some left." Edie took another bite of her po'boy and got up to follow me. "How did it go at the police station?"

I shrugged. "Aunt Yolanda and I signed our statements. Uncle Nestor spent a while with Sullivan, but don't ask me what happened. He's still refusing to answer my questions." I made a beeline for the coffeepot and poured a cup. "I wish I could figure out what's going on with him. Aunt Yolanda said he had a mild heart attack a couple of weeks ago. I'm sure it freaked him out big-time. I don't remember him ever getting sick when I was a kid, not even a cold. But even a shock like that doesn't explain why he's refusing to talk."

Edie shrugged as if to say she had no answer for that and checked the box from Surrey's on the counter. "You're in luck. There's one bagel left. The fixings are in the fridge."

Such as they were. A few smears of cream cheese clung to the edges of the plastic container and two wispy pieces of lox lay limply on a folded sheet of waxed paper. I scraped and spread and arranged until the food looked almost appetizing and then tore into it as if I hadn't eaten in days.

Is there a better bite anywhere in the world? A perfectly boiled bagel, crusty on the outside and chewy on the inside. The sweetly sour burst of cream cheese mixed with the smoky taste of the lox almost made me swoon. I wolfed down half the bagel, pausing only to wag my fingers in farewell as Edie went back to work, and again in hello as Estelle came through the door a few seconds later.

She saw me eating the last bagel and frowned in disappointment. "Oh. You're . . ." She waved a hand as if losing that bagel had flustered her. "That's okay. I had one earlier."

"It's delicious," I said around the last mouthful. "Thanks for bringing them this morning."

She gave her spongy red curls a little flip and crossed to the fridge. "No problem. I thought I should do something. You know. Because of . . . you know. What happened last night."

You betcha. A good bagel is the best cure for a murder hangover.

I sipped coffee, added a dash more sugar, and started toward the door as Estelle pulled a Coke from the fridge. "How are you doing, Rita? Are you holding up okay?" she asked.

I nodded, a little surprised by her question. "I'm fine. I'm sorry for Big Daddy's friends and family, but I didn't really know him."

"Yeah, but —" Estelle reached into the cupboard for a glass and filled it with crushed ice from the refrigerator door. "It's just . . ." Her voice trailed away and she chewed her bottom lip for a moment.

I gave her a verbal nudge. "Just what?"

"Well, you know. Edie told us how your uncle is under suspicion." She twisted the cap off her bottle and concentrated on pouring the soda over ice.

"My uncle is innocent," I said firmly.

"Oh, I know! I'm not saying he's not." She glanced at me and away from her task. It only took a second but the Coke foamed over the side. She grabbed a handful of paper towels and started mopping. "I didn't mean to insinuate anything . . . you know . . . bad." She looked so horrified, I almost felt sorry for her, and I reminded myself that I wasn't the only one at Zydeco feeling the effects of Big Daddy's murder.

"How's Miss Frankie taking all of this? Poor woman. This must be horrible for her."

"I'm sure it's not easy," I agreed.

She tossed the soggy paper towels and checked her soda to ice ratio, then picked up the glass and sipped. "When you're ready, I have some more pictures for the blog."

"More than what you gave me last night?"

"Ox wanted me to get a variety. I tried."

I nodded and tried to look as if I cared, but if the website and blog had been low on my priority list yesterday, they'd slipped off the list completely today. "Just give the memory card to Edie," I said. "I'll get it from her."

"Oh. Sure." Estelle looked at me over the rim of her glass, her eyes expectant and uncertain, as if she wanted to say more but didn't know if she should.

"Is there something else?"

She put the glass down and moved a couple of steps closer. When she spoke again, her voice was almost a whisper. "For what it's worth, I really don't think your uncle did it."

"He didn't," I said again. "And I appreciate the vote of confidence. I just wish I knew how to convince the police that he's innocent."

Estelle's round face creased in a sympathetic smile. "Seems weird to me that they'd be looking at him anyway. Don't they say that it's usually someone close to the victim?"

After I'd finished the other half of my bagel, I threw the empty box and the cream cheese container into the trash. "That's what they say," I agreed. "I wish I knew more about the Boudreauxes. What did Big Daddy have, a couple of ex-wives? A girl-friend?" I liked Mellie when I met her earlier, but what if she wasn't telling the truth? What if she had a grudge against Big Daddy and resolved it by coshing him over the head?

Estelle shook her head. "Bless his heart. Always searching for love and never finding it."

"Is that your way of saying he slept around a lot?"

Estelle didn't give me a direct answer. "It's my way of saying that the poor man never learned he couldn't run his women the way he ran his business." She slanted a sly glance at me and lowered her voice a little more. "I don't like to speak ill of the dead, but I heard him talking to his wife last night and it was downright shameful. No respectable Southern gentleman would say the things he did."

My ears perked up at that. "What kinds of things?"

Estelle put a hand on her chest and glanced at the door. "I probably shouldn't say."

"You'd better say," I warned her. "And right now. If you know something that could help clear Uncle Nestor, you have to tell me."

Estelle sank into a chair and propped her chin in one hand. She looked miserable, but I didn't let it get to me. I sat across from her and made eye contact — which wasn't easy since she seemed determined not to look at me. "What did he say?"

She sighed heavily. "I'm not sure I can help much. The music was so loud."

I was in familiar territory now. If Miss Frankie had taught me anything since I came to New Orleans, it was the dance of Southern gossip. "Yes, it was," I commiserated. *One, two, cha-cha-cha.*

"And of course I wouldn't think of eavesdropping."

"Of course not."

"But I did hear him say that she had no right to worry about being embarrassed by him. That *she* embarrassed *him* every time she opened her mouth."

217

It certainly wasn't nice, but considering the other things Big Daddy had said last night, it seemed almost tame. "Poor thing. How did she react to that?" *Three, four, cha-cha-cha.*

"Well, you can understand why she'd be upset, bless her heart."

"Well, of course. Who wouldn't be?" I imagined myself as Fred Astaire and Estelle as Ginger Rogers. I spun her around with a little sympathy and dipped her by musing aloud and looking innocent. "I wonder what she did to embarrass him."

Estelle leaned in closer. We were conspirators now. "I have no idea about that, but I did notice she'd had a few too many. And I heard her tell him that he had to make things right with Percy."

"Percy Ponter? The guy who was just elected as the krewe's treasurer?" The one who'd been so determined to talk to Big Daddy last night?

"I guess. I don't know who he is, but she said he had to do it last night *or else.*"

"Or else? She actually said that?"

Estelle nodded, her expression deadly serious. "Or else. But don't ask me what was going to happen if he didn't. Like I said, I wasn't eavesdropping."

I felt a little tingle of anticipation. "Do

you remember what time that was?"

"Maybe eleven? It was a while before we served the King Cake. That's all I remember." She delivered the last line with a pointed look that said the dance was over.

I wanted to keep digging, but I knew she wouldn't give me more right now. Getting to my feet, I hugged her quickly. "Thanks, Estelle. At least that gives me a place to start."

"You're welcome." Her cheeks turned pink with pleasure. "Anything I can do to help."

I pondered what I'd just heard as I carried my coffee cup back to my office. I'd had a few questions before, but my conversation with Estelle had brought it up to a full baker's dozen. I tried to sift through them by remembering what I already knew. I thought about Mellie's claim that she'd been looking for Judd by the pool and realized I'd never asked whether she found him. I thought about Big Daddy's connections in Musterion and wondered if someone in the krewe had been responsible for his death. And what about his business empire? After meeting Big Daddy just once, I could easily believe he had a few disgruntled employees in his past, or business deals gone sour, and Mellie had certainly backed up those suspicions.

I knew he had an issue with Percy Ponter, but I had no idea what it was. And now it appeared that the current Mrs. Boudreaux had been unhappy with her husband shortly before he died.

A loud crash sounded from the kitchen, jerking me out of my thoughts. I turned toward it just as someone behind me called my name. "Rita? Thank goodness you're here! Got a minute? We have a problem with the sheeter."

I glanced over my shoulder and saw Isabeau hurrying toward me, her blond ponytail bouncing with every step.

"Sure," I said, trying not to sigh. There were far too many questions and not nearly enough time to find the answers.

TWENTY

I called and left a message for my cousin Santos, asking him to get back to me as soon as he had a minute. Then I began sorting through the top layer of paperwork on my desk — all stuff that hadn't been here last time I looked.

I found a few pieces of mail, some important, the rest junk. An updated calendar for the week and an article clipped from the newspaper about the Hedge-Montgomery wedding. Two e-mails from Edie informing me about consults she'd added to my already crowded schedule and a memo from Ox reminding me that I still hadn't approved the content for the web page he was so up in arms about.

The light on my desk phone flashed on and off, alerting me that I also had voice mail.

Groaning aloud, I buried my head in my arms on top of the paperwork. There simply weren't enough hours in the day.

I indulged in my pity party for about three seconds, then lifted my head, vowing to press on. During those three seconds, Ox materialized in the doorway. Dark stubble had sprung up on his usually clean-shaven head, and his chef's jacket was so wrinkled it looked like origami gone wrong.

I gave a little yelp of surprise and sat up quickly. "You startled me," I said. "I didn't hear you there."

"Napping?" he asked with a sardonic quirk of an eyebrow.

"Hardly," I said, doing my best to quirk back. "Wishing for the world to open up and swallow me whole." I motioned him into the office and waved him toward one of the chairs in front of my desk. "What's up?"

"You have to ask?"

"If it's about the web page —" I began.

He cut me off before I could finish. "It's about the murder last night."

I'm pretty sure the fact that I actually felt a ripple of relief says something strange about me. "What about it?"

Ox cocked an ankle on his knee and rested both burly forearms on the chair's arms. "Your connection to it, however coinciden-tal, it's not good for business."

It took a moment for his meaning to sink in. When it did, I laughed in disbelief. "Surely you're not implying that this is somehow my fault."

"No, but your uncle . . ."

I put the cup down carefully so I wouldn't accidentally fling the coffee in his face. "*What* about my uncle?"

"Oh, come on, Rita. He belted the dead guy in the face last night. He's a person of interest in the murder."

My ears began to buzz. "And? Is that it? Come on, Ox. You know better than that. You were in the same position just a few months ago."

Ox held up both hands in surrender. "I never said I thought he was guilty. I'm just saying that I don't think having you front-and-center is the best thing for Zydeco right now."

I scowled so hard my forehead hurt. "I've already had this conversation with Edie. It's not your call."

"It's nothing personal," he assured me. "Frankly, this couldn't come at a worse time. So if you're thinking that I'm trying to nudge you out of the way, stop. That's not it at all."

I stared at him for a long time, surprised to find that I believed him. "I'm thinking about Zydeco, too," I said. "The staff has already been through enough. If I run and hide right now, it's going to make things worse than if I just take it on the chin."

He wagged his head again. "I don't know —"

"Listen," I said, cutting off his argument before he got started. "I'm still trying to establish myself here with the staff. How I deal with this will either make me or break me. They need to see that I'm willing to stand up and fight for this place — and for them if that's ever necessary." *The way I did for you*, I added silently.

I wasn't sure, but I thought I saw a spark of respect in Ox's dark eyes. "And just how do you plan to do that?"

"Show up. Come inside and do the work." I sounded tougher and more together than I felt, but Aunt Yolanda had been telling me for years to fake it until I could feel it and that's exactly what I was going to do now.

Ox regarded me for a long moment and then changed the subject. "How's your uncle holding up?"

Genuine concern tugged at the corners of his mouth and poked big holes in the anger I'd been feeling. I was worried, and the draw of confiding in a friend was impossible to resist. I told Ox about the heart attack and what I knew about his doctor's orders. "He's supposed to be resting and avoiding stress. Some joke, huh?"

"All the more reason for taking a couple of days off," Ox said. "Stay home. Keep an eye on him. Show both of them the city and party a little. It's your first Mardi Gras, so go enjoy it with your family. It will do you all good."

I laughed. "You don't know my uncle. He's not one for crowds. Really, the best thing for him would be to get him off the police department's radar screen. If I could find a witness who could place him somewhere besides the pool at the time of the murder, I'm sure that would clear him of any suspicion."

Ox shook his head. "To do that, you'd have to interview all two hundred guests and the country club's staff."

"All I need is one reliable witness. What time did *you* leave the party?"

"I don't know. One? Maybe a little after. I don't remember. Why?"

"Were there still guests by the pool? Do you remember? Or had they cleared out by then?"

He gave that some thought before he answered. "There were a lot of people around the pool earlier, but they all started

225

migrating back to the clubhouse around midnight for the captain's speech and the King Cake."

That's how I remembered it, too. "Did you see Uncle Nestor?"

"Not that I recall."

"How about Big Daddy? Do you remember seeing him?"

Ox gave me a look. "Do you really think this is a good idea?"

"What? Asking questions?"

He dipped his head once, a silent affirmation.

"We're talking about my uncle," I reminded him. "The man who raised me. I'm not going to let the police and everyone else treat him like a criminal. So: Did you see Big Daddy before you left the party?"

He gave a reluctant nod. "Yeah."

"Where was he? What was he doing?"

"Upstairs. At the far end of the hall by one of the trophy cases. Big Daddy and his brother were up there together. I got the impression they didn't want anyone to know they were there."

So Big Daddy and Judd had connected during the evening. I wondered how that had gone. "Did they say anything to you?"

Ox shook his head. "No, and I didn't say anything to them. I hit the head and went back to the party. Isabeau and I left about fifteen minutes later." He shifted in his chair, leaning forward to hold my gaze. "Just let the police do their job, okay?"

"Is that what you'd do if *your* uncle was in trouble?"

Ox sighed heavily and looked at me from the corner of his eye. "Yeah. It is."

Sure. And seven-layer double-fudge cake with buttercream icing is low in calories. "I'm not trying to figure out who killed Big Daddy," I argued. "I'm just trying to provide Uncle Nestor with an alibi."

"If he had one, don't you think he'd have told you?"

I shook my head. "He hasn't told anybody anything," I said. "And besides, he doesn't know anyone around here. Even if he was standing somewhere in full view of a dozen guests, he can't exactly name names."

The look in Ox's eyes turned skeptical, which threw cold water on the warm fuzzies of friendship I'd felt only moments before. "He's my uncle," I said again. "I owe him everything. And I'm going to *do* everything I can to clear him."

"I don't like it," Ox said. He stood and crossed to the door, but stopped on the threshold and looked back at me. "Just be careful." His voice was surprisingly gentle.

"Of course." I had no intention of putting myself in danger. I'd just ask a few questions. That's all.

Goes to show how wrong a person can be.

TWENTY-ONE

I spent the rest of the afternoon working alongside the staff in the production line, trying to prove that I was one of them. As it always does, working with my hands relaxed me, and after a while I felt the knots in my shoulders loosen. Even the headache I'd been blaming on exhaustion began to fade.

I'm sure the staff's mood helped. Their excited chatter about their Mardi Gras plans helped me remember that the world hadn't stopped spinning when Big Daddy left it.

Their enthusiasm was infectious, and soon I was caught up in the planning and laughter. As an outsider, I'd had some preconceived notions about Mardi Gras, but I was quickly learning that it wasn't all alcohol and bared breasts. The people in New Orleans love to party, and since Katrina, they've approached life with a unity that's sometimes surprising. As Estelle had pointed out to me a few weeks earlier, the people of New Orleans party for Jesus, for the devil, for any excuse they can find. The party is the important thing.

When Philippe opened Zydeco two years earlier, he'd decreed the Sunday before Mardi Gras an official bakery holiday. The entire staff and their families attended the Krewe of Musterion parade, followed by the Krewe of Bacchus parade, and everyone went in costume. I'd been warned that they took great pains to keep their costumes secret until the great reveal an hour before the parade started.

I'd been meaning to figure out what I'd wear, but somehow work always got in my way. Now, as I listened to the others talk, I realized it wouldn't be a simple matter of stopping by a costume shop and handing the clerk my credit card. If I'd wanted to do that, I should have come up for air weeks ago.

I could feel tension crawling up my spine again, but I did my best to shake it off. I'd learned at Uncle Nestor's knee, and look how that had turned out for him. I didn't want to worry myself into the hospital.

Putting the murder and my ever-growing to-do list out of my mind for the time being, I concentrated on the music playing on the stereo in the corner and tuned out the conversations around me. I lost myself in the scents and sounds of the world I love best. I could hear the phone ringing almost nonstop in Edie's corner, and I hoped that the calls coming in were orders for cakes, not reporters looking for a story. And then I put that worry out of my head, too.

After a while, Isabeau caught my attention and motioned to something behind me. I turned to find Detective Sullivan lounging against the door frame. He gave me a little chin jerk in greeting and pushed away from the wall with his shoulder.

I had a feeling he wasn't here on a social visit, but I told myself not to assume the worst. Maybe he was here to tell me that Uncle Nestor was in the clear. Maybe they'd arrested someone — someone else. Maybe the nightmare was already over.

I motioned for him to come closer and greeted him with the best smile I could manage, considering the nervous tension skating in my belly and the exhaustion dragging at my mind.

Using the dough scraper, I hacked a large ball of risen dough into three pieces. *Whack! Whack!* "Fancy meeting you here."

He sent back a lopsided grin. I noticed that his eyes were a clear blue today, which gave me hope that things were looking up. "Yeah," he said. "Fancy that. That thing you're wielding looks lethal. Should I be worried?"

I waggled it in front of him. "Plastic. The most damage I could inflict is a serious bruise or a broken finger. What's up, Detective? Are you here on business or looking for the best King Cake in the city?"

"Business, I'm afraid."

"Tell me you're here to announce the arrest of Big Daddy's killer."

" 'Fraid not. We've identified the murder weapon, though. Somebody smashed his skull with a small statue we found near the pool."

I shuddered, realizing it must've been the one I'd stepped around on my way to help Big Daddy. "Fingerprints?"

"A couple of partials, but nothing we can use. Actually, I need to speak to a couple of your people. Is this a bad time?"

I was disappointed that the case was still open, but I channeled my frustration into rolling out one of the recently whacked balls of dough. "It's as good as any. Which ones?"

"Sparkle Starr and Dwight Sonntag. Can you spare them for a few minutes?"

"You can take the whole staff if it helps solve the case. Just return them quickly.

We're buried."

"Those two will be fine," he said. "Mind if I use the room upstairs to speak with them?"

"If you don't mind sharing it with a few supplies stored there for carnival season. It's usable. We're still having our weekly staff meetings up there, so make yourself at home."

He didn't need me to show him the way or point out the staff, so the fact that he didn't walk off right away made me look up to see what was going on.

"How's your uncle?" he asked.

I shrugged. "Okay the last time I saw him. Did he happen to mention that he had a heart attack a couple of weeks ago and that he's supposed to be avoiding stress?"

Something flickered in Sullivan's eyes, but I couldn't read it. He shook his head. "He didn't mention anything to me. I'll make a note in the file."

Yeah. That would fix everything.

"Has he been any more forthcoming with you?"

I frowned and shook my head. "I wish. He hardly spoke to me on the way home, and I've been here since I dropped him off. I don't suppose you've managed to clear him of suspicion yet."

"Not yet, but I'm working on it. Don't worry."

Easier said than done. "Any suspects yet?" I asked him.

He shrugged. "One or two."

"Any serious suspects?"

He leaned one hip against the table and watched me work. "C'mon, Rita. You know I can't discuss an ongoing investigation with you. Especially not one where you're related to a person of interest."

I really hated that phrase. "There's no law against me sharing information with *you*, though, is there?"

"Absolutely not. It's your civic duty." He dragged a stool closer and made himself comfortable. "What information?"

"I know why Uncle Nestor was so angry with Big Daddy last night."

"He told you?"

I shook my head. "Someone overheard the conversation. I don't know if he told you about this . . ."

"He didn't tell me much of anything."

I filled Sullivan in on what Mellie had told me in the ladies' room, carefully leaving out how I'd come by the information and rushing on before he could ask me about it. "Uncle Nestor's a traditional Latino, very protective of the women in his family. And

Big Daddy was a traditional sexist pig. It wasn't a good mix."

"Obviously."

"But Uncle Nestor wasn't the only person who had an issue with Big Daddy. Do you know why he and his wife arrived at the party separately? Could there be something important in that? She was with some guy when I met her."

"With? What were they doing?"

"It wasn't what they did," I said with a scowl. "It's the way they looked when they did it. And why was Big Daddy there with his assistant? I'll bet there was something going on between those two."

Sullivan didn't respond to that, which made me think I was right. "You know, don't you, that Big Daddy was treating his wife pretty shabbily last night? You ought to talk to Estelle about what she heard before you leave here."

"Estelle just happened to tell you about this?"

"No" — I gave him a *duh!* look — "I asked her." I hesitated over how much to tell him about Judd. Sure, I'd liked him when I met him, but my loyalty belonged to Uncle Nestor. "Also, I met Judd Boudreaux when I went outside. I got the impression that he had a few issues with Big Daddy, and he didn't seem to like Susannah much. Ox says that Big Daddy and Judd were having a secretive conversation upstairs right before the party ended. And have you talked with Percy Ponter yet? Like I told you that night, he seemed pretty upset with Big Daddy."

Sullivan folded his arms and stared me down. "I've got it under control. Anything else?"

"Not yet," I said, "but I'll keep you posted."

"Rita —"

I interrupted before he could get started. "If this is the part where you warn me to stay out of the investigation, save it. I won't get in your way and I won't interfere, but if I can find someone who can place Uncle Nestor away from the pool at the time of the murder, I'm going to do it."

"Why don't you let me take care of it?"

I planted my hands on the tabletop and met his gaze. "But will you? Or are you focused on finding witnesses who can place him at the scene of the crime? Because those aren't the same thing at all."

"I'm just tryin' to get at the truth," he assured me.

"Yeah. Well. You keep doing that, and if I find out anything that will help, I'll let you know."

He stood, sighing as if he carried the weight of the world on his shoulders. "Right. Guess I'll get on with my interviews if that's all right with you."

"Knock yourself out," I said, adding a thin smile to show that we were still friends.

He smoothed the legs of his jeans so that the hems fell over his boots. "Just in case your uncle didn't mention it, I've asked him not to leave town."

The smile slipped off my face and landed on the floor somewhere near my heart. "You did what?"

"Just for a few days. Until we can clear up his involvement in the case."

"There *is* no involvement," I insisted. Not that my opinion counted for anything.

"As soon as we can prove that, he's free to leave."

"But —"

He arched a brow, waiting for me to offer some protest, but words failed me. Uncle Nestor stuck in New Orleans until the police cleared him? He'd go crazy. *I'd* go crazy.

"Is there a problem?" Sullivan asked.

I shook my head quickly. "No. It'll be fine."

"You're sure?"

My smile had turned brittle, but I flashed

it again. "If I said no, would you let him leave town?"

Sullivan shook his head. " 'Fraid not."

"Then I'm sure."

Sullivan looked at me through eyes narrowed with concern, but he kept his distance. My uncle was on the list of suspects in a homicide case, which I guess made all the friendly sort of stuff that usually fell between us off-limits. He ran those piercing blue eyes over my face and then twitched the corner of his mouth. "Chin up. It's gonna get worse before it gets better."

And on that cheery note, he left to interview my employees.

TWENTY-TWO

Okay, I'll admit it. I was going crazy wondering why Sullivan had wanted to talk with Sparkle and Dwight. They'd come back to work without a word of explanation to me, and my mind had been working overtime running through the possibilities. Even a return phone call from my cousin Santos didn't completely distract me.

Santos didn't tell me anything I didn't already know, but he did reassure me that although Uncle Nestor needed to make some lifestyle changes, he wasn't in imminent danger of keeling over dead. Maybe if I heard it often enough I'd really start believing it.

We bantered back and forth for a few minutes, me giving him grief for not letting me know about his dad's heart attack, him telling me I would have known if I'd stayed in Albuquerque. I was having a great time talking to my oldest cousin until partway through the conversation, when it occurred to me that Santos hadn't once asked about the murder or the trouble his father was in.

And that meant that he must not know.

The possibility that Uncle Nestor and Aunt Yolanda hadn't confided in Santos made me feel better in a way. I didn't like the fact that they were keeping secrets, but at least I wasn't the only person they were keeping in the dark.

Of course, that put me in an awkward position. I didn't feel right hiding the truth from Santos, but I wasn't sure how to break the news to him either. Before I could think through the situation, Edie ran into my office to announce another emergency. One of the temporary workers I'd hired had slipped on the wet floor and it looked like the guy had sprained his ankle. Dwight was taking him to the doctor.

Promising to call back as soon as the crisis passed, I hung up on Santos and hurried into the design room to assess the damage. Losing two more people left us seriously short-handed. It also meant that I didn't get a chance to talk to Sparkle or Dwight about Sullivan's visit for the rest of the day.

By the time I dragged myself home, Uncle Nestor and Aunt Yolanda were already asleep. Yes, I checked to make sure.

They'd left a plate for me in the fridge, but I was more tired than hungry. I fell into an exhausted sleep and didn't wake up until Aunt Yolanda knocked on my bedroom door the next morning, bringing me breakfast in bed.

I took that breakfast tray as a positive sign. If Uncle Nestor had been cooking, maybe things were getting back to normal.

I could have lingered for an hour over the coffee, homemade tortillas, fried potatoes, and scrambled eggs seasoned perfectly with onions and peppers and served with Uncle Nestor's signature salsa. Instead, I wolfed down the meal while Aunt Yolanda told me that Sullivan had stopped by the night before to ask Uncle Nestor more questions — a piece of news that almost took away my appetite.

I peppered Aunt Yolanda with questions about Sullivan's visit, but she couldn't tell me much. He'd shown up at the door. The two men had spoken privately for about an hour, after which Uncle Nestor had gone to bed without a word.

Feeling edgy, I hopped in the shower, dressed, and ran out the door thirty minutes later. Usually, Zydeco is closed on Sundays, but not this month. If the murder and subsequent investigation hadn't been enough to make them regret coming to New Orleans for a visit, I thought, the demands of my schedule certainly would. I needed a day off and a good night's sleep, not necessarily in that order.

Just as the sun crested the horizon, I slung my bag over my shoulder and climbed the steps onto Zydeco's loading dock. It promised to be a beautiful day, and I wanted to be outside enjoying some of the fun.

While coffee brewed, I ran a quick glance over the schedule for the next few days to see if there were any breaks in the lineup that would let me sneak away for an hour or two. I couldn't see any, but I was determined to keep my eyes open for one.

I spent a few minutes prioritizing everything listed on the calendar. A hundred or so King Cakes, a special order for a Valentine's Day party, a meeting later in the week with the website designers to discuss Zydeco's presence on the web, and a three-tier white chocolate cake with white chocolate truffles and henna scrollwork topped by a cluster of white sugar daisies scheduled for a delivery today in the French Quarter. It was due a good two hours before the Krewe of Barkus parade, but crowds would be thick and the police would have blocked off traffic long before we needed to get through. I checked to make sure Edie had picked up a pass to get us through the police barricades. She had, of course, so at least we wouldn't have to carry the cake through the crush of people on foot.

I could have canceled the meeting about the website, which was far from urgent on my priority list. But it would make Ox happy, and keeping morale high was crucial when we were so busy, so I decided to let it stand.

I worked on the three-tier cake, henna piping until the muscles in my hand were cramped from squeezing the piping bag. Finally finished, I stepped back to admire my handiwork, flexing my hand a few times to stretch the muscles. Isabeau had almost finished the dozens of sugar daisies on wire stems needed to top the cake. All we had to do was place them and it would be ready to roll.

I was focused on my work. Really, I was. But I also stayed alert for an opportunity to talk with Dwight or Sparkle about their interviews with Sullivan the day before. What can I say? I'm a caring boss.

It wasn't so easy to find a spare moment, though. Luckily, the temp agency had sent a replacement worker to cover for the man we'd lost. But that meant Dwight had to train the guy while staying on top of his own work, which took him out of circulation for most of the morning. Which left Sparkle doing double-duty in the King Cake production line, which also put her off-limits.

Shortly after the lunch hour passed (completely unnoticed by everyone but a couple of the temps), Ox started fussing about whether to change the schedule for delivery of the henna cake. Dwight had originally been on tap to drive across town. The cake was large and heavy, but not so heavy he'd have needed a second pair of hands.

I had to agree that pulling him away from his work seemed like a bad idea. He'd established a rapport with the new guy, and if he stepped away now, someone else would have to waste time getting up to speed.

While Ox and I debated the merits of sending this person or that, Sparkle stepped up to the plate with an offer that stunned us both. "I'll take it."

I turned toward her, mouth hanging open in surprise. Sparkle isn't much of a team player. She's a good employee, but like Abe, she's usually happiest on her own, just doing her own thing in her own little corner. So her offer startled me.

Ox looked equally stunned. "You'll —" He got that word out but the rest seemed to get stuck in his throat.

Sparkle curled her black-painted lips and peeled off the cap she'd been wearing over her raven black hair. Her eyes were heavily lined, and her stubby fingernails gleamed under a coat of glossy black polish. "I said I'll take it. It's going to be at least an hour before that last batch of cakes is cooled and ready to glaze."

She was right, but Ox and I didn't jump on the offer right away. I can't vouch for his thought process, but I ran a glance over her outfit and tried to imagine how the conservative middle-aged couple who were going to renew their vows after Sunday service at the Life Fellowship Community Church would react to her black corset with its bright red satin ties, the black leather shorts that revealed a long expanse of bare thigh, and the five-inch wedge boots with industrial-strength metal buckles from ankle to knee. Pulling the whole thing together was an ankle-length punk goth coat with leather cross-straps that looked as if they belonged in a torture chamber.

I didn't want her walking into the renewal ceremony as the sole face of Zydeco, but she so rarely volunteered for anything that I didn't have the heart to tell her no. So I did the only thing I could.

"Thanks, Sparkle," I said. "It's a heavy cake, so I'll go with you. Dwight's a lot stronger than either one of us, but I'm sure the two of us can handle it together." Which was true, and would also give me a chance to talk with her about Sullivan's visit the day before. Win-win.

Ox looked at me as if I'd lost my mind. "You want to go on this delivery?"

"Sure. Why not?" I countered with a friendly smile. I felt a little rush of excitement at the prospect of spending some time in the middle of the celebrations, even if I wouldn't get to stay for the parade.

"Right." Ox still looked skeptical.

I turned away before he could come up with an argument and caught Sparkle's eye. "Ready?"

She shrugged a listless shoulder and held out the keys to me. "Whatever. You want to drive?"

I shook my head as a show of faith and kept walking. "You drive. I'll ride along." It would be easier to focus on the questions I wanted to ask her that way. The two of us maneuvered the heavy cake across the design area and out the loading dock, securing it in the back of the van as if we'd done it a hundred times. While Sparkle started the van and cranked the AC to keep the cake cool, I poked my head back through the bakery door and asked, "Anybody need anything while we're out?"

"Food!" Estelle shouted from her corner of the design room. "I'm starving!"

I sketched a mock salute to show that I'd heard the request and hurried back to the van. I scrambled into my seat and we both buckled up for the ride. Sparkle drove in silence, but I'd expected that. She isn't much of a chatterbox.

I gave her a few minutes and then tossed a casual conversation starter into the space between us. "Nice," I said, nodding toward the bondage-worthy belt on the front of her coat. "Where did you get it?"

Sparkle slid a glance at me. "Why? You want one?"

"Maybe."

Her eyes smiled, which was more than I'd hoped for. "There's a store online," she said after a minute. "I can give you the website later."

"Perfect." I was dying to ask her about Sullivan's visit, but I didn't want to push. Sparkle doesn't trust easily, and if I came across as too eager, I could lose my chance. So I pretended to watch the city go by for a few seconds.

We paused at a stop sign near a parking lot filled with food stalls and craft vendors where hundreds of happy-looking people milled about. Some were in costume, some in street clothes, but all were laughing, singing, dancing, and clamoring to spend their money on trinkets. I thought about Ox's suggestion that I take time away to share this with Uncle Nestor and Aunt Yolanda and felt a pang of longing. Uncle Nestor would hate the crowds and the noise, but Aunt Yolanda would revel in the chance to experience something new.

As I so often did, I fell somewhere in between them. But as I looked at the bright colors and felt the beat of the music work its way into my bloodstream, I realized how much I was missing. I needed to learn how to relax and enjoy more. Otherwise, life was going to pass me by.

"What?" Sparkle's droll voice pulled my head around.

"What, what?"

"You want something. What is it?"

I grinned sheepishly. "I'm that obvious?"

"Duh. Whatever it is, just ask."

I turned toward her as far as the seat belt would let me so I could watch her reactions and make sure I wasn't crossing the line.

"I'm just curious about why Detective Sullivan came to see you yesterday."

"He wanted to ask me some questions."

"I kind of figured that."

She took her eyes off the road for a second. "He just wanted to follow up on something I told the other cops I saw."

"Oh?" I tried not to look overly interested even though every one of my nerve endings was buzzing with curiosity.

Sparkle turned her attention back to traffic and we drove in silence for another block or two. "You want to know what it was?"

Yes! Casual shrug. "If you want to tell me."

She processed that for what felt like a very long time. It was all I could do not to unbuckle my seat belt and shake it out of her.

She turned a couple of corners and took us past a rundown strip mall. "That guy who died. Big Daddy? I saw him arguing with that woman he was with."

The buzz turned into a low hum. "Are you talking about his assistant? Violet?"

Sparkle shrugged. "I guess. Dark hair. Glasses."

"Sounds like Violet to me. Did you happen to hear what they were arguing about?"

Sparkle flicked a glance at me as she

braked for a red light. Traffic moving the other way crawled through the intersection at a snail's pace. "I did overhear a few things," she said. "Do you want to know what they were?"

"I would love to know."

Cars stopped moving entirely as a crowd of revelers on foot stepped off the curb and into the street. Sparkle didn't even seem to notice the confusion. "It sounded to me like that girl Violet had just figured out that Big Daddy wasn't going to leave his wife for her after all. She wasn't happy about it."

So I'd been right. They were having an affair. "What did she say?" I held my breath, hoping for something like, *I'll kill you*, or *Stand still so I can hit you over the head.*

The light turned green, but with the intersection full of cars and people, we weren't going anywhere. Sparkle put the van in park, prepared to wait. "She said they were through. And she said that she wasn't going to cover for him anymore."

The hum of anticipation turned to a low-pitched drone that seemed to pulsate in my blood. Or maybe that was the music blaring from some nearby loudspeakers. It was hard to tell. "Cover how? For what? Did she say?"

Sparkle shook her head. "I didn't hear that, but I got the feeling it had something

250

to do with Musterion."

"Why? What gave you that impression?"

Another shrug as the light turned yellow again. A woman dressed as a gigantic purple-and-blue dragonfly floated past the van, followed by another wearing a flower arrangement on her head and then a hairy man in a mermaid costume. "You haven't seen anything yet," Sparkle said with what, for her, passes as a grin.

I must have looked confused, because she nodded toward a couple of harp-playing angels with gossamer wings and said again, "You haven't seen anything yet. We're just getting started."

I laughed and tried to take in the sights, sounds, and smells that bombarded me from every angle. "It's like a gigantic Halloween party, isn't it?"

Sparkle snorted. "Without the ghosts and goblins, I guess, and only about a million times better." We caught a break in traffic and we were moving again — if you can call a slow crawl through the crowded streets "moving." Spectators lined the parade route, waiting for the fun to begin. Music spilled into the air from loudspeakers and street musicians, and we moved from one song to another as we crept along the street.

We made it through the police barrier, but

being one of the few vehicles allowed inside the Quarter didn't make it any easier to maneuver. In addition to the costumed crowds, dozens of street entertainers dotted the sidewalks, artists working in every medium I could have imagined — dancers, singers, jazz musicians, all adding to the experience.

"Is that all you wanted to know?"

Sparkle's question broke through my thoughts, but it took me a few seconds to remember what we'd been talking about. Oh yeah. The murder.

"You said that you thought Violet and Big Daddy were talking about Musterion. What gave you that impression?"

"I can't remember exactly," Sparkle said. "She mentioned a couple of names, but I don't remember what they were. Parry maybe? And Scott?"

I forced myself to look away from the spectacle on the street. "Could it have been Percy?"

Sparkle's black-rimmed eyes widened a bit. "Yeah. I think so. Why? You know him?"

"I know who he is, and I know that he was upset with Big Daddy earlier in the evening. Do you remember what Violet said about him?"

Sparkle inched the van around one last

corner and pulled into the parking lot of the church. She put the van into park and shut off the engine. "She said that she was going to back Percy's story, but I don't know what she meant by that."

Neither did I, but I meant to find out. "What about my uncle?" I asked. "Did you see him anywhere?"

She cut a glance at me. "Yeah, I did."

"Where was he?"

"Out by the pool."

My heart stopped beating for an instant, but I told myself not to panic. I already knew Uncle Nestor had been out by the pool, and so did the police. "What was he doing?"

"I'm pretty sure he was talking to Dwight," Sparkle said, and somewhere in the depths of her dark eyes I saw hope flickering. "I know that probably doesn't help."

"It doesn't hurt either," I assured her as I opened my door. "How did Sullivan react to hearing all of that?"

"He didn't. He just wrote it all down and thanked me for my time."

We closed our doors and met at the back of the van. I had one more question for her before we got back to work. "What time did you hear Big Daddy and Violet arguing? Do you remember?"

Sparkle opened the van's back doors and nodded. "Around midnight. It was just a few minutes after we served the King Cake."

The back door of the church opened and our contact came outside to greet us, and the time for thinking about the murder was past. I had to focus on getting the cake inside without smearing the icing or the piping, or knocking off any of the tiny daisies on the top tier.

I didn't know whether Sparkle's story helped Uncle Nestor or not. The argument she'd overhead seemed more like a motive for Big Daddy to get rid of Violet than the other way around. But it did prove that something was askew in Big Daddy's world — and for now that was enough.

TWENTY-THREE

Sparkle and I maneuvered the henna cake through a narrow gate, across a small children's playground, and into the back door of the church's fellowship hall. In spite of the cool weather, I was red-faced and glistening enthusiastically by the time we finished. Sparkle, on the other hand, looked as cool and pale as ever.

On our way back, we stopped at The Joint for a mess of fall-off-the-bone ribs and tubs of creamy coleslaw and slow-cooked baked beans. It was a little out of our way, but we both agreed it was worth the effort. We loaded a couple gallons of sweet tea into the van with the food and headed back to Zydeco to feed the masses.

Traffic was heavier than ever when we finally pulled out of the French Quarter, but this time we were driving away from the parade zone, so we made better time. We still saw people in costume heading toward the festivities, but the carnival atmosphere faded a little more with every block.

Just as Sparkle stopped for a traffic light, a tall black man stepped off the sidewalk and strode across the street right in front of us. He was surrounded by a dozen other people, but I recognized him immediately. Tall. Dark. Denzelesque.

Percy Ponter.

Since we were stopped already, I made a split-second decision. Unbuckling my belt and grabbing my bag in one continuous motion, I waited until he'd reached the other side of the street and opened the van's door.

"Hey!" Sparkle cried as I hopped out into the middle of traffic. "What are you doing?"

"I just saw someone I need to talk to." The light turned and my sense of urgency spiked. "Ten minutes," I promised. "It's really important."

I could still hear music playing along the parade route, but we were far enough away that I could also hear snatches of conversation as people passed me. The air was rich with scents that should have clashed, but instead worked together in a weird way. Hot grease and the yeasty smell of beignets, spicy polish sausage with onions and peppers, shrimp on a stick, and popcorn, all being sold by street vendors. I thought I caught a whiff of cinnamon and curry powder as well, and it all mixed with the mustiness of old buildings.

"I'll call you on your cell in a few minutes," I yelled to Sparkle.

"What in the hell —" The rest of her question got lost when I shut the door between us.

I darted between cars, earning a couple of shouts, one raised middle finger, and three horn blasts. But I made it to the sidewalk in one piece, and that's what mattered. I slipped behind a chalk artist's easel and around the crowd of people watching him work. I had to walk quickly to keep up with Percy's long stride, but following him was easier than I'd expected. Even if he hadn't topped out at a head taller than almost everyone else on the street that day, his tailored and obviously expensive suit stood out in the mostly jeans-and-a-T-shirt crowd.

I tried to remember if Miss Frankie had told me anything about Percy in the weeks before the party, but the details of two hundred lives were all crammed together in my head. I pulled out my cell phone and dialed Miss Frankie's number. The phone rang a few times and the call went to voice mail. There was no answer at Bernice's house either, which probably meant that the two of them were out somewhere together. I just hoped they were staying out of trouble.

Two blocks later, Percy crossed the street and I got caught by the light. I bounced onto my toes so I could keep him in sight. He disappeared into a narrow building midway up the next block and my spirits sank. I shouldn't have hesitated. Now I might have lost my chance to approach him.

Sighing with frustration, I glanced to my left to check the flow of traffic and realized that Sparkle was sitting at the intersection in the Zydeco van. She was watching me with a strange look on her face.

When she saw that I'd spotted her, she rolled down the window. "What are you doing?"

I glanced back up the street to make sure Percy wasn't on his way back and stepped off the curb between two parked cars so I wouldn't have to shout. "I told you. I need to talk to someone. Please, just go around the block and park. I'll call you in a few minutes."

She chewed her bottom lip, considering. "Are you doing something dangerous?"

"No," I said quickly, even though I wasn't entirely sure I was telling the truth.

Her eyes narrowed suspiciously. The light turned green but she didn't move, even when a driver two cars back laid on his horn. "Let me park this thing and I'll come with you."

I shook my head and stepped back onto the curb. "I'll be fine," I assured her. "Now go!"

She didn't look convinced, but at last she put the van into gear and slowly turned the corner. I hurried across the intersection and began the task of trying to figure out which door Percy had gone through.

I'd passed five or six stores without seeing any sign of him when he suddenly appeared on the sidewalk right in front of me. I let out a nervous yelp and sidestepped quickly to avoid running into him.

He tossed an apologetic smile in my direction and prepared to step around me. While I tried to figure out what to say, I saw recognition dawn in his eyes, followed by a minibattle over whether to say hello or pretend not to recognize me.

After a few seconds his shoulders sagged with resignation, a result of his Southern breeding, I guessed.

He hid his hesitation behind a smile, as if he was delighted to see me. "Don't I know you?"

"Rita Lucero." I popped out a hand for him to shake and returned his smile, trying to look as if I was surprised to see him standing there. I won't ever win an Academy Award for my acting skills, but I think I fooled him. "We met at the Musterion party. I was the hostess. And you're . . . Percy? Is that right?"

Something wary flashed behind his eyes, but he kept that friendly smile in place as he nodded. "Of course. I knew you looked familiar."

I glanced at the building he'd come out of — a small neighborhood market. Nothing particularly sinister there. When I looked back at him, he was already making noises about leaving, so I jumped in with both feet. "I suppose you've heard about Big Daddy Boudreaux."

His smile faded and the wariness I'd noticed before spread from his eyes to his face. "Of course. It's been all over the news. It's a horrible thing. Just horrible."

"I met him for the first time at the party, but my mother-in-law has known him for years." I squinted into the setting sun, still trying to look casual and chitchatty. "His death must have come as a shock to you," I said. "It's not easy to lose a friend."

Percy put his hands in his pockets and glanced up and down the sidewalk, just looking for an excuse to walk away. "It was a shock, yes. But we weren't really friends. We were just both members of Musterion."

"Oh? Why did I think you were?"

"I couldn't say." He checked his watch and tried to look regretful. "It's been nice seeing you again. The party was great. You outdid yourself."

I wasn't finished with him yet, so I just kept talking, counting on his being too well bred to leave midsentence. "I guess this creates quite a problem for Musterion, doesn't it? Next year's captain is dead. What happens now?"

Percy reluctantly looked up from his watch. "It's unfortunate, of course, and the timing is delicate, but there are procedures in place to fill a vacancy. The board will take the appropriate steps after Big Daddy has been laid to rest."

I hadn't even thought about the need for a funeral, but now that Percy had mentioned one, I was pretty sure Miss Frankie would be going and she'd expect me to be there. I hate funerals, but it might be interesting to see how Big Daddy's family and friends handled saying their final good-byes.

I tried to look sad, not curious. "Of course. When will that be?"

"I think Susannah has decided on Wednesday afternoon. It will be in the obituary, of course, and we'll post the details on the krewe's website."

I wondered how many hoops they'd have to jump through to secure a venue large enough for Big Daddy's funeral less than a week before Mardi Gras, but didn't ask. I just made a mental note to talk to Miss Frankie about going together and got back to business. "It's all so sad. And for you especially."

"I'm afraid I don't understand. Why me especially?"

"You had unfinished business with him, didn't you?"

There was no mistaking the way Percy's spine stiffened at that or the cautious way he eyed me while he framed his answer. "That was all a misunderstanding. Nothing important."

"Really? It sounded important. You told him that you were going to settle something between you by the end of the night." It was a bold point to make and I was a little nervous making it, but I wasn't about to let him tell me a blatant lie and get away with it.

All pretense of friendliness vanished. "You must have misunderstood. It wasn't like that at all."

I gaped at him. "I was standing right there

when you confronted Big Daddy. He'd just arrived at the party. You wanted him to talk to you that night. He tried to put you off until Monday. His assistant told you to call and make an appointment. Are you really going to claim I misunderstood all of that?"

He shifted his weight on his feet and glanced around nervously. "Look, Ms. Lucero, it's not what you think."

"Then what was it? What were you so angry about?"

"I wasn't angry. I was . . . concerned."

"Okay. Fine. What were you concerned about?"

"It wasn't important. Just some krewe business. And it's really none of your business."

Maybe not, but I wasn't going to let him sweep that conversation under the rug. "It was important enough for you to issue an ultimatum. What was it you said? Something about taking care of it one way or another?"

Percy forced a laugh and shifted his weight again so that he was facing me more fully. "Okay. Yeah. I know how that must have sounded, but it really wasn't a big deal. It *wasn't important*."

"So then you won't mind telling me what he did to upset you."

"That's confidential," he said, his expression cold. "It was a krewe matter. I'm not at liberty to discuss it with you or anyone else." He paused. Shook his head and smiled with wry amusement that almost looked genuine. "Look, you have to know what Big Daddy was like. He was a hard man to pin down. Sometimes you had to get a little in his face to get his attention. But that's all it was, trust me."

Maybe. But not yet. "Did you talk to him again the night of the party?"

Percy shook his head and checked his watch again. "Not that I remember. Now, if you'll excuse me, I have an appointment."

"Just one more question. Please?"

I could tell that he wanted to leave, but he held back and looked at me with exasperation. "What is it?"

I was feeling some frustration of my own. So far nobody had been able to provide Uncle Nestor with an alibi — or at least nobody was willing to admit they could. Maybe I was barking up the wrong tree. Maybe instead of trying to clear Uncle Nestor, I should be trying to figure out which of these people had the strongest motive to want Big Daddy out of the way.

So I blurted out the question I really wanted him to answer: "If you didn't kill Big Daddy, who did?"

Percy stared at me for a minute before letting out a whooping laugh. "If I — Are you serious? You're standing here in the middle of the street accusing me — Are you *nuts*, girl?"

"I'm just trying to find out who might have had a motive for wanting him out of the way. You knew him. You worked with him at Musterion. If you had to pick a name, whose name would it be?"

Percy put both hands on his hips and turned away so quickly he almost ran into a couple of elderly women coming out of a hair salon. The breeze caught his suit jacket and whipped it out from behind him, making him look like some kind of avenging superhero.

He took a couple of steps away from me, then turned around and came back toward me. "That's a dangerous game you're playing," he said, his voice low.

"It's not a game," I said back. "Who had a reason to want Big Daddy dead? I've heard that he was arguing with both his assistant and his wife that night, and with his brother. And of course, with you. Do you have any idea why he argued with the others?"

Percy barked a sharp laugh. "How would I know that?"

"I just thought you might. Susannah seemed to know about your krewe business. She told Big Daddy that he had to make things right with you that night, or else. And Violet told Big Daddy that she was going to back your story. What did she mean by that?"

Percy's eyes narrowed. "Where did you hear that?" He looked so angry, my heart skipped a beat.

And just in case he was a crazed killer, I wasn't about to give him a name. "From someone who has no reason to lie."

"And you think I do, is that it?" Percy sighed. "Look, Rita, there are a lot of people in this town who aren't exactly losing sleep over Big Daddy's death. But folks in these parts tend to close ranks against outsiders. Take my advice. Quit asking questions."

I didn't know how much of Percy's story to believe. He'd seemed genuinely angry the night of the party, but it was pretty clear he wasn't going to tell me why. He would certainly have the strength to use the statue as a weapon, but was the mysterious krewe business important enough to kill over? Susannah and Violet obviously knew about it, but I wondered who else knew and whether any of them would talk to me about it.

Having delivered his warning, Percy

walked away, and I made no effort to stop him. Which turned out to be a smart decision. I set off in the other direction and pulled out my cell phone just as Sparkle came around the corner on foot. Her coattails billowed out behind her as she walked, and her skin looked paler than usual in the bright sunlight.

"Hey," she said when she saw me. "You all right?"

"Yeah. Fine."

"Did you get what you wanted?"

"Not exactly."

Sparkle and I trudged back to the van in silence. I probably should have been thinking about work, or about the murder, or about Uncle Nestor's health, or even trying to devise a new scheme to get an audience with Ivanka Hedge. But for once, all the other voices in my head were quiet, leaving me time and space to think about the way Sparkle had come to check on me.

I was surprised by my reaction to that. Frankly, it gave me the warm fuzzies, but I wasn't going to tell her that. Sparkle isn't the warm fuzzies type, and I wasn't about to repay her kindness with an insult.

TWENTY-FOUR

The bakery was in chaos by the time Sparkle and I made it through traffic and back to Zydeco. The new temp had moved all twenty-four chocolate roses for the Valentine's Day cake into a sunny spot near the window, which meant it was all hands on deck to make twenty-four more. Even our baker Abe, who typically kept vampire hours but had recently started coming in earlier to help with the workload, got into the act.

By the time we finished, Dwight was in a thoroughly sour mood, so I decided not to ask him about his interview with Sullivan. Maybe tomorrow.

I had plenty of other things to think about in the meantime. I'd been trading phone calls with Miss Frankie for a couple of days, but I hadn't actually talked to her since the night of the party. We finally made a plan for me to go over that night, once I got off work. Now that Percy had reminded me about it, I needed to talk to her about the funeral. Not to mention, with the date of the Bacchus parade approaching rapidly, I had to get serious about finding a costume, and Miss Frankie was my only hope to find anything remotely appropriate.

As I drove across town, I thought about what Percy had said and pieced it together with what I already knew. Presumably, Violet had been under the impression that Big Daddy was going to leave his wife for her. He hadn't exactly seemed lovey-dovey with her in my opinion, but there's no accounting for some people's choices. It appeared that she'd wanted a big jerk who treated her like dirt, and she was upset to learn that she wasn't going to get him all to herself.

Then again, maybe she hadn't actually been in love with Big Daddy. By all accounts, he had money . . . and lots of it. Maybe that's what Violet objected to losing. At some point during the party, she'd found out she wasn't going to get the future she'd been planning on. Either way, that put her high on my personal list of suspects.

And what about Susannah Boudreaux? If she'd found out that Big Daddy was cheating on her, that could give her a pretty strong motive for murder. I put her in the number two spot on my potential killer list and mentally wrote in Percy's name as number three. He wasn't off the hook. Not by a long shot.

I parked in Miss Frankie's driveway a little after ten that evening. She was waiting for me with a warm smile and a welcoming hug. "Come on back to the kitchen, sugar. I started coffee after you called, and I'm so glad you did. We've been needing to talk. I've warmed some rolls left over from lunch so we can nibble on those."

I was still pleasantly full from the ribs and slaw, but Miss Frankie's homemade rolls are a taste sensation not to be missed. I trailed after, admiring her black silk lounging pajamas with a birds of paradise design that exactly matched the shade of her hair. A pair of black sandals showed off her feet — the recipients of a recent pedicure — with toenails painted the same shade of burnt orange. Which, naturally, matched the shade of polish on her fingernails. At least I knew how she'd been keeping herself busy since the party.

I sat in the kitchen and inhaled the rich aroma of chicory coffee. It's the little things.

Miss Frankie splashed in the condensed milk and filled a mug for me, then put a plate with two steaming dinner rolls and a generous pat of butter on the table in front of me. She gathered some for herself and sat across from me, giving me a look. "So what is it, sugar? What brings you to my door in the middle of the night?"

"It's only ten," I said with a rueful smile. "But if you're ready for bed, I'll come back tomorrow."

"Not on your life. I've been wantin' to see you for a couple of days now. How you holding up?"

"I'm fine," I assured her. "Just a little tired. I'm hoping you can help me with my costume for the Bacchus parade next weekend."

"You don't have one?"

"Not yet," I admitted. "I know, I should have taken care of it weeks ago."

Miss Frankie smiled gently. "Don't you worry. I have plenty of things in the attic. We'll fix you up. Now are you going to tell me why you're here, or are you going to keep me guessing?"

"I left you a message about Big Daddy's funeral. Do you want to go together?"

"You know I do. Shall I pick you up around ten on Wednesday?"

"Perfect." I tore off a piece of roll and smothered it in butter. "What's on your calendar for the next couple of days? Would

271

you and Bernice have time to show Uncle Nestor and Aunt Yolanda around the city? They're stuck here in town, and I'm not going to have time to spend with them."

"Of course. I'm sure Bernice will be delighted. I'll call her first thing in the morning. Is that all?"

I nodded, then stopped and shook my head. "You could tell me what you know about the current Mrs. Boudreaux."

"Susannah?" Miss Frankie wrapped her hands around her mug and stared at the ceiling for a minute, gathering her thoughts together. "Susannah's an interesting woman," she said after a few minutes. "She was Bradley's third wife, you know."

"So I've heard. How long were they married?"

"Oh, goodness. I don't know. Four years? Maybe five."

"Was it a good marriage?"

"I always assumed it was. Bradley seemed content enough. At least he was as content as he ever got."

"But he was cheating on her," I said. "He was having an affair with his assistant."

Miss Frankie dismissed my comment with a wave of her hand. "Bradley wasn't the kind of man who does well in a committed relationship. He had a tendency to stray, but I'm sure Susannah knew that before she married him. After all, that's how she met him."

My lips curved slightly. "That doesn't necessarily mean she'd be okay with him cheating on her."

"If they'll do it with you," Miss Frankie said, "they'll do it to you."

"That's true," I said with a smile. "What about her? Was she faithful to him?"

Miss Frankie sipped, then put her cup on the table. "I wouldn't know about that, sugar. She and I don't exactly run in the same social circle."

"Really? I thought you did."

"Gracious no. She's young and energetic and interested in all sorts of things I'm not. The only time I see her is at charitable events or Musterion functions, and then only to say hello. I've always suspected she's the reason Bradley didn't make it to Philippe's funeral."

"He did say they were on a cruise," I pointed out.

"Yes, I know. At times I thought she seemed a little threatened by Bradley's past, as if she felt the need to keep all his attention focused on her."

"So you think she purposely kept Big Daddy away from Philippe's funeral?"

"I'm saying I don't think she'd have rushed home for it, even if they could have."

That made her unlikeable, but not necessarily homicidal. I decided to get right to the point. "Do you think she could have killed her husband?"

Miss Frankie's eyes narrowed thoughtfully. "Of course she *could* have. The question is why would she?"

"Because he was cheating on her," I said. "And because he'd done something she was very unhappy about, and it had something to do with Musterion. Or at least with that guy Percy. Anyway, she gave Big Daddy an ultimatum to make it right, or else."

Miss Frankie's thoughtful expression turned grim. "Are you sure about that, sugar?"

"That's what Estelle overheard. Percy denies it, of course. He claims it was all about some unimportant Musterion business. But you heard what he said to Big Daddy at the party. It sure didn't sound unimportant to me. Did it to you?"

"Percy did seem upset," she admitted. "When did you talk to him about it?" she asked, looking a little worried.

I waved off her concerns. "I ran into him while Sparkle and I were delivering a cake. It was no big deal. The question is, why was

Susannah Boudreaux so eager to throw suspicion on my uncle? She had to know Uncle Nestor didn't kill her husband."

Miss Frankie looked skeptical. "How would she know that?"

"Well, because . . . if she saw him do it, why didn't she stop him? Or at least let the rest of us know that something horrible was happening? Why wait until the police were there to make her big, dramatic accusation?"

"That's a good question."

I thought so, too, but neither of us had answers. I finished off one roll and changed my tack. "What can you tell me about Judd Boudreaux? Why would Big Daddy have been upset with him that night?"

Miss Frankie sighed softly. "There's a lot to be upset with when it comes to Judd, I'm afraid."

"He was Philippe's friend?" At her nod, I asked, "Why haven't I heard of him before? Why didn't Philippe ever mention him?"

"Probably because Judd's life is such a sad, sad story. Back when they were boys, Judd was a golden child. Smart. Funny. And so good-looking. He had a way with people and everyone loved him."

I could easily believe that. "He sounds like Philippe," I said, and for the first time I

275

wondered if that's why I'd felt drawn to him when we met.

Miss Frankie nodded again. "They were very much alike, and they bonded almost the minute they met. They went everywhere together, like two peas in a pod. And they both looked up to Bradley."

I made a face. "Please tell me he was different back then."

She laughed a little. "Oh, yes. Both Boudreaux boys were. They got a little older and Judd started playing the guitar and writing music. He was talented, a rising star, and we all thought he'd end up being signed to some big-time record label. Thought we had us our own version of Elvis or something."

I tried to reconcile that dream with the Judd I'd met. If he'd been sober, it would have been easier. "So what happened?"

Her smile faded and deep sadness flooded her eyes. "It was such a terrible tragedy. He was driving a car late one night. He'd been drinking, of course, and he went off the road. The car flipped a few times and he was thrown free. The young woman with him wasn't so lucky."

My breath caught, and the pain I'd sensed in Judd flashed through my mind. Shades of Ted Kennedy, only apparently Judd hadn't bounced back. "She died?"

"Yes." Miss Frankie sighed, reliving a time that obviously still had the power to wound. "It turned out she was younger than she'd claimed to be. Only seventeen. Her parents were devastated. His parents were devastated. And Judd . . . well, that boy has never been the same."

"That's tragic," I said softly.

"You don't know the half of it, sugar. Judd pushed everybody away after that and started drowning his future in a bottle. Their mama took it hard, poor thing. Bradley stood by him, bless his heart. He was just about the only person Judd would let get close. Philippe tried to help, but Judd turned him away time and time again. Bradley never gave up though, even when their daddy threatened to disown Judd if he didn't straighten up, stop drinking, and get his life together."

"Which Judd refused to do?"

"I think he tried a few times, but his heart was never in it. I don't think he's ever forgiven himself for that girl's death. I'm not sure he ever will. For all his faults, Bradley stuck with him. He's bailed him out of trouble more times than I can count."

I tried to reconcile *that* image with the Big Daddy I'd met at the party, but it was even harder to do. One last question hovered on my lips. I didn't want to ask it, but I knew I had to. "Do you think Judd could have killed Big Daddy?"

"I can't imagine why he would," Miss Frankie said. "Big Daddy was just about all Judd had left."

TWENTY-FIVE

Monday passed in a blur of work. I was at Zydeco by sunrise and crawled into bed well after midnight. Tuesday flew by as well, and it was Tuesday evening before I found a chance to ask Dwight about his interview with Sullivan and the conversation Sparkle said he'd had with Uncle Nestor. Before I could, though, Edie informed me that I was tardy for the website meeting, and that Ox was already upstairs with our website designers. I rushed into the meeting room, conveniently forgetting that I'd opted not to cancel the meeting and cursing Ox under my breath for scheduling the appointment at all. Frankly, there was no reason for me to be there, and not being all that web savvy, I found that most of what they talked about was over my head. But maybe that's because I was struggling just to keep my eyes open. By the time we all stood up to shake hands and declare our mutual delight to be working together, they'd been discussing meta tags, pixels, and search engines for an hour. That was an hour of my life I'd never get back. But Ox was smiling as he walked them to the front door, so I guess it was worth it.

The sun had gone down and most of the staff had packed it in for the day while Ox and I were otherwise occupied. "Isabeau and I are heading over to the Duke for a drink," he said. "Want to join us?"

I almost said no, but it occurred to me that (1) the Duke served a killer jambalaya, and (2) Dwight was probably there. So I nodded and said, "Sure. Sounds great." You know, for the greater good.

Uncle Nestor and Aunt Yolanda would be waiting for me at home, but I promised myself I'd be quick. Thirty minutes tops.

The Dizzy Duke has been the staff's after-hours hangout since the bakery opened almost three years ago. It's an ancient red-brick building squatting in the midst of a bunch of aging, sagging buildings two blocks east of Zydeco. The whole neighborhood smells faintly of rotting wood. That's not a smell I'm used to, coming from the western half of the country, where dry, not damp, is our cross to bear, but I'm learning to like it.

Ox held the door and I trailed Isabeau

inside, pausing for a moment to let my eyes adjust to the low lighting and neon. Here, too, carnival season had left its mark. The whole bar looked as if it had been dusted with Mardi Gras colors. I spotted my favorite bartender, Gabriel Broussard (whom I've mentally dubbed "Hot Cajun"), behind the polished wood bar and waved a greeting. He scooped a lazy hank of dark hair off his forehead and grinned back. The house band was playing a low-key jazz number I didn't recognize — which wasn't saying much. I'm still new to that world, too.

Near the bandstand, someone had pulled a couple of tables together, and most of my staff lounged around them along with a couple of the temps. I was embarrassed to realize I'd forgotten their names. In my defense, I maintain that the brain can only hold so much information at one time. Mine was already chock-full.

I could see Dwight in the center of the group, his usually rumpled clothes looking worse than ever, his face gaunt and pale. We were all burning out fast, and I wasn't sure what to do about it. I made an executive decision and headed for the bar. Maybe I couldn't cut their hours or lessen the workload, but at least I could let them know how much I appreciated what they were doing.

Gabriel spotted me coming, tossed a towel over his shoulder, and leaned on the bar in a sexy sort of way to wait for me. I don't mind admitting that his obvious interest does a little something to my insides, but I was far too tired right then to dwell on it.

I hitched onto a bar stool and offered him a weary smile in response to the slow grin he aimed at me. "Well, well, well," he said as I tried to wrangle my purse onto the bar beside me. He ran a glance over me from head to toe. "Busy day?"

"Little bit," I said. "Why?"

"No reason, except you're a mess."

"Thanks. That means I look better than I feel." I patted the hair I knew had probably frizzed up like a Chia Pet and swiped at a couple of unidentifiable spots on my jeans.

"So what's going on to put that look on your face?"

I shrugged. "Just the normal stuff, times about ten. Surprise out-of-town guests and way too much work."

"You work too hard," Gabriel said. "You need to let your hair down and have a little fun."

"You're not the first person to tell me that," I said, struggling to hold back a yawn. "It's not as easy as it sounds."

"Sure it is. Just let yourself relax."

I propped up my chin in my hand and sighed. "I was raised by a professional worrier. It's in my genes."

"That's a cop-out."

He might have been right, but I was also too tired for self-examination. "Are you going to take my order, or what?"

"Fine. What can I get for you?"

"A virgin margarita," I told him. "And make *sure* it's a virgin. I'm driving." He started to turn away but I called after him. "And jambalaya. Please tell me you have some left."

"Sorry. It's shrimp étouffée tonight." The Duke isn't a restaurant, but the owners throw together a pot of something wonderful almost every night and serve it on a first-come, first-served basis. I miss out far more often than I actually score a meal.

"That's just as good," I assured him. "Make it a small bowl," I said, knowing there was probably a plate of something waiting for me at home. "And send a round of whatever everyone's having over there, on me," I said, jerking my chin toward the staff's tables. "They deserve it."

Gabriel wandered away and returned a few minutes later with a frosty glass on a fragile stem, filled with sweetly sour frozen slush. He knows me pretty well by now, so he doesn't have to ask if I want salt on the rim. If you ask me, drinking tequila without salt is almost sacrilegious; the rule also holds for anything that should have tequila in it, but doesn't.

I sipped cautiously. Not that I don't trust Gabriel to leave the alcohol out . . . but I don't. He's been known to pour with a heavy hand around me, so it's always better to be safe than sorry. When I didn't detect any tequila, I took a healthier swallow and sighed happily. I appreciate a skilled artist, no matter what medium he may work in.

Gabriel filled an order for one of the cocktail waitresses and gravitated toward me again carrying a bowl of étouffée brimming with shrimp, onions, jalapeños, and just enough rice to give it body. I dug in with gusto.

Étouffée-loving foodies have been known to debate certain aspects of the dish. Is it acceptable to use more than one kind of seafood, or does that make it gumbo? Should étouffée be made with a roux (flour and oil whisked together over heat until it's perfectly smooth) or without? Does a proper étouffée contain tomatoes or not? Personally, I loved the Duke's version: single seafood, includes a roux, and excludes tomatoes. It was a well-balanced and flavorful dish with just the right amount of kick to it.

While I shoveled shrimp, peppers, garlic, and rice into my mouth, Gabriel got to work on the order for the staff. "So I hear Big Daddy Boudreaux met his demise at your party," he said.

I stopped eating just long enough to stick out my tongue at him. "It was my party in name only, and I had nothing to do with his untimely demise." I plied a napkin over my mouth to make sure I hadn't left any unsightly bits. "What did people see in him anyway? I don't get it."

"You weren't blown away by Big Daddy's charm and sex appeal?"

I pretended to stick my finger down my throat and made a little gagging noise. "Seriously. I don't get it. What *did* people see in him?"

Gabriel laughed and added 7-Up to the whiskey in Ox's glass. "Money is power, baby. And power is sexy. It's always been that way."

I made a face. "That's a stupid rule."

"It's not a rule," he said. "It's a universal truth. Rules you can break or change. The truth just is. You can't avoid it."

I put down my spoon and took another

mouthful of slush. "So you're a philosopher now?"

"I'm a bartender. It's part of the job description."

I licked a little salt from the rim of my glass. "Yeah? Well, I sure hope you're right. Otherwise, my uncle might be paying a very high price for a mighty big lie."

Gabriel pulled a couple of beers from the cooler behind him. "What lie would that be?"

He looked genuinely interested, so I unloaded on him. Bartender, remember? The next best thing to a therapist.

I told him about Big Daddy's behavior at the party and, in the interest of honesty, gave him a brief summary of the fight between Uncle Nestor and Big Daddy. I told him about meeting Judd and overhearing his conversation with Mellie. About finding Big Daddy floating in the pool. About the conversation between Big Daddy and Judd that Ox had witnessed and Mellie's search for Judd later by the pool.

I topped the whole thing off with a second virgin margarita and an account of the Widow Boudreaux making it sound like Uncle Nestor had killed her husband. By the time I'd finished sharing, I felt much better. "She has to know it's not true," I said as I wound down. "Uncle Nestor barely knew the guy. He had no reason to kill Big Daddy."

Gabriel had listened to my whole diatribe without interrupting. Now he cocked his head to one side and asked, "If she knows it's not true, why would she say it?"

"Your guess is as good as mine," I said, yawning again. "Because she's crazy? Because living with Big Daddy drove her nuts? Because she had to be out of her head to get involved with him in the first place?"

Gabriel cashed out a tab for a regular customer I recognized by sight and wiped a spill from the bar, glancing at me from the corner of his eye. "You're not thinking clearly. The woman's not crazy. She might not be the brightest star in the sky, but she's not stupid either. I'm guessing either she believes it's true, or she's lying to divert attention."

I sat up a little straighter and a couple of heavy gray clouds floated out of my head. "You mean, like, from herself?"

"Could be. My understanding is the Boudreauxes weren't getting along all that well."

I started to say something, but sudden realization wiped whatever it was right out of my head. "Wait a minute. Do you know them?"

"Sure. Doesn't everybody?"

"No, I mean, like really *know* them? Not just from the TV? That stuff you said about her not being stupid. How do you know that?"

He dropped a cherry into a tequila sunrise and gave me a half-grin. "I've spent some time with them."

"They're friends of yours?"

"Acquaintances."

"From where? How do you know them?"

He spritzed soda into a glass and reached for a straw. "We're all members of the same krewe."

You could have knocked me off that barstool with a feather. "You're a member of Musterion? Why weren't you at the party?"

"I'm not on the board this year. Not involved in the planning either, thank God. But I'll be there for the ball and for the parade."

"In costume?"

He grinned. "That information's on a need-to-know basis."

I was getting distracted, so I finished my étouffée and licked my spoon — discreetly, of course. With my stomach pleasantly full, I managed to string a few coherent thoughts together. "Does that mean you also know Ivanka Hedge and Richard Montgomery?"

"I do. I was on the parade committee with Rich a couple of years ago."

My exhaustion fell away and I bounced up in my seat. "Are you serious?"

He arched an eyebrow. "Would I lie to you?"

I shook my head quickly. "Not if your life depended on it. Could you introduce me to them?"

"I suppose I could."

"Will you?"

"That depends."

"On what?"

"On what's in it for me."

Everybody has an angle. "How about my undying gratitude?"

He did a little shruggy-thing with his mouth. "That's the best you can do?"

I shrugged back. "I don't know. Maybe." When he didn't relent, I did. "If that's not good enough, what *do* you want?"

"I'll think about it," he said.

"Come on, Gabriel. You have no idea how important this is to me."

He cleared away my bowl, but he didn't say a word.

"This could make or break me," I said. "I really need this."

He turned to a middle-aged man on a barstool a few feet away, pointedly ignoring me.

"Seriously?" I demanded.

He gave the man a beer and turned toward the kitchen. "I'll let you know," he said over his shoulder.

I stood on the rungs of the barstool to make myself taller. "*Seriously?* Oh, come on!" I called to his retreating back. But he just kept walking.

TWENTY-SIX

When Gabriel didn't come back after a few minutes, I picked up my glass and carried it across the room alongside the cocktail waitress who carried the tray laden with drinks for my employees. The group hailed me like some conquering hero and lifted their glasses in salute. I laughed, pleased with myself for doing the right thing. My ex-husband, their former boss, had been fun-loving and gregarious. Picking up the tab for a round of drinks had been second nature to him. I had to work a little harder at making those kinds of friendly gestures, so I always felt a little rush of pleasure when one of them worked out well.

The Duke had a respectable-sized crowd tonight, but it wasn't so busy that I felt claustrophobic. Laughter and chatter rose and fell all around me, but the group clustered around Zydeco's tables was by far the loudest. I positioned my chair close enough to Dwight's to get his attention easily, then waited through two or three songs before I made the effort. "Hey!" I said in the relative silence that fell between songs. "Could I talk to you for a minute?"

Dwight looked puzzled, but he nodded. "Sure. What's up?"

"Not here," I said. "Outside?"

He got to his feet and we wove our way back through the tables while the band's lead singer, an aging man with a graying ponytail and a shaggy Fu Manchu mustache, announced the band's next selection.

Outside, I led Dwight toward a park bench barely illuminated by a nearby streetlight.

He sat next to me, groaning a little from the effort. "I'm getting old," he said with a grin. "I'm starting to sound like my old man."

I scowled at him. "Don't say that. We're the same age."

He laughed and stretched his legs out in front of him. "It's gonna happen to us sooner or later. Might as well accept it."

"Never!"

He laughed again and linked his hands behind his head. "So what do you want to talk about?"

I didn't want to keep him away from the

others for long, so I launched right in. "Sparkle told me that she saw you talking to my uncle by the pool the night of the murder. Do you remember what time that was?"

Dwight stretched then linked his hands together behind his head. "A little after midnight, I think. We'd already served the King Cake."

That matched Sparkle's memory and it gave me hope that I was on the right track. We hadn't discovered Big Daddy's body until after two. What were the chances that Uncle Nestor had stayed in the same spot for two hours? "Did you see anyone else out there?"

"Lots of people," Dwight said, cutting a glance at me. "Are you interested in someone in particular?"

"Yeah. Whoever killed Big Daddy."

Dwight grinned and settled more comfortably on the bench. "Wish I could help you, but I wasn't around when he was killed."

"Kinda figured that," I said. "Otherwise, you'd have told Sullivan and there'd have been an arrest by now." A breeze rustled the leaves overhead, a soft, soothing sound. Somewhere nearby a dog barked and music floated out from the Duke as the band began another song. "So what did you and

Uncle Nestor talk about?"

"Nothing much. I asked how long they'd be staying, he asked whether you seemed happy."

"How did he seem?"

"You mean was he agitated or did I think he was about to rush off and kill somebody? No. Neither. He seemed normal. Like a guy at a party he didn't particularly want to be at."

"How drunk was he?"

Dwight gave me a funny look. "He wasn't. He might have had a little buzz on, but he wasn't drunk. In fact, when I saw him, he was nursing a ginger ale. Said it was doctor's orders."

That surprised me, but maybe it shouldn't have. I should have known that cutting out alcohol would have been on the same list as "take up jogging." I was just having trouble wrapping my mind around the idea of Uncle Nestor following those orders without argument. But had I actually seen him drinking a lot, or had I just assumed he was drinking because of his behavior? "Did he say anything about the fight he had with Big Daddy?"

Dwight shook his head. "Nope. In fact, he acted as if it never happened."

"I wish it had never happened," I said.

"So that was it? That's all you two talked about?"

Again with the funny look on Dwight's face. "Not exactly."

I nudged him in the ribs with my elbow. "Would you just tell me? I'm too tired to pry it out of you."

"He's worried about you, Rita. He's afraid you're . . . how did he say it? Forgetting who you are and where you came from."

"That's ridiculous," I said, but I felt something tugging uncomfortably at my heart. The last thing I wanted to do was hurt Uncle Nestor or Aunt Yolanda, and I hated knowing that he felt that way. "What did you tell him?"

"I told him that you're cool," Dwight said. "That you've got it together and he shouldn't worry so much."

I grinned and slouched down on the bench so that I matched his posture. "Thanks. Did he believe you?"

"I doubt it."

So did I. We sat there for a moment in companionable silence before I asked the other question that had been nagging at me. "So what did Sullivan want to talk to you about?"

"He didn't tell you?"

I snorted a little. "Are you kidding? He

295

hasn't said two words to me about the investigation. So what was it? And please don't tell me it was something that makes my uncle look even guiltier."

Dwight shook his head. "Nope. He wanted to know about an argument I overheard between Big Daddy and Judd Boudreaux."

"What argument? Where? When? Were they upstairs in the clubhouse?"

Dwight shook his head. "They were outside."

So not the secretive conversation Ox had seen them having. That made me sit up a little straighter. "Did you hear what they were arguing about?"

"Not the whole thing, but enough. Big Daddy was furious about something. He grabbed Judd by the shirt and shoved him up against the wall. Looked like he wanted to rip him apart."

The Big Daddy who'd been his brother's protector for all these years? What was that about? "You don't know why?"

Dwight shook his head. "I heard Big Daddy tell Judd that he'd crossed the line big-time this time, but that's about it."

I tried to imagine the soft-spoken Judd under assault from his big brother, and wondered what Judd had done that had made Big Daddy slip from protector to attacker. "What line?"

"I have no idea. Sorry."

"So what did Judd say?"

Dwight lifted one shoulder. "He was pretty sloshed. Kind of hard to understand. He just kept telling Big Daddy that he'd pay him back."

"Pay him back? Like get even?"

Dwight shook his head. "It sounded like they were talking about money to me. Judd said he'd pay Big Daddy back, and Big Daddy told him he'd better get it together by the next day or their asses would both be on the line."

"Judd owed Big Daddy money?"

"That's what it sounded like to me."

For the first time, I gave some serious thought to what the financial situation was in the Boudreaux family. According to Judd, they'd been members of The Shores since he was a boy, so I assumed they were old money. But how was that money split, and who controlled it?

"Then what?"

Dwight shrugged again. "They argued like that for a while and then Big Daddy told Judd he was sending him to rehab. He said this was the final straw."

I couldn't imagine the Judd I'd met getting angry enough to whack his own brother over the head and push him into the pool, but could I have been wrong? "How did Judd react to that?"

"I don't know. Estelle asked me for help with something she did to her camera, and I went back inside. By the time I went back outside, they were gone."

I sat there for a minute, taking that all in and weighing it against what Miss Frankie had said about the relationship between Judd and Big Daddy and what Ox had already told me about the two of them the night of the party. "What about Uncle Nestor?" I asked when I couldn't make all the pieces fit. "Did you see him after that?"

Dwight shook his head. "Sorry."

"How late did you stay?"

"It took me half an hour or so to figure out what Estelle did to the camera. I left right after that." He got to his feet and stood over me for a moment. "Just do me a favor, okay?"

"What's that?"

"Be careful. If you ask me, all the Boudreauxes are crazy as loons. If one of them did kill Big Daddy, they won't hesitate to hurt anyone else who gets in their way."

His warning sent a chill up my spine, but I nodded. "Don't worry about me."

"I'm serious," he said. "The police know

everything I just told you. Just let them do their jobs."

"I'm not trying to get involved in their investigation," I assured him. "I'm just trying to clear my uncle."

He walked away a minute later, and I stood there trying to decide whether to go back inside or head home. I craved some alone time, but Uncle Nestor and Aunt Yolanda had been on their own too much. I was quite possibly the world's worst hostess. It was time to do something about that.

TWENTY-SEVEN

I parked three doors away from my house at a little after nine, relieved to see that the lights were still on. I found Uncle Nestor and Aunt Yolanda at the dining room table, talking about something over a pot of decaf. Aunt Yolanda bounced up when I came through the door and spent the next few minutes warming me up a plate, bringing me silverware, and fussing over me in a way I hadn't been fussed over in months. Uncle Nestor didn't say much, but I caught him watching me fondly a couple of times. I hoped that meant that we were okay again.

After I was finally tucked in with a plate of homemade tamales, chili *verde*, and tortillas, all my doubts about their feelings for me faded away. I ate quickly, a little embarrassed that I could put away so much of Uncle Nestor's food after the étouffée at the Duke. In my defense, it had been a small bowl, and the only other thing I'd eaten all day was a blueberry streusel muffin so long ago it seemed like I'd had that in the previous century.

The chili was perfect, flavorful and garlicky, with a bite from the jalapeños that came with a slow after-burn. The tortillas were soft and warm. I tore off one piece after another, using them to scoop up the chili in the time-honored fashion of my childhood. I peeled away the hot corn husk wrapping from the tamales and enjoyed an entirely different taste sensation as the rich flavor of chili *rojo* exploded on my tongue. It was spicy without being hot, and the bland *masa* wrapping acted as the perfect complement.

If ever a meal expressed love, that one did. My stomach was comfortably full as I wiped up the last of the chili with a scrap of tortilla, and so was my heart. I missed my childhood home and the life I'd had in Albuquerque, but I loved living on my own for the first time ever, and my new career was more satisfying than anything I'd ever done. I suppose there are no easy answers to life's hard questions.

They filled me in on their day — a stroll around the neighborhood, a stop at the corner market two blocks down, and phone calls home. I filled them in on mine, minus the stop at the Duke.

The mood was warm and cozy and I hated to disturb it, but there were too many unanswered questions between us. Besides, Uncle Nestor was in a good mood, and I didn't want to let the opportunity to ask a few simple questions slip away. While Aunt Yolanda told me about Santos's oldest son taking a tumble from his bike, I carried my dishes to the sink, rinsed them, and stacked them next to the dishwasher. When she'd finished, I broached the subject uppermost in my mind as gently as I knew how.

"I've been talking to a couple of my employees, Sparkle and Dwight. They had some interesting things to say about the night Big Daddy Boudreaux was killed."

"Sparkle," Uncle Nestor said. "She's the one with the dark hair, am I right?"

"That's right. And Dwight's a friend from pastry school."

"The dirty one," Uncle Nestor said.

I was impressed that he'd made an effort to put names with faces. Resuming my seat, I put my feet up to take some of the pressure off the waistband of my jeans, which had suddenly become too tight. "He's not dirty. He's just . . . cleanliness challenged. And he's very talented."

Aunt Yolanda smiled indulgently. "He

seems like a very nice young man."

"He is," I agreed. "But that's not what I want to talk about." I made eye contact with Uncle Nestor and said, "I know why you fought with Big Daddy. You might as well tell the police. If I found out, they will, too."

He looked back at me with an expression of supreme innocence. "What makes you think I haven't already told them?"

"Oh, I don't know. Maybe the fact that Sullivan told me you hadn't."

"And you believe him over me?"

"He has no reason to lie about it," I said without blinking. "So what's up, *Tío*? Why are you still refusing to talk about it?"

Uncle Nestor made a noise like a low growl and turned his attention to my feet on the chair. "Why are your feet on the furniture? Didn't we teach you better than that?"

"My house, my rules." I grinned broadly as I repeated the phrase I'd heard too often as a kid. He was trying to distract me and I wasn't going to let him get away with it. "Now, answer my question."

He scowled up at me and blinked a couple of times. "What question?"

"The one about why you're still refusing to talk about the fight you had with Big Daddy the night he died."

Blink. Blink . . . Blink.

Aunt Yolanda shot me a warning glance. "I don't think we should talk about that just now."

"Well, I do," I said as gently as I could. "Staying silent isn't helping him, *Tía*." I turned back to Uncle Nestor. "If you're trying to protect Aunt Yolanda, she's not as delicate as you might think. She can handle whatever you have to say."

Blink, blink.

I sat up and put my feet on the floor, but only because I was too agitated to sit still. "How about I start then? Big Daddy made some disgusting comments about Aunt Yolanda and about me. You heard them. Maybe he even said them right to you. It made you angry and you blasted him in the face. How am I doing so far?"

Aunt Yolanda looked from Uncle Nestor to me and back again. "What comments?"

Blink.

"You got into that fight because of me?"

Blink, blink.

"Look," I said, hanging on to what little patience I had left, "I understand that you're kind of freaked out after your heart attack — which is another thing we need to talk about, by the way. And I understand that you're worried about me, which you

304

don't have to be. And I can understand losing your temper, especially if you were drinking."

Aunt Yolanda rounded on him, eyes flashing with anger. "You were drinking?"

Uncle Nestor shot me a look, and his wife a smile, clearly intended to placate her. "I wasn't drinking, sweetheart. I promised I wouldn't."

"I just meant that I could almost understand what he did *if* he had been under the influence," I assured her. "But I don't understand starting a fight with one of Miss Frankie's guests if you were stone-cold sober. And not just a fight. You hit him twice while I was standing there, and you went after him again later. *And* somebody heard you threaten to kill him."

His eyes flashed to mine, and for the first time I thought he actually looked worried.

"That's right," I said, pressing my advantage. "Have I got your attention now?"

He sat ramrod straight, his chin held high, his dark eyes narrowed in disapproval. "I was raised to respect women, and that means that there are some subjects a man won't discuss in front of them."

Aunt Yolanda made a noise with her tongue. "What did that stupid man say that you think I can't handle?"

Blink.

He was good, but I wasn't buying it. "If that's the case, why aren't you talking to the police? Sullivan's not a woman. You could tell him what happened."

Uncle Nestor's gaze flicked to mine quickly. "Didn't I teach you to respect your elders?"

"Didn't your mother teach you to tell the truth? Come on, *Tío*. What's really going on?"

He stood, and for a moment I thought he was going to leave the room. To my surprise, he took a couple of steps, then turned back to face us both. "It was that wife of his," he said after a lengthy pause. His haughtiness had evaporated and he looked downright miserable. "I don't know what was going on between the two of them, but she . . ." He slid an unhappy look at Aunt Yolanda. "She kissed me."

My mouth fell open and it was my turn to stare. *Blink, blink, blink.* "She *what?*"

"I didn't know who she was at the time," he said as if that explained everything.

Aunt Yolanda got to her feet, walked across the kitchen, and slapped him across the face. Hard. I was still trying to process what he'd just said, and I waited for her to laugh, to smile, to give some indication that

306

she found the whole thing amusing.

She muttered something under her breath and swept up the stairs before I could wrap my mind around what was happening. When she'd disappeared, I turned my startled gaze back to my uncle and whispered, "What was that?"

Uncle Nestor looked unhappier than I'd ever seen him. "I didn't want her to know. It wasn't anything. It didn't mean anything."

"Well, of course not. Susannah kissed you, not the other way around. Right?"

He nodded, but he didn't exactly look at me, and that gave me a bad feeling inside. "What's going on, *Tío*? What don't I know?"

"It's nothing."

"Are you kidding me?" I jumped out of my chair so fast it rocked back on two legs before slamming onto all four again. "Aunt Yolanda just slapped you. She's royally pissed. It doesn't take a rocket scientist to see that something's wrong here."

"We'll work it out," he said, his voice barely audible.

"Work what out? What's there *to* work out?"

"It's nothing," he said. He turned away, grabbed his jacket from the back of a chair, and disappeared out the front door, leaving me gaping after him.

I had no idea what was going on between them. I'd never seen them like that, not with each other and not with anyone else. But there was one thing I knew for sure — it most definitely wasn't "nothing."

TWENTY-EIGHT

Miss Frankie sailed into Zydeco Wednesday morning wearing a tan linen suit, serviceable pumps, and a wide-brimmed hat that looked as if it belonged at the Kentucky Derby. Her nail color had been changed to match, and her hair had been teased and sprayed, artistically arranged around the hat. She looked sensational.

I looked noticeably less spectacular in a plain navy dress and a pair of low heels, hair pinned up haphazardly, and a whiff of makeup and lip gloss. I hadn't slept well after my conversation with Uncle Nestor and Aunt Yolanda the night before. I was so tired, my eyes felt gritty, and I ached all the way to my bones. I didn't want anyone to ask me why, so I kept a smile on my face and tried to act as if my most pressing concern was how much modeling chocolate we'd need for the next month.

I'm not sure I actually fooled anybody,

but at least the members of my staff pretended not to notice. Miss Frankie went along just until we drove out of the parking lot. "What's wrong, sugar? You look like something the cat dragged home."

I rolled a look of mock annoyance in her direction. "Thanks. Nothing like a sincere compliment to start the day off right."

She waved a hand in the air and weaved between two slower-moving cars. "You know what I mean. You want to talk about it?"

She knew me too well. I hesitated over how much to tell her about Uncle Nestor's encounter with the third Mrs. Big Daddy, but reasoned that the more she knew, the more she could help me. "I found out last night that Susannah Boudreaux kissed Uncle Nestor at the party."

Miss Frankie looked away from traffic for a split second. "I see."

"*She* kissed *him*," I said, wanting to be very clear on that point. "He didn't even know who she was. At least not at the time. He found out later, of course."

"Did he happen to mention why she kissed him?"

I shook my head. "We . . . uh . . . we didn't get that far."

Miss Frankie seemed to understand the

rest without being told. It's one of the things I love about her. She took one hand off the wheel and covered one of mine in a comforting gesture. "Well, I'm sure it was nothing."

"Yeah," I said. "Nothing."

"Your uncle is very much in love with your aunt," Miss Frankie said. "It's obvious to everyone."

"Except maybe to her," I mumbled.

She darted in and out of traffic again, taking chances I never would have taken. When she put on her turn signal, I planted my feet to keep my balance as we sailed around the corner. "I take it Yolanda wasn't pleased by the news?"

"That's an understatement. They're not even speaking this morning."

"Well, I know it's hard on you to see them at odds, but I wouldn't worry. They've been together a long time. I'm sure they've weathered storms before, and they'll get through this one, too."

I put on a brave face and offered up a smile, but it felt as fragile as spun sugar. "I'm sure you're right." There was nothing else either of us could say about that, so I changed the subject and told her about my conversation with Dwight the night before. "If Big Daddy was so protective of Judd," I said when I'd finished, "why would he

311

threaten to send him to rehab the night he died? Tough love?"

Miss Frankie let up on the gas a little and shook her head. "That doesn't sound like Bradley. He believed in handling such things privately, and he always thought that Judd would come around if he had the support of his family."

"I think he was a little misguided on that score," I said. "And anyway, I hear he *did* threaten Judd with rehab, and told him that he'd helped for the very last time."

"That's odd," Miss Frankie said, and our speed dropped a little more. We drove in silence while she tried to process the idea of Big Daddy and Judd at each other's throats. "Whatever it was Judd got himself into," she said after a while, "it must have been big. Bradley wouldn't have threatened him that way if it wasn't."

That's exactly what I was thinking. Neither of us said it, but I knew we were both wondering the same thing: Was the trouble Judd got himself into big enough to kill over?

Reporters were camped outside the church, trying to capture the faces of the mourners who'd gathered to say a last farewell to Big Daddy. Luckily, they had no real interest in

Miss Frankie and me. We sailed past the cameras and into the cool, dark foyer of the church, where friends were gathered, greeting one another with the appropriate amount of somberness.

Miss Frankie hugged and kissed her way toward the sanctuary, and within minutes, I was following her down the center aisle toward a pew near the front. Flowers filled the room with a scent I'd prefer never to smell again — that odd mix of mums, carnations, and roses that always brings back memories of my parents' funeral. I'd have preferred a seat in the back, but I wasn't going to argue with her.

Bernice Dudley had saved us a seat directly behind the single row that had been reserved for family. We barely had time to agree what a tragedy Big Daddy's death was before the organist began playing and the side doors opened.

We all stood while the pallbearers, none of whom I recognized, carried Big Daddy in for his last public appearance. It seemed that Judd should be one of them, but he shuffled behind the coffin with a black-veiled Susannah on his arm.

The look on his face made my heart twist. I knew how it felt to be alone in the world. It's a feeling I wouldn't wish on anyone.

Mellie came in next with two boys and a young girl, who I assumed were her children from her marriage to Big Daddy. When they were settled, the pastor rose to the pulpit and began the service.

I wish I could say that I figured out who killed Big Daddy while I sat there, but the truth is that it was an entirely unremarkable funeral service. A couple of Musterion members spoke about all the good things Big Daddy had done for the krewe, making it sound as if he'd almost single-handedly planned and executed a fund-raiser last month for the krewe's favorite charity and gushing over how much money he'd raised on their behalf. One longtime employee told us all about Big Daddy's generosity toward the people who worked for him, and another related the story of how Big Daddy had given him a second chance after a brush with the law.

Trying not to be obvious about it, I looked around for the other people on my list of suspects. I spotted Violet a couple of rows back, mostly hidden behind the handkerchief she was using to mop up the tears. I didn't see Percy in the very back row until the service was over and I stood to leave.

The family was ushered out behind Big Daddy, and the rest of us followed slowly.

Miss Frankie stopped just outside the doors to speak to an old friend but I slipped away, hoping to find Judd and offer a word of condolence before he left for the cemetery.

I circled around the church toward the side entrance, where the hearse was parked. Apparently, I turned too soon because I found myself in a little garden area between two wings of the E-shaped church. I was trying to decide whether it would be quicker to cut through the inside or go around the outside when I heard voices. One of them belonged to a woman, the other to a man. The choked sobs in the woman's voice made me instinctively slip behind a flowering shrub so I wouldn't intrude on her grief.

"I'm sorry," she said, hiccupping slightly. "It's just that I don't know what I'm going to do now. He was my whole world."

After hearing that, I just *had* to peek around the bush to see who she was. I was a little surprised to see Violet and the dark-haired man in horn-rimmed glasses, whom I recognized from the party with Susannah. I hadn't noticed him inside during the service, but here he was, acting all best-friend-forever-like with Violet.

He gave her a there-there pat on the shoulder, but he seemed almost distracted as he did. "Well, you weren't *his* world. But

I guess you finally figured that out."

That was harsh. Even if I did agree with him.

She wiped a fresh batch of tears from her cheeks and sighed. "I know what you thought of him, Tyson. But he wasn't a bad man. He was just . . . busy. Preoccupied. Important."

"In his own mind," Tyson muttered. When she gave him a look of hurt mixed with horror, he relented slightly. "You're going to be okay, Violet. She doesn't hate you. I'll talk to her and make sure she lets you stay on."

She? They had to be talking about Susannah. Interesting.

Violet choked out a disbelieving laugh. "She's not going to want me around, Tyson."

"What I know," he said, "is that you worry too much. Let me take care of it."

Definitely Susannah. I was sure of it. But who was this guy and why did he think he could influence Susannah's decisions? And what was his connection to Violet?

Their voices dropped and the noise of car doors slamming and engines starting drowned out whatever they said next, but eventually Tyson reached for the door handle. "Are you okay now? They're going to be wondering where we are."

316

"Not *we*," Violet said with a tremulous smile. She let out a sigh that seemed to come from the depths of her soul. "She'd be happy if I fell off the face of the earth."

Tyson clenched his jaw. "Don't be so melodramatic, Violet."

But Violet couldn't help herself. She blew her nose and lifted her chin, but shudders, the residue of her bout with tears, shook her shoulders. "She's got it all now, doesn't she?"

Tyson pulled open the door and waved her inside. "That's the part you never understood, kid. She always did."

The family limousines were gone by the time I got to the parking lot, and Miss Frankie was waiting for me wearing a worried frown. "Gracious, sugar, you gave me a start. One minute you were there with me, and the next you were gone. Wherever did you go?"

"I was hoping to say a few words to Judd," I told her. "I didn't make it."

I told her about the conversation I'd overheard between Tyson and Violet. "Who is he anyway? Do you know him?"

She thought for a minute before shaking her head. "I can't say. Not anyone I know. He's probably an employee at one of Big Daddy's auto dealerships."

That made sense. But no matter who he was, the conversation had convinced me of one thing. Violet might have had a strong motive for killing Big Daddy, but I believed that her motive to keep him alive was even stronger.

TWENTY-NINE

Uncle Nestor and Aunt Yolanda were asleep when I got home that night and barely speaking when I left for work on Thursday morning. When they did speak to each other, I almost wished they hadn't. The sharpness in their voices reminded me of the way Philippe and I had spoken to each other before we separated. It saddened me.

I tried to hold on to Miss Frankie's assurance that my aunt and uncle had weathered other storms and come out together on the other side, but the knowledge that Philippe and I hadn't made it, as so many couples didn't, frightened me. I'd seen Uncle Nestor and Aunt Yolanda at odds with each other over the years, but I'd never seen them like this.

Thankfully I hit the ground running when I got to Zydeco, leaving me little time to think about family issues or the murder. Since we had only one more weekend until

Mardi Gras, everyone gathered in the large room upstairs for our second production meeting of the week. We ran through the schedule, parceling out the work that needed to be done and haggling good-naturedly over who got to do what. I tried to rotate people in and out of the production line, giving everyone an equal chance to work on other orders.

I put Sparkle and Isabeau to work on a butter cake with blueberries and a Bavarian cream filling for a baby shower coming up next week: two tiers, stacked, covered in baby blue fondant and a myriad of white fondant stars. On the top tier they'd attach a molded gum-paste cow jumping over a sculpted cake moon. An adorable design, if I do say so myself. Getting the faces cute enough for a baby shower would have been challenging for most of us, but Sparkle should be able to knock them out easily.

Ox and Estelle would be tackling a tart orange divorce cake with orange custard filling scheduled for delivery on Wednesday. Two tiers again, but this cake wouldn't be stacked. The design called for a flat bottom tier sporting a gum-paste groom with one foot on the top tier, as if he was kicking the bride and her half of the cake to the curb. The little gum-paste bride would be clinging to the side of her tilting tier.

The design was Ox's suggestion, given that the fellow throwing the party was a jilted husband, and I'd approved it wholeheartedly last week. Today, with Aunt Yolanda barely speaking to Uncle Nestor, I didn't find it nearly so amusing.

Dwight and I would work on a four-tier tropical cream cake in a Mardi Gras design. We'd start with sponge cake, lightly dab each layer with coconut syrup, and then spread Bavarian cream, fresh mangoes, and pineapple between the cakes to create each tier. We'd stack the tiers and cover the whole thing with white fondant, then finish the design by applying stripes and harlequin shapes on alternate layers and topping the cake with a gum-paste Mardi Gras mask.

With those details settled, I dismissed the staff so they could get to work and gathered up my notebook and coffee cup, intending to do the same. As I stood, I realized that Ox was still sitting at the end of the table, watching me.

"Have you had a chance to look at the web page?" he asked.

I groaned aloud and shook my head. "Don't start. Please. You have no idea how crazy things have been since my uncle and aunt showed up."

"I'm asking you for fifteen minutes. Thirty tops. Why is that so difficult?"

"Because it is." I shoved a stray lock of hair out of my face and sighed. "Why don't you just approve it yourself? It will save us all time."

"Are you sure you're okay with that?"

"I wouldn't have suggested it if I wasn't." I shoved my chair in the general direction of the table and started toward the door.

"And the blog?"

"Is going to have to wait," I said. He made a noise and I whipped back around to face him. "Seriously, Ox, I can't do it right now. You're just going to have to be patient."

He held up both hands in surrender. "Fine. Whatever. Do I dare ask about the photos from the party?"

It was on the tip of my tongue to say no, but the sudden thought that Estelle might have captured something useful made me cut myself off before I got the word out. Admittedly, it was a long shot, but it was worth a look. "I'll get to them tonight. Will that be soon enough?"

Ox's eyes narrowed as if I'd confused him. "Really? You don't want me to take them? I probably have more time than you do."

"I'll do it," I said as I sailed out the door.

He came after me. "Why so cooperative

all of a sudden?"

I grinned at him as I started down the stairs. "You've been complaining because I don't want to help. Now you're complaining because I do?"

He clattered down the stairs behind me, his big feet in their heavy boots making enough noise to raise the dead. "Call me cynical, but I'm highly suspicious of this sudden turnaround."

We reached the bottom of the stairs, so I turned to face him. Edie was away from her desk, leaving us alone in the foyer. "Okay, so it's not entirely about the website. It just occurred to me that Estelle might have gotten some shots of Big Daddy and his killer. I figured I might as well kill two birds with one stone — so to speak."

He frowned so hard wrinkles ran from his eyebrows to what used to be his hairline. "I knew it."

"What's the big deal?" I asked. "I'll look at the pictures. Pick out a few for the website and check for evidence at the same time. You'll get what you want, and hopefully I'll get what I want. We both win."

"Right."

I turned to walk away and another idea hit me squarely in the face. "Hey, Ox?"

He was halfway to the door already, but

he wheeled around when I called him. "Yeah?"

"You did such a great job with the design for the divorce cake. How'd you like to throw together something that says, 'Sorry for your loss'?"

The worry wrinkles reappeared on his forehead. "You want a bereavement cake?"

"Yeah. Just something simple. Something appropriate for a recent widow who may or may not have murdered her husband."

"You're going to take Big Daddy's wife a cake?"

"Why not? Where I come from, taking food to the family after a funeral is the socially accepted way to deal with death. Don't they do that around here?"

Ox gave a grudging nod. "But it's still a bad idea, Rita."

"Maybe. But it's the only one I've got. I need to get a foot in her door somehow."

"No. You don't."

"Yeah. I do. I can't explain why, but I really need to talk to her. Can you have it ready for me by this afternoon?"

Ox took a step toward me, his eyes clouded with concern. "Let the police handle it."

"They can't handle this," I told him. I held up my right hand, as if I were taking an oath. "I swear, it's not about the murder. I need to talk to her about something else."

And it was true. Mostly. I really did want to ask what happened between her and Uncle Nestor. Maybe I could help smooth things over for my miserable *tío*. And if the subject of Big Daddy's murder came up? Well . . . I'd have to talk to her about it, wouldn't I? I wouldn't want to be rude.

THIRTY

After work that evening I found Big Daddy's address on the guest list and followed my GPS instructions to a house set back from the road behind a grove of trees. Now that I was here, I started second-guessing my plan.

The cake Ox had pulled together for me in between his regular duties sat on the seat beside me in a box bearing Zydeco's cartoon alligator logo. The cake itself was nothing fancy. He'd found a spare hummingbird sheetcake — a local favorite — in the kitchen and he'd decorated it tastefully with a few pastel peach flowers in one corner. No cheesy hand-piped sentiment. Just cake. It was perfect for what I had in mind.

I turned onto the driveway and wound through forest until the house came into view. A handful of cars were scattered around — two parked in front of the house on a circular drive, two more in front of a garage at the side of the house, and a huge white SUV nosed up next to a serene-looking garden with a lighted fountain surrounded by some exotic-looking broad-leaved shrubbery.

I gathered up the cake and put on a sympathetic expression as I approached the door. A tall, thin man with horn-rimmed glasses and an impatient expression answered my ring and glared down at me from a step above.

Tyson. Well, well, well.

"Yes?"

"I'm here to see Mrs. Boudreaux. Is she in?"

"She's in, but she's not available. Is there something I can help you with?" The look on his face said he'd rather do anything but.

I shook my head, but I didn't back down. Now that I'd run into him, my curiosity was in overdrive. "I really need to see her," I said. "It's important." And when that didn't impress him, I added, "I only need five minutes of her time."

He glanced over his shoulder — the first sign that maybe he didn't actually rule the world and had to take orders from someone else. "I'll see if she's up to seeing you. Your name?"

"Rita Lucero."

Nothing.

"From Zydeco Cakes." I held up the cake box as if that might make a difference.

He still didn't move away from the door.

Desperate times call for desperate measures, so I tried a different strategy. "Her husband passed away at my party," I explained. "I feel so horrible I just won't be able to rest until I offer my condolences."

"The funeral was yesterday," he said.

"That's why I waited until today," I said back.

He still looked hesitant, but he motioned me inside and shut the door behind me. But that's where he drew the line on hospitality. He held up a hand to indicate that I wasn't to come any farther inside and said, "I'll see if she's feeling up to visitors."

I wondered if he'd be so bristly if I told him I'd been in the church garden yesterday. Even if Susannah didn't actually hate Violet, she still might not like learning that her cabana boy was on friendly terms with her husband's mistress.

He kept me cooling my heels for a good fifteen minutes before he came back. His expression was so sour, I expected him to show me out the door again. I could feel aggression pouring off him in waves. Instead, he growled, "Come this way."

I kept my own face expressionless, but inside I did a little skippy dance of joy and followed him through the house and onto a screened porch filled with potted ferns and wicker furniture. Susannah Boudreaux sat on a swinging daybed suspended on chains from the ceiling.

She wore black clam diggers and an open sweater of soft, draped material over a pastel pink tank top. Her legs were tucked under her, and she looked pale and wan, as if sitting was almost too much for her. But her burgundy-colored hair had been carefully teased and sprayed, and her makeup appeared flawless. Which made me think she was stronger than she was letting on.

She offered me a limp hand when I approached, and waved me toward a chair.

I put the cake box on the coffee table and sat. "Thank you for seeing me. I'm so sorry for your loss."

"Thank you." Her voice was soft. Barely above a whisper. A far cry from the fishwife shriek she'd used when she told the world about Uncle Nestor attacking Big Daddy. "You brought me a cake?"

"Just a little something," I said. "It's what I do."

She smiled sadly. "Well. Thanks." She blew her nose and tucked the tissue into her pocket. "Tyson said you wanted to see me about something important?"

I nodded and glanced toward Tyson, who stood in the doorway, arms crossed and glaring at me from behind his glasses. I took a page out of Miss Frankie's book and dusted my next comment with sugar.

"It must be so comforting to have your family around at a time like this."

Her gaze shot to Tyson and they shared a look. "Tyson's a friend," she said when she looked away. "A family friend."

I wondered whether Big Daddy had been aware of his wife's friendship with Tyson. I'd have bet half of everything I owned that he hadn't. "Friends are good, too," I said, smiling as if I believed her. "The important thing is that you're not alone."

"Yes," she said. "Well. What is it you wanted to see me about?"

I decided it might be best to ease into the subject of that kiss, so I said, "Please understand that I don't mean any disrespect. And I don't want to bring up painful issues, but I'd like to ask you about your brother-in-law. I understand he had a disagreement with your husband the night Big Daddy died."

"He may have," she said. "I don't know anything about that."

"Your husband didn't mention it to you?"

She smoothed one hand down the leg of her pants and I spotted a slight tremor in her hand. Nerves or grief? I couldn't be sure. "No," she said. "And neither did Judd."

"So you don't know anything about the trouble Judd was in?"

She pulled her hand away from her leg and clasped both hands in her lap. "What makes you think he was in trouble?"

"Someone overhead him promising to pay Big Daddy back. In that same conversation, Big Daddy told Judd he was going to put him in rehab. You don't know anything about that?"

She shook her head slowly. "No, but I suppose I shouldn't be surprised. It's no secret that Judd has issues with alcohol. He makes a habit of getting himself into scrapes and my husband was constantly bailing him out." Her voice was hard and flat, and so were her eyes.

"I take it you didn't approve?"

"Approve? Hardly. Judd's behavior is destructive and selfish. But he's family, and my husband was very protective of him."

"And that's why you gave your husband an ultimatum?"

She shot flaming daggers at me with her

331

eyes. "I did no such thing."

"You didn't tell him he had to make things right with Percy — and I quote — or else?"

"I have no idea what you're talking about. My husband was a softhearted and generous man. His brother sometimes took advantage of that."

"His alcoholism?"

"Everyone knows it's a disease," she said. She looked at me through a set of snake eyes. "Big Daddy and I were both very sympathetic toward his brother's illness."

"Until the night he died," I pointed out. "How do you think Judd would have reacted to the threat of being sent to rehab?"

"He would have been angry and upset, but he would have gone. He always did anything Big Daddy asked him to do." She narrowed her eyes and looked to Tyson for direction. He gave an almost imperceptible shake of his head, resuming his position as king of her world.

"I don't understand why you're asking all these questions about my brother-in-law," she said, shifting position slightly. "What's it to you?"

"I'm just trying to figure out what happened."

"Isn't that a job for the police?" Tyson said from his post at the door.

"Yes, of course. But Mrs. Boudreaux practically accused my uncle of killing her husband." I turned away from Tyson and addressed Susannah again. "I'd like to know what led you to believe that."

She looked stunned and angry. "That man is your uncle?"

"Visiting from out of town," I said with a nod. "He arrived just a few hours before the party. He didn't even know Big Daddy."

"Apparently he knew him well enough," Tyson put in.

Yeah. Thanks, buddy. I stayed focused on Susannah. "Why do you believe my uncle killed your husband?"

"I believe that," she said, "because it's true."

Liar. "You saw him do it?"

She shot another look at Tyson and said, "No. But I'm sure it was him."

"With all due respect, Mrs. Boudreaux, that wasn't my question. I asked why you think that."

Her spine stiffened and the softness around her mouth disappeared. "I think that because he attacked my husband. Twice. And he did it in front of everyone."

"He confronted him because your husband made inappropriate suggestions." At least that's why they'd fought the first time.

I still wasn't sure what had caused the second fight, but I assumed it had something to do with the kiss.

She rolled her eyes. "Oh, please. Big Daddy made a little joke. What's the harm in that? That's just the kind of man he was."

I'm not a violent person, but I wanted to get up out of my chair and show her the harm with the flat of my hand. What can I say? I *am* related to my uncle. I gripped the arms of the chair to keep myself where I was. "It was no joke," I said. "And not everyone found your late husband amusing."

She waved away my comment as if it were a pesky fly. "Clearly, your uncle has anger issues that he's incapable of controlling. I can't help but feel sorry for his wife. To live with that kind of a monster must be horrible."

She really was too much. "If you felt that way," I said, getting to the crux of the issue, "why did you kiss him?"

Tyson's head jerked up as if someone had a string attached to it, but he didn't say a word. Family friend, my ass.

Susannah's eyes glinted, but her hard edges disappeared under a coating of Southern sweet ganache. "Oh, sweetie," she purred. "Someone's been lying to you. I didn't kiss him, he kissed me."

THIRTY-ONE

Tyson showed me to the door, and I held my head high as I walked back to the Mercedes. I drove half a block before anger and frustration forced me to the side of the road. I put the car into park and leaned my forehead against the steering wheel while emotions churned around inside.

Somebody was lying to me. That much was obvious. I just didn't know whether that somebody was Uncle Nestor or Susannah Boudreaux. Gut instinct told me to believe Uncle Nestor, but the way he'd been acting, so secretive, made me begin to wonder.

I don't know how long I sat there before I began to calm down and think rationally again. My family was waiting for me at home. But I wasn't ready to talk to Uncle Nestor just yet. I still needed to process what Susannah had told me.

There was another reason I didn't put the car in gear and head for home. In all the conversations I'd had over the past week, nobody had told me anything that would clear Uncle Nestor for good. But I couldn't just give up. Especially now, with things so rocky between Uncle Nestor and Aunt Yolanda. My uncle might be a lot of things, but he's not a murderer. Somebody out there knew something that would prove that. I just had to keep digging until I found it.

I pulled the guest list out of my bag and flipped through the pages until I found the address I was looking for. I programmed it into the GSP, made a U-turn, and drove to Judd Boudreaux's apartment. He lived in a picturesque complex on Lake Pontchartrain, which consisted of half a dozen three-story buildings scattered across a well-trimmed lawn, all posed in front of the lake and harbor like something that belonged on a postcard.

The road wound around through the buildings, edging off into small parking lots here and there. I followed it until I found the right building and made the rest of the journey on foot.

Unit 203 was on the middle floor, set back from the common staircase to give the illusion of a private entrance. A couple of old newspapers and some dry leaves littered the entryway, and the light over the door flickered on and off as if it was on its last legs.

I rang the bell and the sound of scuffing footsteps reached me a few seconds later. I felt the pricking of nerves and a sudden rush of adrenaline. What was I thinking, coming here alone?

He'd been drinking, and pretty steadily. My clues? The smell, the way he wobbled on his feet and squinted to figure out who I was, and the bottle in his hand. Oh, and the fact that he was still wearing the clothes he'd had on at the funeral yesterday — minus the tie.

He looked tired and sad. Dark circles had formed under his eyes, and thin spider veins were visible across his nose and cheeks. The charm that had so affected me the first time we met was subdued tonight, diluted by grief and whiskey.

"Well," he said with weak attempt at a grin. "If it isn't the lovely Cinderella. Looking for your shoes again?"

"I have them tonight, thanks. I wonder if you'd mind answering a few questions."

He eyed me curiously. "Questions? What are you, a police officer?"

I shook my head. "Just a friend."

He took a deep drink from the bottle and stepped away from the door, bowing elaborately at the waist. "Well, in that case, come on in."

Inside, the place was a far cry from Big Daddy's home. It was sparsely furnished with a threadbare couch, two lopsided easy chairs, and a coffee table dotted with cigarette burns. Early Goodwill.

He swept a hand toward one easy chair. "Make yourself at home."

I perched on the edge of the seat to avoid a spring I could see coming through the cushion. Judd dropped heavily into a matching chair next to a cluttered TV tray. He bounded to his feet again almost immediately, his once-handsome face clouded. "My mama would have my hide for not offering you something to drink. Can I get you a beer, or would you like something stronger?"

"Nothing," I said with a scant smile. "Thanks."

"You're sure?" He shrugged at my nod and sat. "So what can I do for you?"

"I'd like to ask you about the night your brother died, if you don't mind."

"What do you want to know?"

"First, let me say how sorry I am for your loss. I understand that you and Big Daddy were close. I know this must be difficult for you."

He didn't say anything, but a muscle in his cheek jumped and I knew he was feeling something.

"I wonder if you could tell me if your brother had any enemies. You know, was there anyone angry with him? Anyone who might have wanted to hurt him?"

Judd let out a deep breath. His cheeks puffed out a little as he exhaled, and he wiped one hand across his eyes. "Bradley had a lot of friends," he said when he finally spoke. "But he also had a lot of enemies. People either loved him or hated him."

"He had a strong personality," I said, trying to put a positive spin on it. "Do you know if he was having any issues at work? Did he ever mention any issues with an employee, or maybe a disgruntled former one?"

Judd shook his head. "Not that I know of. Nothing serious, anyway. I've done some work for him off and on over the years. People came and went. A few people got upset over having to work weekends and late night hours, but that's the nature of the business. Some people stuck around for a while, but some got out of there as fast as they could. With Bradley, it was his way or the highway. You either did what he said, or you walked."

"And people were okay with that?"

Judd shrugged. "It was what it was. He made it clear from the beginning, so nobody could ever say they were surprised."

He seemed to be dodging the question, and I wondered whether he was consciously avoiding the answer or if his brain was just too pickled to form a straight answer. "Did anybody ever try to say they were surprised? Maybe someone he fired?"

Judd shook his head slowly. "Not recently."

I filed that away in case I needed it later. "What about his marriage? What was that like?"

Judd took another drink and capped the bottle slowly. "You ask a lot of questions, Cinderella. Has anyone ever told you that?"

I smiled. "A few people. I do that when I'm trying to help someone."

"That's admirable, but hardly justification for me to spill all of my brother's secrets."

"If those secrets were responsible for his death, I think you'd want to bring them to light."

Judd didn't say anything to that, so I gave him a little more to think about. "I just came from Susannah's house. She accused my uncle of killing your brother. Uncle Nestor didn't do it. I'm trying to help him prove that."

That brought Judd's head up quickly. "Your uncle's the old man? The one who took a couple of swings at Bradley?"

"Yes, but he was only reacting to something Big Daddy said about my aunt."

"That would be the lovely older Latin lady?"

I nodded. "How did you know about Uncle Nestor and your brother?"

"Word gets around quickly. Bradley thought it was kind of a kick, you know. Since nobody actually got hurt and all."

"He didn't seem all that amused at the time."

"Well, that was my brother for you. He could change his mind faster than anyone I ever knew."

"Does that mean that you don't think my uncle killed your brother?"

He flicked something from one pant leg and looked up at me as if the idea of that surprised him. "I guess I don't."

I could have kissed him, and I might have if he hadn't smelled so bad. "What happened after the fight? Did you see where your brother went or who he talked to?"

Judd cleared a space for his bottle on the TV tray and spent a moment getting it to balance in the small spot. "I didn't see him again after that. I don't know where he went or who he talked to."

Well, that was a big fat lie, but I didn't say so. I had a few more questions to ask before I called him on it. "Why was Susannah upset with your brother that night?"

He scowled. "She was always upset with him. That's not news."

"Are you saying they fought a lot?"

He flicked a glance at me. "It would be hard not to fight with Susannah. She's not exactly easy to get along with."

That was a nice way of putting it. "She gave your brother an ultimatum. Do you know anything about that?"

He yawned, but I had the feeling it was just for show. "Sorry. Can't help you. Ultimatums are her thing. It's how she rolls." He put on a falsetto voice and mimicked Susannah. "Get me that car for Christmas or there'll be no sex for you. Take me to Cancún for our anniversary or I'll spend everything in your bank account."

Interesting, but not surprising. "This ultimatum had something to do with a man named Percy. Do you know anything about that?"

Abruptly, the smile slid from his face. "No, and I'm finished answering your questions." He tried to get up, but he lost his balance and fell back into the chair with a thud.

My heart pounded in my chest at the sudden change in him, but I refused to cut and run. "A friend of mine heard her tell Big Daddy that this was the last straw. That she wasn't going to let him embarrass her. Do you have any idea why she'd say that?"

"I just told you," he snapped. His eyes had taken on a strange focus, and the bleary-eyed drunk turned into something raw and powerful right in front of me. "I don't know anything about what happened between the two of them. I don't care what happened between the two of them." He stood, this time without trouble. "I think you'd better leave now."

He didn't have to tell me twice. I got up and scurried toward the door and freedom. But as I stepped out onto the dimly lit landing, I couldn't leave without asking one more question. "Another friend of mine says he heard you arguing with Big Daddy a little before one in the morning. You promised to pay him back, and he told you he was sending you to rehab. You owed him money. For what?"

"I don't mean to be rude, darlin', but that's none of your damn business." The door slammed between us, and I bolted down the stairs, cursing myself for taking such a stupid chance and grateful that he'd done nothing worse than growl at me.

Judd hadn't exactly been a font of information, but I knew one thing that I hadn't known when I arrived: Susannah wasn't the only Boudreaux lying about what happened the night that Big Daddy died.

THIRTY-TWO

I thought about my conversations with the Boudreauxes all the way home. I was convinced that one of them had killed Big Daddy, but which one? Had Big Daddy found out about Susannah's relationship with Tyson? Maybe he'd confronted her and gotten himself killed in a fit of passion. But if he really was sleeping with Violet, would he have cared that much about Susannah's sexual activities? I might have been wrong, but I doubted Susannah had killed him in a jealous rage.

Their sleeping arrangements must not have been what they'd argued about, I reasoned. Susannah was the one who'd drawn the line in the sand. Whatever upset her, it was something Big Daddy had done, not the other way around.

Judd was clearly lying about his argument with his brother. He'd owed him money, and while he'd promised to pay it back, that hadn't been enough for Big Daddy, who'd threatened to put Judd in rehab. Why? After covering for him all these years, after bailing him out from one trouble situation after another, what had Judd done that had driven Big Daddy to change the way he'd been handling his brother?

I went round and round the questions all the way home, but I wasn't going to find the answers in my own head. I wanted to talk with Violet and find out if she could shed any light on what Big Daddy had going with Percy, but I couldn't do it tonight. It was too late, and I was too tired.

The lights were out on the main floor, so I started upstairs to my bedroom. The door to the guest room was open and I saw Aunt Yolanda on the bed, curled up with a book. Alone. I stopped for a moment to talk with her as I climbed the stairs to my room. We'd done the same thing so many times when I was younger that things felt normal for a moment. If we'd been in Albuquerque, I'd have assumed that Uncle Nestor was at the restaurant. But we weren't, and he wasn't.

Aunt Yolanda might be able to pretend that everything was normal, but I couldn't. I asked her where he was, and she nodded toward the ceiling. "Upstairs on your terrace. He's been up there for hours."

"Is he all right?"

She frowned and gave a little shrug. "I'm sure he is."

That answer was so out of character for her that I moved into the bedroom and sat on the foot of the bed. "How long is this going to go on, *Tía*?"

She kept her eyes on her book. "I'm only going to finish this chapter. It's late, and I'm tired."

"That's not what I'm talking about, and you know it."

She flipped a page, pointedly refusing to look at me. "What I know is that it's never a good idea to get involved in someone else's relationship. I'm sure I've mentioned that to you before."

"Yeah. You have. But this is ridiculous. You know how much Uncle Nestor loves you."

Her gaze finally left the book. She locked eyes with me. "This is between your uncle and me," she said, her voice harder than I'd ever heard it. She marked her place with a bookmark and set the book aside. "I'm tired. I'd like to go to sleep."

Her reaction confused and frightened me, but I stood up and went back to the door. "I'll see you tomorrow," I said.

She mumbled something, but her voice

was too low and I couldn't hear it. With my heart aching, I climbed to the third floor, but instead of going into my own bedroom, I kept going to the rooftop garden.

It's a beautiful space filled with large planters holding trees and flowering bushes, a wrought-iron railing allowing a view of the street below, and a stone table with chairs in the center. Twinkling white lights in the trees and along the railing make the whole thing feel like a fairy tale.

Almost losing my life here last summer had turned the fairy tale into a nightmare, but I was slowly learning to relax in this space. New Orleans is never a quiet city, and during carnival season the noise level multiplies. I could hear the revelry all around me. Parties. Music. Laughing. Fireworks in the distance. One of the smaller krewes was having its parade a few blocks away, and the sounds from that hit me softly, as if they'd been wrapped in cotton.

Uncle Nestor sat in a patio chair with his back to the door. He held a glass of water in one hand, but he ignored it and stared up at the sky. I didn't want to startle him, so I cleared my throat as I stepped out onto the rooftop.

He didn't move a muscle. "I wondered

when you'd come looking for me. You're home late. Again."

"It's the nature of the business," I said as I walked toward him. "You know what it's like."

He dipped his head a fraction of an inch. "You're very busy. Maybe too busy."

"Only for a few more days," I reminded him. "Once Mardi Gras is over, things will slow down."

He nodded. Sipped. Let out a sigh that came from somewhere near the bottom of his soul.

I worried about how all this stress was affecting his heart. "How are you holding up, *Tío*? Are you feeling okay?"

"Physically?" He darted a glance at me. "I'm fine."

"But . . ."

He turned back to the sky. "Your aunt is angry with me."

"I noticed." I pulled a chair around and sat beside him. "Does she have reason to be?"

He shook his head slowly, leaning forward slightly and resting his arms on his thighs. "For what happened at the party? No."

I didn't like that answer. It was too open-ended. Too full of negative possibilities. The twelve-year-old I'd been when Uncle Nestor took me in after my parents' death wanted to let it go. Since the accident he'd been my rock. My protector. I wanted to protect him now. But my adult self knew I couldn't leave his answer lying in the dark.

"But there's some reason she feels this way." It wasn't a question.

Uncle Nestor let out another of those soul-wrenching sighs. "I suppose so."

"You *suppose* so?"

"It happened a long time ago. It doesn't matter now."

I gaped at him. "Aunt Yolanda is downstairs in bed. Alone. You're up here staring at the stars. Alone. Apparently it matters."

He tried to work up some irritation, but it lacked steam. "It's between your aunt and me."

"Yeah. Right." I let out a sigh of my own and leaned back in my seat. Maybe the stars would have some answers for me. Nobody else seemed willing to give me any. "You know, I'm doing my best to help you, but you sure don't make it easy. I understand you're not big on sharing everything you feel, but would it hurt so much to talk to me?"

He turned his face to the sky again and I figured that was that. Our bonding moment was over. I was just about to give up and go downstairs to bed when he started talking.

"It was a long time ago. Before you came to us."

I didn't breathe for a few seconds. I didn't want to do anything that would make him shut down again. Part of me wanted him to rip the bandage off the wound quickly, but I forced myself to wait.

"It was after Aaron was born," he said. "I made a mistake. A stupid mistake. It meant nothing, but things were rough between Yolanda and me. She was exhausted. Tired from a difficult pregnancy and trying to care for four little boys who had way too much energy. I was exhausted and worried about the money. I had no idea how we'd make it, and every time I turned around, she was telling me about something else we needed to buy."

"So you turned to someone else."

He nodded miserably.

I didn't know what to feel. He'd cheated on his wife. He'd betrayed her, and even though it had happened years ago, I felt as if he'd betrayed me. The idea of him being with someone else made me physically ill. But the pain on his face landed on my heart like a rock. "Did you love her?"

"No!" He dropped his head as if he simply didn't have the strength to hold it up any longer. "It wasn't about love. It was about fear. I hated the way I felt at home. I wasn't making it. I didn't think I *could* make it. Every time I walked through the door and saw Yolanda and the kids looking at me, I felt like a failure."

I put my feet on the cement border in front of me. "That's no excuse, you know."

He laughed without humor. "Not an excuse, just an explanation. It only lasted three months, but I've been paying for it for the past thirty years."

"She hasn't forgiven you?"

The back door of the Thai restaurant next door opened with a loud squeak, followed by the clang of metal as someone tossed trash into the Dumpster. Uncle Nestor waited to speak until the door closed again.

"She's forgiven me as much as it's possible to forgive, I guess. Her God won't let her do any less. But she hasn't forgotten."

"I'm not sure it's possible to forget something like that," I said. "At least, I don't think I could. Not really."

"Well, that's fair," he said with a sad smile. "I haven't forgotten it either. And she's a step ahead of me. I haven't forgiven myself. I'm not sure I ever will."

I put my hand on top of his and we sat in silence for a moment. But we weren't finished. I still had questions to ask. "I went to see Susannah Boudreaux this afternoon."

He looked confused. "Who's that?"

"The woman you kissed at the party."

"I didn't kiss anyone at the party, *mija*. It was the other way around."

I needed to hear him say that, but I couldn't get distracted by sentiment. "That's not what she says."

"Then she's lying."

"Yeah. That's what I thought." I pulled my hand away from his and scooted my chair closer. "Tell me what happened that night. Why did she kiss you?"

"I have no idea. I was standing by the pool, and all of a sudden she was there. We started talking."

"About what?"

"About nothing. About the weather. About the food in the buffet. Small talk. I had no idea who she was. I didn't care."

"Then what? Think about it carefully. What happened right before she kissed you?"

He tilted his head to one side and gave that some thought. I waited, holding my breath until he shook his head. "I just don't remember, *mija*. I wish I could."

I wasn't going to give up so easily. "Think, *Tío*. Did you see anyone else there?"

"There were many people there," he said a little impatiently. "It was a party. But don't ask me who any of them were, because I don't know."

"Did you see her talking to anyone else before she started talking to you?"

He looked up at me from hooded eyes. "She was arguing with Big Daddy. I remember feeling a little sorry for her. And I'll confess that I was amused. He started to walk away in the middle of their argument, and she shouted that she'd show him. I can only guess that's why she did what she did."

"So, was this what your second argument with Big Daddy was about?"

Uncle Nestor rubbed his forehead. He looked tired, and I felt a pang of guilt for pushing him so hard. "Yes. He came back a few minutes later, just as that woman kissed me, and he was very angry. Called me a hypocrite."

"Why?"

"He said I had some nerve blowing up when he made an innocent little comment about my wife, and then trying to . . . you know."

"Hit on his wife?"

He nodded. "It wasn't like that, *mija*. I didn't want anything to do with her."

"I believe you," I said. "But I'm not the

one who matters. Aunt Yolanda is really hurt."

"I know."

"What are you going to do about it?" I asked.

He shook his head and got to his feet with a groan. "I don't know. But I'll think of something."

I wanted desperately to believe him. I knew how easily a marriage could unravel, and I needed the two of them to show me that it didn't have to be that way. "It would probably help if you told the police about what happened," I said.

He gave me a thin smile. "I talked with your Detective Sullivan again yesterday. But I don't want anyone else to know. Your cousins don't know about the past, and I don't want them to know."

I could understand that, I suppose. At least he'd told Sullivan the truth, and that made me feel better than I'd felt in days.

"And you're not to worry about this. It's my life, Rita. My problem. I'll deal with it." He crossed the patio and disappeared through the door, no doubt believing that I'd back off.

I'd said the same thing to him more times than I could count while I was growing up, and it had never stopped him from sticking his nose in where I didn't think it belonged. If he saw me in trouble, he was there whether I wanted him there or not.

I loved him enough to repay the favor.

THIRTY-THREE

I couldn't sleep. I just kept thinking about Uncle Nestor and Aunt Yolanda and wondering whether they'd be able to work through their issues. They'd worked through trouble before, I reminded myself several times. But there's a big difference between forgiving someone for a single mistake and forgiving him for appearing to make the same mistake twice. I believed Uncle Nestor's account of what happened with Susannah Boudreaux, but I wasn't the one who mattered. If Aunt Yolanda thought Uncle Nestor's eyes were wandering, he'd have a hard time convincing her otherwise.

After a long time, I got up and booted up my laptop. I found the memory card Estelle had given me at the party and began the arduous task of looking through more than two hundred pictures. I'd left the second memory card in my desk at work, so there were at least this many pictures waiting for me at Zydeco. I figured my odds of finding something useful were relatively high.

Since Ox wanted pictures of the party for the website, I kept that in mind as I scrolled through the images Estelle had captured, but frankly, photos for the website weren't my top priority. I scanned shots of the crowd, looking for any of the major players in Big Daddy's life. I spotted Big Daddy himself in several pictures, laughing with a group of men, flirting with a handful of women. I saw him heaping a plate at the buffet and putting an arm around Miss Frankie.

It was a little creepy looking at those pictures of a man who'd been killed just a few hours after the images were captured. I wondered if he'd had any sense of impending doom, or if he'd been surprised when the attack came.

I paid close attention to the pictures Estelle had taken near the pool, but I didn't see anything that seemed either important or out of place. Frustrated, I downloaded the files to my computer, jotted down the file names of a handful of pictures I thought Ox might like, and tucked the memory card into my wallet so I could return it to Estelle.

By the time I'd finished, I was tired enough to sleep — or at least give it a good try. I tossed and turned all night, waking myself every time I turned over. I was up again with the sun and walked through the door at Zydeco a few minutes after six.

I spent the morning working on the carved Mardi Gras mask for the cake we had to deliver next week, first sculpting the general shape using a serrated knife, then concentrating on the details until I was satisfied with the size and shape. I made a fresh batch of fondant, stirring together corn syrup and shortening, adding salt and vanilla, and finally blending in the confectioner's sugar and stirring until I had stiff dough. I bypassed the electric mixer and kneaded the fondant by hand. It's the best way I know to work through my frustrations.

I spent the rest of the morning cutting out shapes for the Mardi Gras cake, measuring carefully, and storing them in airtight containers so they'd still be pliable when I was ready to use them the next day.

After grabbing a quick lunch from the market down the street, I took my place on the King Cake line, and finally moved into my office around four to check the second memory card. It was slow going and tedious work, but I wouldn't let myself quit until I'd gone through every shot.

I hit pay dirt after only two hundred and fourteen pictures. I'd started zoning out, paying more attention to the headache forming behind my eyes than the images on the screen in front of me. And then, suddenly, there it was.

Estelle had been shooting one of the outdoor tables, but she'd caught Susannah Boudreaux at the edge of the picture. Susannah stood near the swimming pool, her face rigid with anger, her eyes filled with fury. In front of her was Big Daddy's assistant, Violet, who jabbed at Susannah's chest with one finger. Violet's mouth was open wide, giving the impression that she'd been shouting.

I'd fallen into a rhythm as I moved through row after row of photographs, and my finger clicked on the mouse button to move on almost before my brain registered what I'd just seen. I sat up with a jerk and clicked the back button on the browser window so I could study the picture more closely.

I focused on the two women at first, studying their expressions and body language. Clearly, there was no love lost between them. As my focus broadened, I began to notice other details. There, just behind Susannah, the blurry face of Judd Boudreaux.

And to her right, Ivanka Hedge.

My heart beat erratically as I sent the image to print and moved on. I had less than a hundred photographs to go, but my hopes were higher than they'd been in days. If Estelle had captured one argument with her camera, maybe she'd inadvertently caught another one.

Luck was with me just twenty-one pictures later when I found a picture of Big Daddy and Percy standing a little apart from the rest of the crowd. That was interesting enough, considering the fact that Percy denied talking with Big Daddy again before he died. But what I found most interesting was the look on Percy's face.

He looked angry enough to kill.

It wasn't yet five o'clock, so I printed both pictures and tucked them into my purse, then drove across town to the address I found online for Big Daddy's corporate office. It was located in a single-story building that squatted between two of his car dealerships.

Inside, the scent of stale coffee filled the air, and a brunette receptionist who looked all of sixteen sat behind a small desk and tapped slowly on a computer keyboard. She looked at me with bored disinterest, and I told her why I was there.

She made a couple of calls in an effort to track down Violet's whereabouts. After the second one, she pointed me toward a waiting area consisting of a handful of plastic chairs near a coffeepot in the corner and assured me that Violet would be with me in a few minutes.

I thanked her and started away. Big Daddy's operation wasn't what I'd call classy, but it was certainly big. From where I stood, I could see cars in every direction. Chevrolet to the left of me, Nissan to the right, and a large used car lot across the street. These weren't his only enterprises either, and for the first time the sheer scope of his business struck me. I wondered who'd take up the reins now that Big Daddy was gone. Would Judd inherit? Would it all pass on to the next generation of Boudreauxes? Or would Susannah get it all? Getting control of that fortune might have been a motive for murder.

I changed my mind about the stale coffee midstep and turned back toward the receptionist with what I hoped looked like a friendly smile. "I'm sorry about your loss, by the way. It must be difficult to come to work after what happened."

She looked away from the computer

screen as if my comment confused her, but she nodded and swept a lock of hair from her shoulder. "I still can't believe it. I mean, who'd want to kill Big Daddy?"

That's what I wanted to know. "So he was a good boss?"

"Yeah. Sure. He was a real nice man."

Yeah. Sure. "I guess his death has made things kind of difficult around here," I said. "Do you have any idea what's going to happen to all of this now that he's gone?"

The girl's expression sobered. "I don't know. We're supposed to have a meeting next week, and I guess they'll tell us then."

I was pretty sure Sullivan would know who inherited Big Daddy's fortune. I just wondered if he'd share that information with me. "Have the police been around asking questions?"

She rolled her eyes as if to say I'd asked a foolish question. "They were here for a couple of days, looking in all our files, checking stuff on the computer. It was awful."

I started to say something sympathetic, but I heard the sharp staccato of rapid footsteps approaching, and an instant later Violet rounded a corner. She looked curious and hesitant until she spotted me. Then her expression turned sour and wary. She nudged her glasses up on her nose and scowled as if I'd just ruined her day. "Can I help you?"

I pretended not to notice the way her mouth puckered up as if she'd tasted something bitter. "I don't know if you remember me," I said. "I'm Rita Lucero. We met at the Musterion party."

She dipped her head slightly. "I remember you. What can I do for you?"

"Is there somewhere we could talk privately? I'd like to ask you a couple of questions if that's okay."

Her mouth puckered a little tighter. "This is a really bad time. If you'll call tomorrow, I'll see if I can arrange a time to meet with you."

I was pretty sure that if I walked out the door, I'd never get this close to her again. "It will only take a minute," I said.

She turned to leave. "Not now. Call to make an appointment."

I wasn't about to let her walk out on me, so I called after her. "Why was Percy Ponter so upset with Big Daddy the night of the murder?"

She stopped walking and turned around wearing an icy expression. "I don't know what you're talking about."

"Would you like me to refresh your

365

memory here, or would you rather talk privately?"

Her nostrils flared slightly. "I can give you five minutes," she snapped. She started walking again, and I had to jog a little to keep up with her.

I trailed her down a narrow corridor to a corner office with windows lining both outside walls. I guessed that it had been Big Daddy's office when he was alive. She sat behind a massive desk that had probably been just right for her former boss, but dwarfed her.

"I don't know what game you're playing —" she began.

I cut her off before she could finish. "It's not a game. Susannah Boudreaux is trying to accuse my uncle of killing Big Daddy, and I'm going to prove her wrong. What do you know about Big Daddy's dealings with Percy Ponter?"

"Nothing."

Nice try. I held her gaze and said, "I don't believe you. I have a feeling you knew just about everything there was to know about Big Daddy's business dealings. How does Percy fit into the picture?"

"Why should I tell you?"

Her attitude was starting to get on my nerves. "Why not tell me? Unless you have something to hide. Why was Percy so upset with Big Daddy the night of the murder?"

"Why don't you ask him?"

"I have. Now I want to hear what you have to say."

She smirked, and I saw some of her tension fall away, as if she'd just dodged a bullet. "It wasn't anything important," she said. "Percy's . . . excitable. He tends to overreact to things."

"What things? Were they in business together?"

"Big Daddy and Percy? No."

"So then why did Susannah tell Big Daddy he had to make things right with Percy before the end of the night?"

Hostility flashed across her face. "How would I know why Susannah did anything?"

I ignored her question and asked another one of my own. "And why did you tell Big Daddy that you'd be backing Percy's story?"

Her face froze, and her eyes took on a deer-in-the-headlights look. She blinked and it disappeared. "That was about an upcoming krewe meeting. Nothing important."

"And Susannah's ultimatum?"

Her lip curled. "I have no idea."

"I take it you don't like her."

"I didn't say that."

"You didn't have to." I pulled the picture of the two of them arguing from my purse and put it on the desk in front of her. "What was going on here?"

She glanced at the picture, then up at me. "Where did you get that?"

I still didn't know if she'd conked Big Daddy over the head with the statue, so I wasn't about to give up Estelle's name. I said only, "That's not important. What were the two of you arguing about?"

Violet's gaze went back and forth between the picture and me a few times before she finally responded. "So we were arguing. So what?"

I bit back the sarcastic retort that rose to my lips and explained what should have been obvious. "I'm trying to piece together what was going on in Big Daddy's life before he died. I'm going out on a limb here, but I think this argument had something to do with him."

Violet rolled her eyes and sat back in her chair. "Yeah? Well, you're right. It did."

"Let me guess," I said. "She found out that you and Big Daddy were sleeping together."

Her cheeks flushed and her gaze faltered. "You make it sound so cheap."

Yeah, well, if it walks like a duck . . . "So

368

you were having an affair."

"Bradley and I were in love. We were going to be together once Mardi Gras was over."

"I'm guessing that Susannah found out about you?"

"That's right. She wasn't too happy about it either."

I didn't know whether to believe that or not. None of these people seemed to truly love each other. But what did I know? "She certainly looks like she was angry with you. Was she also angry with him?"

Violet nodded and her expression sobered. "She was furious with him. He'd been intending to tell her about us for a few weeks, but every time he got ready to have the talk, she'd come up with some emergency so he wouldn't. First it was something with his brother. Then it was something with one of his kids. They live with their mother, but they used to stay with their father on the weekends. I swear, Susannah knew what was coming and she did everything she could to keep it from happening."

"Even though she was seeing someone else on the side?"

Violet's posture grew rigid. "Who told you that?"

I shrugged. "I don't remember. Did Big

369

Daddy ever say anything about her cheating on him?"

"No," Violet admitted reluctantly. "But I wouldn't be surprised. If you ask me, she probably killed him. She's a real piece of work."

I couldn't disagree with that. "What about Big Daddy's relationship with his brother? What was going on between them?"

"Judd?" Violet seemed surprised by the change of direction.

I nodded. "Big Daddy threatened to send him to rehab the night he died. Do you know why?"

Her gaze flickered away from mine for a moment. "That's not true. He would never have done that."

"But he did," I insisted.

Her gaze locked on mine. "Big Daddy would never have done that," she insisted. "He worried about Judd. He took care of Judd. Big Daddy risked everything for him —" She cut herself off abruptly, eyes wide as if she'd said too much.

I felt a slow flush of excitement. "How so?"

Violet stood, shaking her head angrily.

"What did he risk, Violet?"

She came out from behind the desk and opened the door. "Your five minutes is up.

370

Please leave. I have work to do." I was disappointed but I wasn't going to argue with her. I knew I'd struck a nerve and I was leaving with more than I'd had when I came in. I stood and walked toward the door, thinking back over everything I'd learned in the past week. Susannah had given Big Daddy an ultimatum last Friday evening at the party. She told him he had to make things right with Percy before the end of the night. A few hours later, Big Daddy told Judd that he was through covering for him and threatened to send him to rehab. I didn't think that was a coincidence. "Just one more question," I said. "Who gets all of this now that Big Daddy's gone?"

Fear and anger rippled across her expression, but they were gone in a flash. "As far as I know, Susannah inherits everything as his widow."

THIRTY-FOUR

"Susannah did it," I told Gabriel an hour later at the Dizzy Duke. "I know she did. I just can't prove it. Yet."

It was the dinner hour and the bar was nearly empty, which meant that he had time to talk. He leaned on the bar in front of me and listened while I sipped a Diet Coke and laid out my theory. "She found out about his affair with Violet. Big Daddy was going to leave her, but she couldn't let him do that. She'd have lost everything. With him dead, she gets it all. And she accused my uncle to throw suspicion off of herself."

It was nice and tidy, all the loose ends tucked in neatly, and I was proud of myself for piecing it together on my own.

Gabriel didn't look so sure. "So she picked up a statue and whacked him with it?"

"It was what she had. A crime of passion. I don't think she planned it, or she'd have brought her own murder weapon along."

"Why not wait until they got home?"

"Duh! Because then it would have been obvious. She saw an opportunity to pin the murder on a stranger, and she grabbed it."

Gabriel rolled his eyes toward the ceiling for a moment, then looked at me again and shook his head. "I don't know. I don't buy it."

"What's not to buy? It's what happened."

He shook his head again and straightened up, reaching for a couple of dirty glasses someone had left on the bar. "First of all, you're assuming that Violet's telling you the truth. How do you know she is? How do you know Big Daddy really planned on leaving his wife? Do you have anyone else's word to back that up?"

Okay. He had a point there. Big Daddy hadn't seemed all that interested in Violet when I saw them together. Was there any truth at all in her claim?

I'd give Gabriel that one. "No, but if it's true, I'm sure someone will be able to corroborate her story. Why else would Violet and Susannah have argued?"

"I can think of at least half a dozen reasons off the top of my head. One, Violet knew that Susannah was cheating on Big Daddy. You know how protective she was of him. Maybe she got in Susannah's face over that. Or two, maybe Big Daddy told Violet that he *wasn't* going to leave Susannah." He ticked off his ideas on his fingers as he went. "Three, maybe Susannah broke Violet's fingernail or Violet accidentally bumped into Susannah. I've seen people go after each other over less, especially when booze is involved."

I made a face at him. "Funny. Okay, I'll grant you the first two, but this was about more than a fingernail or a misstep." I pushed the picture across the bar toward him, a visual reminder of the incident in question. "Look at their faces."

He glanced. Shrugged. "That doesn't prove anything. You take that idea to the police, they're going to laugh you out of the building. You don't have a single piece of real evidence to prove your theory."

So he had another point. So what? "At least it might convince the police to scratch Uncle Nestor off their list for good so he can go home." They'd been in New Orleans a week already and Uncle Nestor was getting antsy. I hoped that getting back to the restaurant and their own house might help the two of them patch things up.

Gabriel wiped something from the bar and tossed the rag into the sink behind him.

"What makes you think they haven't already considered the wife as a suspect? You know what they say. The spouse is always the first person they look at. If the police haven't arrested her, it's probably because they've eliminated her as a suspect."

And just like that, my heart dropped to the floor. I hated to admit it, but he was right. "Fine then," I said grudgingly. "Who do you think did it?"

He shook his head and grinned at me as if we were playing a game. "I have no idea, *chérie*. If you ask me, the best thing you can do is to back off."

"Not while Uncle Nestor is still a suspect." I propped my chin in my hand and ran through my own list of potential killers once again. "How about Judd Boudreaux? In financial trouble and threatened with a stint in rehab. Did he kill his own brother, either because he couldn't pay him back or to avoid being locked up in a detox center for a few weeks?"

Gabriel shook his head. "I don't buy it. I've known Judd for years. He's a mess, but he's not violent."

"You didn't see his face when I was at his house the other night." Gabriel gave me a *didn't I warn you?* look, which I ignored. "Judd stays on the list, at least for now. What about Percy Ponter?"

"As far as I can see," Gabriel said thoughtfully, "he doesn't even have a motive."

"Oh, he does," I insisted. "I just don't know what it is yet. Whatever was going on between him and Big Daddy, nobody's talking about it. And that makes me think it must have been something big."

"Okay, but Susannah's off the list, right?"

"Not even close," I said. "And let's not forget about Tyson. Maybe he wanted Big Daddy out of the way so his girlfriend would inherit all that money. And, of course, Violet," I went on. "She's capable of murder, even if she didn't have a reason to commit one."

Gabriel laughed and walked away to help another customer. When he came back, he put a fresh Diet Coke in front of me and changed the subject. "You still want that introduction to Ivanka Hedge?"

Thoughts of murder melted away like a mouthful of meringue. "Are you kidding me? Of course!"

"All right then. If you'll drop all this murder business, you can go with me to the Musterion Ball. Interested?"

Wow. I had to think about that for a few minutes. It was short notice, but it was also a chance to land a contract for Ivanka's wedding cake and that was huge. But by asking me to stop looking into Big Daddy's death, he was asking me to turn my back on Uncle Nestor.

I chewed my thumbnail for a moment, torn between the biggest opportunity that had come my way professionally and the biggest trouble to hit my family since my cousin Julio told us he'd gotten his girlfriend pregnant.

"Are you in or out?" Gabriel asked. "Make up your mind now or the invitation's gone."

"Hey! That's not fair. Give me a minute."

"Who cares about fair? You asked me for a favor. I'm willing to do it, but you've got to do me a favor in return. Stop poking around in this murder investigation before you get yourself killed."

When he put it that way, what else could I do? I smiled my most agreeable smile and lied through my teeth. "All right," I said. "You win. It's a deal."

He picked me up Saturday evening, just like a real date, and I don't mind admitting that seeing him on my front porch in a tux made me sit up and pay attention. He cleaned up even better than I'd expected him to, and I'd had some pretty high expectations to begin with.

Aunt Yolanda had helped me get ready, which was a good thing, since I'm fashion-challenged. I'd picked up a silk chiffon A-line dress with spaghetti straps and pleating in the front. It was cut so low I felt exposed and vulnerable, but the look in Gabriel's eyes when he saw me made it worth a little discomfort.

Aunt Yolanda and Uncle Nestor greeted him together, which I took as a good sign. They both seemed charmed by his easy smile and laid-back personality, but I wondered if Uncle Nestor would have something snarky to say later.

Gabriel and I made the short trip to the historic Belle Grande Hotel and walked together through the lobby, just like a real couple. Chatter from groups of people in formal evening dress rose and fell all around us, the cacophony of sounds amplified by the hotel's high gilt-edged ceilings. The hotel is a beautiful place, all glitter and opulence — the perfect venue for a formal ball during carnival season.

We walked what felt like two miles through the hotel to the escalator leading to the brilliantly lit mezzanine, where the party seemed to be in full swing already. I waved to Miss Frankie, who was laughing with Bernice and a few other friends across the room. I'd called to tell her that I'd be coming to the ball with Gabriel, and she'd seemed delighted with the idea . . . but I could tell it was hard for her to think of me moving on with my life. She still held on to the belief that Philippe and I would have gotten back together, had he lived. But I was in no real hurry to get involved, and I knew that she'd come around eventually.

Gabriel seemed to know everyone, and to my surprise, everyone seemed to know him. I wondered how he'd come to be so comfortable in a social class that I'd pretty much automatically assumed was as far over his head as it was mine. My old insecurities rose up to lodge in my throat for a moment, but I shoved them aside. I was going to have a good time tonight.

I still didn't feel like I belonged here, but I had to at least learn to fake it. If I couldn't do that, I'd never make Zydeco a success.

Squaring my shoulders and holding my head high, I walked with Gabriel through the crowd. I smiled at people I recognized and indulged in so much small talk, I thought my head would burst. At last, I spotted Ivanka Hedge and her fiancé, Richard Montgomery, a few feet from where we stood. They weren't alone; it took me a few seconds to realize that the couple with them was Susannah Boudreaux and her brother-in-law, Judd. I felt a flash of disappointment I couldn't entirely explain, and I thought Judd looked a little uncomfortable when our eyes met. Hovering a few feet away and trying to look discreet, Tyson looked on with storm clouds in his eyes.

Gabriel put his hand on the small of my back and steered me toward them. He greeted the women by kissing their cheeks and spent a few seconds shaking hands and slapping backs with the men. To my surprise, Judd seemed almost sober — or at least not too drunk yet. Susannah seemed unpleasantly surprised to see me there, but she greeted me with a nod before pointedly ignoring me.

My ears were buzzing, but I couldn't tell if it was because I was nervous about meeting Ivanka and Richard, or if some sixth sense was telling me to beware. I decided on the former, if only because I couldn't figure out where Susannah would have hidden a weapon in the slinky black gown she wore.

Gabriel officially introduced me to Ivanka and Richard. She gave me a cool hello and a limp-wristed handshake. Richard greeted me more warmly, and even asked me a few questions about Zydeco. And then it was over. Ivanka turned away from me as if I was of no more interest to her than a gnat, and I wondered for a minute why I'd wanted to make her wedding cake in the first place.

I thought about Big Daddy's advice the night of my party. I could almost hear his big, booming voice when he said, "You can make yourself crazy chasin' after people who don't give two hoots about you. Don't do it. Just relax. Be yourself. That's what I do." And I realized that in spite of all his faults, he might have been right about that.

Gabriel glanced down at me and grinned as if he understood my disappointment. "Got what you wanted?"

"Yeah," I fibbed. "Thanks." And then I turned my attention to more important matters. I nodded toward Susannah and hissed in his ear, "What's she doing here? Shouldn't she be somewhere pretending to mourn or something?"

Gabriel's smile vanished. "Don't start."

"I'm not starting anything," I assured him. "It just seems a little odd, don't you think? Her husband's barely in the ground and she's partying — with his *brother*. What's up with that?"

Gabriel tugged me a few feet away from their cozy little group. "It's Mardi Gras. You're not from around here. You wouldn't understand."

"You're right," I said, making a face. "I don't get it. I'm not sure I want to. What do you think is up with the two of them?"

Gabriel shook his head and propelled me a few more feet away. "You promised. No more with the murder."

"I lied." He rolled his eyes in exasperation, and I said, "Oh, come on, Gabriel. That little nothing introduction was hardly worth the price."

"You," he said, "cannot be trusted." And then he pulled me into his arms and swept me out onto the dance floor.

It was a brilliant move on his part. I didn't think about the murder again for hours.

THIRTY-FIVE

I'm not easily impressed, but even I have to admit that the Musterion Ball was a magical event. Gabriel and I danced until we were overheated, then slipped outside and walked together in the moonlit courtyard. He took my hand as if it was the most natural thing in the world, and I surprised myself by not freaking out over it.

Unfortunately, reality has a way of popping even the most dream-filled moments. As we came back into the hotel, I excused myself to answer the call of nature. And that's when the trouble started.

I wandered around for a few minutes looking for a ladies' room that didn't have a line halfway to Biloxi. By the time I found a nearly deserted hallway with a small restroom at the end, the need was truly desperate. I walked past an elderly couple moving slowly toward the lobby and skimmed past a couple of women who were chatting about a new dress shop.

I raced into the ladies' room, took care of business, and was just about to step back into the hallway when I became aware of voices on the other side of the door. I didn't pay them much attention until one of the men said, "Damn it, Percy. This has gotten out of hand."

I froze with the door partway open, just wide enough for me to peek through into the hallway. Percy Ponter and two other men were so deep in their conversation, none of them noticed me. Which I counted as a good thing.

Glancing behind me to make sure I was really alone in the lavatory, I pressed my ear to the opening so I could hear what they were saying. After all, I was stuck here. Even Gabriel couldn't blame me for this.

"I know it's gotten out of hand," Percy mumbled. "I'm telling you, we need to just own up to this."

I recognized Stanton Meyer, Musterion's first lieutenant, a short, round man with ruddy skin and neatly trimmed salt-and-pepper beard. At Percy's words, his ruddy skin turned even redder. He reared back, as shocked as if Percy had suggested they all run naked through the ballroom. "We are *not* going public with this," he barked.

"We're going to get the money back from Boudreaux and that will be that."

"How?" Percy demanded. "Judd doesn't have it. He used it to pay off the gambling debt. There's no way he can get the money back now."

Norman Costlow, the krewe's second lieutenant, made a noise of derision. He's a tall, thin man with a shock of red hair and a hook nose. "There's money in Big Daddy's businesses," he said. "Judd can take the money out of there if he has to. I'm sure Susannah would be willing to write a check to shield the family from embarrassment."

I almost choked when I heard that. So that's what Susannah had been talking about when she warned Big Daddy not to embarrass her. That must have been why she'd issued the ultimatum. Protect the family from embarrassment, *or else*. But had *or else* meant murder?

"I've already talked to her," Percy said in a low voice. "If there was money available in one of the businesses, Big Daddy would have skimmed it from there in the first place. There's a reason he pocketed the money from the fund-raiser, gentlemen. I say we just swallow our pride and admit what happened. It will sully Boudreaux's name, but he did embezzle the funds. I don't think we should hide that from the members."

Pieces to the puzzle clicked into place and I had to press my lips together to keep from squeaking with excitement.

Costlow shook his head firmly. "I will not drag his name through the mud now that he's dead. It wouldn't be right."

"I don't give two hoots about Boudreaux's reputation," Meyer snapped. "But I sure as hell care about mine, and I'm not going out there and telling those people that a million dollars of their money disappeared during my watch. Get it back from Boudreaux," he ordered. "I don't care what you have to do."

My heart was pounding so hard I almost missed what he said, and they moved away before I could figure out what to do about what I'd just heard. Big Daddy had stolen money from Musterion to protect his baby brother. That's why his ass was on the line. That's why he was so angry he'd threatened Judd with rehab.

But had Susannah been so determined to protect her own reputation that she'd killed Big Daddy? Had she really thought she could pin the murder on someone else and get away with it?

I had to call Sullivan and let him know what I'd just heard. Trembling with excitement, I fished my cell phone out of my evening bag, but I had no service. Not even a partial bar.

Checking my phone as I walked, I hurried down the hall and out into the crowd. Still nothing.

Gabriel was waiting for me near the escalator, and the smile slid from his face when he saw the look on mine. "You look serious. Is everything okay?"

"I'm fine," I assured him. "But I need to call Detective Sullivan. I just heard something he needs to know about. Any idea where I can get service in this hotel?"

"Not off the top of my head. Shall we go outside? You should be able to get reception there."

I nodded and we moved toward the escalator, but before we could begin our descent, Richard Montgomery stopped us. "I've been looking all over for you," he said to Gabriel. "I need you to settle a bet for me."

Gabriel hesitated, but I waved him off. "This will only take a minute," I promised. "I'll be back before you know it."

He strolled away with Richard, and I rode the escalator to the main floor, then headed toward the lobby, looking for a signal or a side entrance as I walked. The broad corridor was mostly deserted, but there were a few people around. I hadn't gone far when a laughing couple came through a set of glass doors a few feet in front of me.

I veered toward it and checked to make sure I could get back inside — I'd learned my lesson at The Shores — then let the door shut behind me and moved away from the building until a couple of bars showed up on my screen. I punched in Sullivan's number — or at least the first four numbers. That's as far as I got before I spotted Judd and Susannah leaving the hotel by an entrance about thirty feet away.

Judd strolled slowly, hands in his pockets, as if he hadn't a care in the world. Susannah's movements were more furtive. She glanced over her shoulder twice in thirty seconds, and she held one arm in front of her, her evening wrap tossed loosely over her hand.

I had a bad feeling about what I was seeing, so I finished punching in Sullivan's number and waited impatiently for him to answer. "Get over to the Belle Grande Hotel," I said when I heard his voice. "Susannah Boudreaux has a gun. I think she's about to kill her brother-in-law."

Sullivan didn't waste time asking annoying questions, which is one of my favorite things about him. He asked exactly where they were, ordered me to get back inside, and put out a call to dispatch.

I had no desire to get between a crazy woman and her gun, but I couldn't just go back inside and leave Judd on his own. Besides, if I went back into the hotel, I wouldn't be able to call for help if things got worse.

Scarcely breathing, I moved a little closer, keeping to the shadows so they wouldn't see me.

"They know," I heard Susannah say. "They *know*! And they're demanding the money back. They're threatening to destroy Bradley — and me in the process."

Judd sat on the edge of a raised flower-bed. "How can they destroy you, Susannah? You had nothing to do with it."

"Do you think I can hold my head up if this gets out? Do you think anybody in this town will invite me to anything? I'll be a laughingstock. Or worse, they'll feel sorry for me."

Judd smiled sadly. "Now that would be a shame."

"Well, it's not going to happen," she said, her voice growing a little louder. "I'm not going to let it happen. You've embarrassed this family for the last time."

"I sincerely doubt that," Judd said. "Embarrassing the family is the one thing I'm truly gifted at."

Susannah shook her head. I could only see the side of her face, but I thought she was beginning to look a little wild around the eyes, so I moved closer still. "I don't know how I'm going to manage it, but I'm going to get that money back to the krewe. I'll sell one of the businesses if I have to. But I won't do this again. Big Daddy carried you all these years. He protected you from yourself. He bailed you out, using all of *our* money to do it." She swung her hand and the wrap covering it fell away.

"You're going to leave. Tonight. And you're never coming back. Do you understand me?"

"Why not just let me confess to what really happened the night of the party? They'll lock me up for the rest of my life, and you'll be finished with me for good."

Wait a minute. *What?* My heart stopped beating for an instant and then hammered in my chest so hard I couldn't hear anything else.

Susannah leveled the gun at him. "Never. I'm tired of the pitying looks on my friends' faces when your name comes up. I'm tired of everything always being about you and your *sickness.*"

Judd ran a slow glance over her hand and the gun she held. "You'd rather kill me than turn me in?"

"In a heartbeat."

He held out his arms, daring her to take a shot. "Then do it, Susannah. I know I panicked when Bradley died, but this week has been hell and I've realized I can't go through this again." She shifted uncertainly and he pushed harder. "Come on, Susannah. Do you think I care what happens to me now? Life in prison or no life at all, it's all the same to me."

She shook her head and refocused her aim. "I think you're the *only* person you care about, you selfish bastard. I think you used your brother up for his whole life, and you never gave one single thing back to him." Anger twisted her features, making her pretty face almost unrecognizably ugly. "He didn't love you, you know. He took care of you because he *had* to."

Pain seared Judd's face. Her hateful words had found their mark.

"If you cared about him at all, you'd leave," she shouted. "Let me salvage his name. Let me keep this story from getting out. Let me protect his reputation the way you never would."

Judd dropped his head and stared at the

ground. When he lifted his head again, he looked different. Resigned. "Why don't you just tell them the truth? Why don't we just get it over with now?"

"Because the truth won't help anything," Susannah shouted. "Do you really think I want to be known as the woman whose husband was murdered by his own brother?"

She'd almost convinced me that she cared about her husband, but that question snapped me back to reality. This wasn't about Big Daddy. It had always been about her.

"I told you, it was an accident," Judd said, but his voice was so low I almost missed it.

"Oh, I know. You didn't *mean* to. You never mean to, Judd. That's the problem, but you still ruin everything for everybody."

I hated knowing that Judd had killed Big Daddy, and I hated Susannah for caring more about herself than she did about either of them. But knowing that she'd tried to throw my uncle to the wolves to protect her reputation made my blood boil.

Sirens split the night, and Judd lifted his head to listen. "Someone knows we're out here," he said. "Looks like I'm not going anywhere."

Panicked, Susannah raised the gun. I

didn't have time to think about what I did next. I'll never know whether she intended to shoot him or not, but I threw myself on her before she had the chance.

I stumbled a little as I grabbed for her hand, and I lost my balance. We fell to the ground together. Pain shot through my knees, and the pavement tore the skin from my arms. My elbow throbbed, but I stayed focused on Susannah's hands and the gun. I just had to keep her from using it until the police arrived.

I expected Judd to run, but he didn't move.

Susannah surged upward, trying to shake me. I jabbed an elbow into her stomach and heard the breath rush from her lungs. Judd still didn't move.

"What's the matter with you?" I shouted at him. "Either get out of here or help me with her. Don't just stand there."

That seemed to rouse him. I could hear the heavy footsteps of New Orleans's finest pounding as help came. I could hear Sullivan shouting my name. But I couldn't tear my eyes from the sight of Judd walking away and leaving me to fight Susannah on my own.

THIRTY-SIX

The news of Judd Boudreaux's fatal accident hit the news early Sunday morning and spread like wildfire. He'd been drunk when he drove his car into a tree. The police estimated his speed at around ninety miles an hour.

Everyone said it was inevitable. The way he drank, they'd been expecting something like this for years. I couldn't prove it, and I didn't even want to try, but I suspected it was no accident.

With Big Daddy's murder solved, Sullivan cleared Uncle Nestor and Aunt Yolanda to travel, and they wasted no time booking their flight. My heart was heavy as I drove them to the airport. It had been a hectic week, but it had been great to see them again. And at least they were on speaking terms again.

I pulled into the passenger drop-off and we kept busy unloading their bags from the trunk, avoiding "good-bye" for as long as possible. When we couldn't put it off any longer, I hugged Aunt Yolanda tightly and blinked back tears.

"Are you *sure* you want to leave this morning?" I said, trying to laugh around the lump in my throat. "You should stay until after Mardi Gras."

"You might be able to convince me," she whispered, "but Nestor is anxious to get home again." She pulled back and I could see that her eyes were shimmering, too. "We're going to miss you, *mija*. Come home for a visit soon."

"I will," I promised. I sniffed. Dug in my pocket for a tissue.

And looked up just as Uncle Nestor pulled me into his arms. "I am so proud of you, Rita. Never forget that."

I couldn't see his face. My own tears blinded me. "I love you, *Tío*."

And then they were gone. I watched them walk across the lanes of traffic and into the airport before sliding behind the wheel of the Mercedes and driving away. As painful as saying good-bye was, I still didn't regret the choice I'd made to stay here in New Orleans.

That was good to know.

■ ■ ■ ■

Memories of the confrontation with Susannah, and Judd's subsequent death, had sparked one of life's clarifying moments for me. I wanted to laugh more and worry less. I wanted to dare more and fear less. I didn't think that was too much to ask. And there was no better time to start relaxing and having a little fun than right then.

I'd spent the past couple of days immersing myself in the Mardi Gras experience with Miss Frankie, Bernice, and the Zydeco crew. Despite Big Daddy's murder and Judd's suicide, Musterion put on a great parade on Sunday. Even the scandal of Big Daddy's embezzlement wasn't enough to dampen Mardi Gras spirits.

I was learning that New Orleans moves to its own unique rhythm, and that's never truer than during Mardi Gras. The music, the crowds, the noise and laughter, the unlikeliest costumes on the unlikeliest people can almost lead to sensory overload. There's nothing subtle or understated about Mardi Gras. The louder, brighter, and more garish the costume or float, the better. It's all about self-indulgence during carnival and self-denial once carnival is over and Lent begins.

I'd had a great time, but I think mostly I enjoyed feeling as if I'd belonged in our little group and being part of a tradition that dates back hundreds of years. I'd spent some time on Bourbon Street, with its beautiful old buildings and iron lacework standing side-by-side with neon signs advertising XXX entertainment. It's an experience, but not my favorite.

I'd been happier at the Uptown parades, where people lined up six or seven deep, and the back rows were made up of people standing on ladders to see over the crowds. I'd loved watching the delight on the kids' faces when someone on a passing float tossed a trinket or stuffed animal their way. And I'd been completely charmed by the people on the West Bank, who'd thrown their arms wide and welcomed me as if I'd always belonged there.

After the intense revelry of Fat Tuesday, I woke up to a quiet, empty house on Ash Wednesday morning. It was the first time I'd been alone in my own home for a long time, and I was enjoying the solitude. For a few hours, nobody needed me and even I couldn't work up anything to worry about. I rolled over and pulled the covers over my head, settling down for another hour of sleep.

The entire staff at Zydeco had been out late the night before, so I'd given everyone the morning off. Which left me free to putter around the house and catch up with some of the chores I'd let slip for weeks. Aunt Yolanda had taken care of the most pressing issues, so I started a load of laundry, whipped up some French toast with cinnamon, and made coffee — strong and black — to kick-start my morning.

Just as I carried my plate and a mug to the kitchen table, the doorbell rang. I cinched my robe around my waist and opened the door to Sullivan. I can't say I was surprised to see him. Along with the rest of the police force, he'd been working double shifts throughout the celebration, but I knew he'd pay me a visit when he could.

He looked good. Strong. Handsome. Steady. After I'd spent the better part of Saturday evening dancing with Gabriel, my reaction to Sullivan confused me. But then, so did my reaction to Gabriel. I'd always been a one-man woman.

I didn't waste time dissecting my feelings. I invited Sullivan in, poured coffee and made him a plate, and then sat across from him. I like my time alone, but I still had unanswered questions, and I hoped Sullivan could clear those up for me. And besides, he's easy on the eyes. "So," I said, "what brings you here?"

He dug into the French toast like a man who hadn't eaten in days. "I thought you'd like to know that Susannah Boudreaux has been charged with two counts of aggravated assault. With your testimony, we should be able to make the charges stick."

"So she'll go to prison? Good. It seems only fair."

He lifted one shoulder and mopped up some syrup with a wedge of toast. "If all goes well. I wouldn't be surprised if her attorney tries an insanity plea, though. She's . . . disturbed."

"Ya think?" I grinned and settled back in my seat, cradling my mug in both hands. "Has she explained how she knew that Judd killed Big Daddy?"

Sullivan nodded. "Apparently, she and Tyson stumbled upon the scene as Judd was running away."

"Who *is* Tyson, anyway?"

"He's the general manager at one of Big Daddy's car dealerships. That's how he met both Susannah and Violet."

"So was he sleeping with both of them?"

Sullivan shook his head. "As far as I know, just Susannah."

"So he and Susannah were together when they found Big Daddy? But they just left him there?"

"That's right. They both say that they didn't actually see Judd hit Big Daddy, but it was pretty obvious what had happened."

"So instead of turning her brother-in-law in, Susannah tried to throw suspicion on Uncle Nestor? The woman really is certifiable, isn't she?"

"I think she was desperate to protect the Boudreaux family, and by extension, her standing in the community. She liked her life, and she saw Big Daddy's name and reputation as her key to keeping it. And I'm pretty sure alcohol was a factor. She'd been at that party for several hours by that time, and the witnesses I've talked to have all said she was drinking heavily. She had a knee-jerk reaction when she found her husband dead. After that, she was afraid to come forward with the truth."

Somehow I thought her decision had been more calculated than that. "Judd said Big Daddy's death was an accident," I said. "Do you think it was?"

Sullivan nodded. "I do, but without Judd's testimony we'll never be able to prove it."

And with his past, Judd's memory would probably always be under a cloud of suspicion. I shook off the slight melancholy that settled on my shoulders at that thought and told Liam about Uncle Nestor and Aunt Yolanda and how Susannah Boudreaux had kissed him at the party. "I still don't understand why she did that," I said. "I even asked her about it, but she claimed that my uncle kissed her. I know she's lying."

"She and Big Daddy had a twisted-up relationship," Sullivan said. "They were both sleeping around, and yet they both seemed to genuinely care about each other in an odd way." He held up both hands to ward off the argument he could feel coming and added, "Hey, I don't get it either. I took a statement from Susannah's friend Tyson the other day. He claims that Susannah was trying to show Big Daddy that she meant business. Apparently, she used to threaten to leave him on a regular basis. This time, she wanted him to believe she was serious. So she kissed your uncle right in front of Big Daddy just to prove a point."

"What a crock. Do you believe that?"

"I believe that's what she told Tyson," Sullivan said with a shrug. "But I don't think she had any intention of leaving Big Daddy."

Neither did I. I hated her for involving

Uncle Nestor in her mess. He'd had the misfortune of being in the wrong place at the wrong time, and it had come very close to destroying his own marriage, not to mention his life.

"If you ask me," I said, "Big Daddy had already tarnished the name. Other than the way he took care of his brother, he didn't have a lot of redeeming social value."

"He wasn't all bad," Sullivan said.

"He wasn't all good either."

"Who is? If it makes you feel better, I heard from the Boudreauxes' attorney this morning. Susannah had assumed she was going to inherit Big Daddy's estate, but it turns out he left a will dividing almost all of it between his children. He also left some property a few miles north to Judd. I guess the kids — meaning Mellie, since none of the children is yet of age — have decided to turn that land into a treatment facility: the Judd Boudreaux Memorial Rehabilitation Center."

The melancholy lifted a little further. "I like knowing that," I said.

Sullivan finished his breakfast and sat back with a sigh of satisfaction. "You sure can cook."

I actually felt myself blush. "I'm glad you enjoyed it. Would you like more?"

He patted his stomach and shook his head. "Thanks, but I shouldn't." He glanced around the kitchen. His gaze landed on a pile of sequins and feathers, the costume I'd worn on Bourbon Street. He arched an eyebrow and grinned, leaning over to hold it up in front of him. "New outfit?"

I laughed and nodded. "Yeah, but it was a one-time-only deal. That thing will never again see the light of day with me in it."

He ran another glance over it and looked back at me slowly. "So your aunt and uncle are gone?"

I swallowed. Hard. And tried not to over-react to the way his eyes suddenly turned smoky gray. "They flew out on Sunday. Aunt Yolanda would have liked to stay for Mardi Gras, but Uncle Nestor was ready to get home. He's not really into crowds and noise. They make him nervous."

"I'm sorry their visit was ruined by the investigation," Sullivan said. "I really did try to find someone who could provide him with an alibi."

"Yeah. Me, too." But that was all water under the bridge. The important thing now was that they were speaking to each other when they left New Orleans. As long as they were talking, I trusted they could work through anything.

Without another word, Sullivan got up and came around the table toward me. He pulled me out of the chair with more gentleness than I would have imagined for a man his size, and put his arms around me tenderly. "I'm glad you called me the other night, but you had me worried sick. Don't do that again, okay?"

I wrapped my arms around his waist and leaned my head on his solid chest.

"Rita? Promise?"

I wanted to oblige, but I don't like making promises I might not be able to keep. "I promise that if I'm ever in trouble, I'll call you."

He pulled back and scowled at me. "That's it? That's all I get?"

"I'm afraid so." I had no idea what the future held for any of us, but I deliberately pushed aside the worry that was so natural for me and let myself enjoy the moment.

I have to admit, it felt pretty good.

He didn't stay. Which was probably a very good thing. If he'd asked, I might have said yes. But I wasn't sure I was ready for that. I had plenty of time to figure out where I was headed. I didn't have to have all the answers today.

After he left, I climbed the stairs to my office and booted up my computer. And then, because Sullivan's visit had left me in such an agreeable mood, I pounded out my first blog entry and e-mailed it to Ox before I could change my mind. Life's too short to quibble about the small stuff, and yeah, it's all small stuff.

RECIPES

RITA'S BREAKFAST CASSEROLE
Serves 12

3 cups chopped onion
3 tablespoons margarine or butter
1/4 to 1/2 teaspoon salt
1/4 teaspoon pepper
2 (12-ounce) cans refrigerated buttermilk
 biscuit
6 slices bacon, crisply cooked, crumbled
2/3 cup whipping cream
1/2 cup dairy sour cream
3 eggs
(1/2 cup) shredded white cheddar or
 Monterey Jack cheese
Additional pepper for sprinkling, if desired

Preheat the oven to 375° F.

In a large skillet, cook onions in margarine until tender but not browned. Stir in salt and 1/4 teaspoon pepper.

Separate biscuit dough into 20 biscuits

and place in an ungreased 15 × 10-inch jelly roll pan. Press over bottom and 1/2 inch up sides to form crust. Spoon onions over crust, and sprinkle with bacon.

In a medium bowl, combine whipping cream, sour cream, and eggs until well blended. Stir in cheese. Spoon evenly over onions and bacon. Sprinkle with additional pepper.

Bake for 24 to 30 minutes or until crust is deep golden brown.

Serve hot. Store leftovers in refrigerator.

This is a great dish for brunch or when relatives drop in for a weekend visit.

Dizzy Duke Shrimp Étouffée
Serves 4 to 6

Étouffée is considered one of Louisiana's crown jewels when it comes to cuisine. The word étouffée *basically means "smothered," and it's a common cooking technique here in the South. Shrimp étouffée brings together all the greats of Louisiana cooking: seafood, a flour-and-oil roux, and a mirepoix, otherwise known as the holy trinity: onion, celery, and green pepper. Add some traditional Cajun seasoning and hot sauce, and you can't beat it.*

You can make this dish two ways: either by peeling the shrimp yourself and simmering the stock in your own kitchen, or you can choose the short version, which will cut your prep time to about 20 minutes.

Note that while this recipe calls for shrimp, you can also use crawfish or crab.

Optional Shrimp Stock

Shells from 2 pounds of shrimp
1/2 large onion, chopped
Top and bottom from 1 green pepper
2 garlic cloves, chopped
1 celery stalk, chopped
5 bay leaves

Étouffée

1/4 cup vegetable oil or lard
Heaping 1/4 cup flour
1/2 large onion, chopped
1 bell pepper, chopped
1 to 2 jalapeño peppers, chopped
1 large celery stalk, chopped
4 garlic cloves, chopped
1 pint shrimp stock (see above), or clam juice or premade fish or shellfish stock
1 tablespoon Cajun seasoning
1/2 teaspoon celery seed
1 tablespoon sweet paprika
Salt
2 pounds shrimp, shell on (remove shells for use in the shrimp stock; if not making

your own stock, you can get shrimp already shelled)

3 green onions, chopped

Hot sauce (Crystal or Tabasco) to taste

For Shrimp Stock

Pour 2 quarts of water into a pot and add all the remaining stock ingredients. Bring to a boil. Reduce heat and simmer the stock gently for 45 minutes.

Strain stock through a fine-meshed sieve into another pot over low heat. This recipe makes a large amount of stock, which you can use for other recipes. It lasts in the fridge for a week.

For Étouffée

Begin by making a roux. Heat the vegetable oil or lard in a heavy pot over medium heat for 1 to 2 minutes. Stir in the flour well, whisking to make sure there are no clumps. Cook for 10 minutes or so, stirring often, until it turns a pretty brown color.

Add the onion, bell pepper, jalapeño, and celery. Mix well and cook over medium heat for approximately 4 minutes, stirring occasionally. Add the garlic and cook another 2 minutes. (Do not overcook the garlic at this stage.)

Slowly add the hot shrimp stock, stirring

constantly so it incorporates. The roux will absorb the stock and thicken at first, then it will loosen. Add stock in small amounts until your sauce is about the thickness of syrup. It should be about 1 pint of sauce.

Add Cajun seasoning, celery seed, and paprika, and mix well. Add salt to taste, then mix in the shrimp. Cover the pot, turn the heat to its lowest setting, and cook for 10 minutes.

Add the green onions and hot sauce to taste. Serve over white rice. Great with a cold beer or lemonade.

ZYDECO KING CAKE
Serves 10 to 12

King Cake is a tradition that came to New Orleans with the first French settlers. It's been a part of the culture ever since, though during the early days, the King Cake was part of a family's celebration. It really didn't take on a public role until around 1870.

The sides of the dough should pull away from the sides of the mixing bowl as you knead this dough. If it doesn't, the moisture content in the flour has fluctuated with the humidity, so add a spoonful or two more flour.

Cake

1 cup lukewarm milk (about 110° F)
1/2 cup granulated sugar
2 tablespoons dry yeast
3 3/4 cups all-purpose flour
1 cup melted butter
5 egg yolks, beaten
1 teaspoon vanilla extract
1 teaspoon grated fresh lemon zest
3 teaspoons cinnamon
1 teaspoon grated fresh nutmeg (more or
   less to taste)

Icing

2 cups powdered sugar
1/4 cup condensed milk
1 teaspoon fresh lemon juice
Purple, green, and gold decorative sugars
1 plastic baby to hide in the cake (can also
   use a fava bean)

For Cake

Pour the warm milk into a large bowl. Whisk in the granulated sugar, yeast, and a heaping tablespoon of the flour, mixing until both the sugar and the yeast have thoroughly dissolved. Once bubbles have developed on the surface of the milk, and the yeast causes it to foam, whisk in the butter, egg yolks, vanilla, and lemon zest. Add remaining flour, cinnamon, and nutmeg, folding the dry ingredients into the wet ingredients. A large rubber spatula works great for this step.

After the dough is mixed well and pulls away from the sides of the bowl, shape it into a large ball. Then knead the dough on a floured surface until it is smooth and elastic, which takes about 15 minutes.

Put the dough back into the bowl, cover with plastic wrap, and set aside in a draft-free place to let it proof, or rise, for 1 1/2 hours or until the dough has doubled in volume.

Preheat the oven to 375° F. Once the dough has risen, punch it down and divide the dough into 3 equal pieces. Roll each piece of dough into a long strip, making 3 ropes of equal length. Braid the 3 ropes together and then form the braid into a circle, pinching ends together to form a seal.

Carefully place the braided dough on a nonstick cookie sheet and let it rise again until it doubles in size, about 30 minutes.

Once the cake has doubled in size, place the cookie sheet in the oven and bake until the braid is golden brown, about 30 minutes.

Remove the cake from the oven, place on a wire rack to allow air to circulate, and cool for 30 minutes.

For Icing

While the cake is cooling, whisk together the powdered sugar, condensed milk, and lemon juice in a bowl until the icing is smooth and spreadable. If the icing seems too thick, add a bit more condensed milk; if it's a bit too liquid, add a bit more powdered sugar until you have the right consistency.

Spread the icing over the top of the cooled cake and sprinkle with purple, green, and gold sugars while the icing is still wet.

Tuck the plastic baby into underside of the cake and, using a spatula, slide the cake onto a serving platter.

CHILE VERDE
Serves 6

In all my life, I've never known anyone to make chile verde from a recipe. It's usually made with inexact measurements, and adjusted to taste, so take these approximate measurements and then adjust as you like:

3 pounds pork roast
Lard or olive oil to sauté
3 tablespoons flour
3 large onions, chopped
3 cloves garlic, minced

1 tablespoon oregano, crumbled (this is entirely optional; I usually don't include it)
1 cup green chilies, chopped
1 to 2 jalapeños, deseeded and chopped (optional)
Water
Salt and pepper

Trim away as much fat as possible from the pork roast and cut into cubes. Brown meat in lard or olive oil. Remove from pan and sprinkle meat with the flour. Brown onions and garlic in frying pan until transparent, but not brown. Add meat, oregano, chilies, and jalapeños to the onion mixture and then add water to cover. Simmer 2 to 3 hours. Add salt and pepper during last half hour.

Cool and degrease stew.

Serve with flour tortillas.

FLOUR TORTILLAS
Makes approximately 2 dozen
4 cups all-purpose flour
1 teaspoon salt
2 teaspoons baking powder
2 tablespoons lard
1 1/2 cups water

Whisk the flour, salt, and baking powder together in a mixing bowl. Mix in the lard with your fingers until the flour resembles cornmeal. Add the water and mix until the dough comes together; place on a lightly floured surface and knead a few minutes until smooth and elastic. Divide the dough into 24 equal pieces and roll each piece into a ball.

Preheat a large skillet over medium-high heat and add 2 to 3 drops of oil. (Using more oil will make the tortillas greasy and cause smoking in the kitchen.) Use a well-floured rolling pin to roll a dough ball into a thin, round tortilla. Place into the hot skillet, and cook until the exposed surface begins to bubble. Flip and continue cooking until golden on the other side.

Place the cooked tortilla in a tortilla warmer or between the folds of a clean kitchen towel to keep it moist until serving. Continue rolling and cooking the remaining dough.

The employees of Thorndike Press hope you have enjoyed this Large Print book. All our Thorndike, Wheeler, and Kennebec Large Print titles are designed for easy reading, and all our books are made to last. Other Thorndike Press Large Print books are available at your library, through selected bookstores, or directly from us.

For information about titles, please call:
  (800) 223-1244

or visit our Web site at:
  http://gale.cengage.com/thorndike

To share your comments, please write:
Publisher
Thorndike Press
10 Water St., Suite 310
Waterville, ME 04901